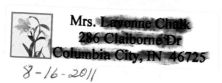

Manners, Alexandra
Wildford's daughter

DATE DUE		
JUL 3 '86	FE 3 '89	SE 16 '94
AUG 1 2 '86	FE 17 '89	MR 8 '95
NOV 4 '86	MR 3 '89	AP 25 '95
APR 2 '87	MR 25 '89	MR 27 '96
OCT 2 2 '87	JON 6 1989	
FEB 6 '88	JE 28 '89	
APR 2 2 '88	OCT 0 2 1981	
JUN 7 '88	OC 26 '90	
JUL 1 4 '88	AP 5 '91	
AUG 2 4 '88	AP 24 91	
JA 3 '89	SE 30 '91	
	AG 25 '93	

Wildford's Daughter

Other Books by Alexandra Manners

THE STONE MAIDEN
CANDLES IN THE WOOD
THE SINGING SWANS
CARDIGAN SQUARE

Wildford's Daughter

by
Alexandra Manners

G. P. Putnam's Sons
New York

Copyright © 1978 by Alexandra Manners

All rights reserved. This book , or parts thereof,
must not be reproduced in any form without permission.
Published simultaneously in Canada by Longman
Canada Limited, Toronto.

SBN: 399-12198-6
Library of Congress Cataloging in Publication Data

Rundle, Anne.
  Wildford's daughter.

  I. Title.
PZ4.R9425Wi 1978 [PR6068.U7]   823'.91'4   78-2636

Printed in the United States of America

For Isa, with love

Wildford's Daughter

CHAPTER ONE

It was the strangest journey she had ever undertaken. The night was full of sound , the rumble of coach wheels and the creak of harness and the clops of the horses' hooves. If she stretched her neck out of the window she could see the animals' hindquarters straining under the weight of the vehicle, smooth and glossy from the ministrations of Papa's grooms. Beyond the light shed by the coach lamps, the horses' heads were lost in obscurity, all but the manes that tossed in the wind, their edges caught in fitful irradiation. Bare arms of trees were thrown into brief prominence, furred with pale green. But it was the moths that were magic, tiny scraps of white enticed by the candle glow, flittering, hovering, drawn to oblivion by the beckoning flame.

Emma could no longer remember how many had died and was possessed by a sick excitement that was part shame because there was no way in which she could stop the relentless pageant of death.

Mama was weeping hysterically in the opposite corner. Maybrick had one arm around her possessively, but his cold gaze was on Emma. She remembered how, when she had refused to accompany them, he had seized her and thrust her, protesting, into the dark maw of the carriage. "Let your father sweat for a little," he said curtly, his fingers hurting her upper arms. "Why should he go free of worry?"

"I'll never go back to him. Never!" Mama cried, looking beautiful in spite of the tears and dishevelment.

"Of course not," Maybrick agreed. "The man's a brute. Always was."

"Papa is not a brute," Emma said loudly and clearly. "If there is blame, Mama must share it."

Maybrick favored her with another bleak look as Mama shook in a fresh storm of crying. "How are you supposed to judge?"

"You see," Mama said between sobs, "how he has managed to estrange us? Put me in the wrong?"

"I see."

Studying her mother's pretty, tearstained face, Emma decided she was never going to marry, never fall in love. If this was what blond curls and blue eyes got you, she was glad she was plain. She put her hands over her ears to stifle the sound of Mama's hiccupping distress, which she was certain was mostly for Maybrick's benefit. Then she leaned out of the window to look once more at the fat candles in the brass lamps and the moths' dance of death. Even if she shouted at them they would not understand. They would keep on coming, sizzling, and dying in the hot wax.

The trees and fields gave way to scattered houses, to streets and boulevards, to a blue frieze of chimney pots and lights like cats' eyes, cobbles filmed with damp and the wash of the river. She knew she was now within reach of her grandparents' house, and she prepared herself for the imminent encounter. Maybrick was a distant cousin of Mama's and therefore, being one of the Hunts, would be in the right, whatever happened as a result of today's flight from Staves.

It was exactly as Emma had anticipated. Grandmama, a grayer version of her mother, still youthful in ruffled peignoir, baby-blue eyes shrewd and bright as marbles, sat her daughter on a sofa and wasted no time in demanding an explanation from Maybrick who replied in a chill, quiet voice that could not be heard above the comings and goings of curious household staff. But Emma did hear him say it would be better to wait until the child was put to bed before beginning the serious discussion about what was best for Amelia.

Grandpapa appeared at this juncture, having apparently been roused from bed. Emma disliked him for many things, but in particular, his intolerable snobbishness.

"I'm not tired, and anyway, I know all about it," Emma said distinctly, enjoying the variety of conflicting emotions her pronouncement aroused.

"A pity she takes so strongly after Wildford," Grandmama pronounced arctically.

"The child's difficult," stated Maybrick as he shot another bleak look at Emma.

"She must obviously be disciplined," Grandpapa agreed self-importantly.

"If Papa is so terrible, why did you let Mama marry him?" Emma asked clearly. "Because he has lots of money, I expect. I'd rather live with him and he is sure to know that. He'll come looking for me, you may rest assured. And I will go."

"Discipline! There must be a firmer hand kept on the girl!" Grandpapa thundered, the effect spoiled by the sight of his thin shanks under the hem of the embroidered house robe. Emma hated the white nightcap he wore. Her father had none of these affectations. He wore his own abundant black hair loose in bed and spurned popinjay garments. Everything about him was masculine which was more than one could say for Maybrick in spite of his cold ferocity and handsome profile. Something about him repelled.

"You let him wed Mama because he has the wealthiest

bank in Norwich," Emma continued inexorably. "And she's too much of a child for a real man." She had heard Mrs. Bott say this several times on her way back to the kitchen. Emma always enjoyed the downstairs gossip.

Mama fainted artistically—none of her emotions was ever unstudied—and Grandmama called shrilly for feathers and a taper. Maybrick set down his glass and rushed to catch Amelia.

Grandpapa's face took on the look of resentful obstinacy Emma secretly feared. His displeasure could cast a tangible cloud over the entire household. But she would not have her father vilified without at least attempting to speak up on his behalf. Mama would receive most of the sympathy over the breakdown of the marriage but if Papa had turned to mistresses it must be because of some fault in his wife. Happily married men, Mrs. Bott said, did not require distractions and Emma knew this to be the truth.

"She's like some changeling," Mama sobbed.

"You only took me with you to spite Papa," Emma remarked, unable to help herself. One day she was going to encounter terrible trouble because of her forthright speaking but she could not bear lies and evasions. She also found it hard to tolerate fools. Mama was so—empty. Surely Papa must have known? But she was also divinely attractive. How she must have hated the first sight of her unrewarding baby. Emma experienced a twinge of pity for her mother's perfectly understandable disappointment.

"Ashcroft!" Grandpapa was bellowing in the direction of an anonymous maidservant who hovered in the background. "Take Miss Emma away and see that she's settled for the night in the nursery. Without supper."

Emma's heart sank. She was desperately hungry after the journey and insufficient food en route. Yet she realized that honesty was not always comfortable and principles were worth the ensuing suffering. At least Papa was not without support. She had a sudden heartwarming picture of him in breeches and long boots, his thick hair tied back with black ribbon, the hairs on his chest visible through the gap in his shirt. He would never leave her here. And she was far too old for the nursery!

Ashcroft, her face shrouded by a mobcap, came silently, waiting for Emma to accompany her. The girl could see only the maid's mouth and chin but she looked young.

Mama was by this time stretched out on the chaise longue and feathers were being burned under her nose. The smell was abominable. Emma said , "Father is certain to come and he'll be very angry."

The Parthian shot exchanged, Emma moved away in the wake of Ashcroft. The girl's shoulders heaved as though she were either crying or amused. Grandpapa was in full flood about ingratitude and pertness but Emma regretted nothing. At least she would be spared the drawing room and possibly the dining room during her sojourn, and once Papa came she'd be rid of them all for good. One would not be allowed to take a child from its father. There must be laws to prevent this, Emma decided, and she was at peace.

Ashcroft pattered up the stairs in the direction of the nursery. Emma noticed that her stockings were darned and her shoes were worn down at the heel. She looked little older than herself and would probably have to work harder than usual in an establishment like Grandpapa's with its pretensions and lack of money. Father's staff was much smarter, all in livery or proper uniforms, and they looked more cheerful than the servants here in Freer Street.

The nursery was uninviting, dingy with brown paint and linoleum and beds like sarcophagi.

Emma knew a great deal because Papa talked to her and encouraged her to read. At fifteen she was educated far beyond the normal for a girl of the age.

"I'm hungry, Ashcroft," she announced, throwing her cloak onto a chair and running to stare out of the attic window. The moon had risen and the chimney pots stood like people listening. She moved away reluctantly from the hint of magic.

The girl ceased her turning back of the prim covers and stared at Emma. The light of the candle showed Emma a face both intelligent and astonishingly presentable. There was none of Mama's useless prettiness but the strong features were pleasing and the wide eyes very blue, rather like the gentians she had seen in the mountains while holidaying on the Continent. "How pretty you are, Ashcroft."

"Am I, miss?"

"You must know you are."

"It's not for me to say."

"I suppose not. What's your other name?"

"Jess."

"Jess. It suits you."

"We must put up with names. It's not a question of whether it suits. Can't say nothing about likes and dislikes by the time *we're* old enough to have opinions, miss. Too late for that."

"Now, what am I to do about this hunger of mine?" Emma was intrigued that Jess Ashcroft appeared to be a philosopher and was not afraid to speak her mind.

"Can't rightly do nothing about it. Not my place to go into the larder, miss. Cook would skin me. Most I can do is fetch a warming pan to air the bed proper."

"Couldn't you put something in your pocket when you do bring it?"

Jess hesitated and Emma knew instinctively that the girl was remembering the reasons for Emma's present disgrace, and approved of her rebellion. "Please," she coaxed.

"Can't make no promises, miss."

"But you'll try?"

"Well—" Ashcroft pattered away, leaving Emma in a dispiriting silence. She went to the press and extracted one of the nightgowns always kept for her unwilling visits. There was water in the ewer and a piece of harsh soap—Wildfords were too common to warrant anything better—so she washed and took off her clothes, then pulled the gown over her head. Her tiredness was abated by a scream. Several screams.

She rushed to the stairs and ran down to the drawing room where she and Mama had been received. Mama was sitting up now with Grandmama beside her on the couch. Maybrick was holding Ashcroft while Grandpapa struck the girl across the back with the younger man's cane and all the force in his arm.

"What are you doing?" Emma cried.

"The girl's a thief. Your grandmother saw her trying to pass the door with a leg of chicken filched from the larder—"

"I ordered her to bring it," Emma said. "It's hours since I've eaten and I could not endure till breakfast."

"Ashcroft should not have stolen the food. She'll be so well beaten, she'll not do it again should the devil ask her." Grandpapa raised the cane and Emma, with a shout of anger, darted between him and the girl so that the stroke fell on her own shoulders. Tears sprang to her eyes but she would not allow them to escape.

"The child's a savage, Amelia," Grandmama pronounced stridently. "She's as bad as Ashcroft."

"Wildford has always allowed her too much license," Amelia observed with a fragile smile in Maybrick's direction.

"Quite so," Maybrick agreed and tightened his grasp on the half-fainting girl.

"In the name of God," Papa said suddenly from behind Emma. "What do you think you are doing?"

"I knew you'd come!" Emma was conscious of a painful stickiness between her shoulder blades. Amelia whimpered and shrank back against the satin cover of the chaise longue while her mother flushed and sat up straighter.

"It was a mistake," Grandpapa mumbled and laid down the stick.

"Oh, it was certainly a mistake," Papa agreed grimly.

"The child's back is bloody and I've a mind to use the cane on a few others before I leave. How dare you remove my daughter from Staves, Maybrick!"

Maybrick had turned pale and glowering. "Amelia thought she should come here. They did not seem suitable conditions for a growing child—"

"And these are, I suppose? The stink of burnt feathers. Two grown men beating children while the women look on. Bodily punishment is so much more acceptable than fornication? An odd scale of values."

Grandmama gasped. Her face colored unattractively.

"Get out of this house," Grandpapa insisted a little tremulously. Luke Wildford did hold the stage most magnificently. "Amelia has left you and we cannot blame her. You'll not get her back."

"Who wants her back?" Papa answered contemptuously, and there was a look on his dark, harshly angled face that made Emma want to cry, so much bitterness and self-detestation were mirrored there.

"Now, look—" Maybrick began.

"There was one thing I'd planned to do before I left," Papa said with dangerous softness and snatched up the cane to strike Maybrick heavily across the cheek. Another blow crisscrossed the first and the skin was split deeply. Blood welled from the open gash to stain the white cravat. "Make what you want of that, but any man who can help thrash a servant girl into that state deserves a horsewhipping. Can you stand, child?"

Maybrick did not move, only held his face, the blood running through his fingers to drop with soft "plops" onto the carpet.

Jess pushed herself upward painfully. The blue color seemed washed out of her pupils. "I—I think so."

"Come back with me to Staves. There's no such punishment where I live."

"There's only Sodom and Gomorrah," Grandmama snapped vitriolically. "You'll go to hell."

"I'll come wi' you, sir," Jess said as though she had not heard.

"Can you go up for your things, Emma? I've a few things to say down here."

"Yes."

"Then go and dress quickly. Fetch what was brought for you. Have you anything to say to me, Maybrick?"

Maybrick glared out of slitted eyes. It was a terrible look. "You'll get my reply one of these days, Wildford. When you least expect it."

"Have you anything of value, girl?" Wildford asked Jess. "Anything you don't wish to leave?"

"Ain't got nothing, really," Jess murmured, then slumped forward in a faint. The back of her gown was tinged with thin, crimson stripes.

Wildford restrained himself with difficulty. "What was her crime?"

"I was to be sent to bed supperless. I told Jess— Ashcroft—and asked her to fetch me food. Grandmother saw her," Emma said.

Wildford's gaze came to rest on the chicken leg reposing on top of the copper warming pan on the table. "You'd do that for so slight a cause? To a child of Emma's age?"

"The girl stole. She needed a lesson," Grandpapa insisted.

"I'd not leave a dog in your charge," Wildford said grimly. "And to think I once thought you charming and gentle. You're monsters. I should ram that drumstick down your throat."

"We never thought you anything but crude and distasteful," Grandmama told him, standing up, her body interposed between daughter and son-in-law.

"Yet you allowed me to take your daughter for the benefits that would surely follow?"

"Just as you anticipated the introductions of the wealthy and titled to Wildford's Bank," she retorted spitefully. "Hopes that were fully justified."

"Touché," Wildford whispered, "but there was at least

honesty on my side. Amelia was never led to expect anything that was not on display. If I was coarse, I did not conceal it under false gentility. You were under no misappre-
hension, any of you." He bent to pick up the unconscious
girl. "I'll have to rouse some quack to attend to her. It's the
last time you'll clap eyes on Emma, you may be certain."

Emma, smarting but satisfied, ran upstairs to collect her
belongings. If only Maybrick had not looked so vengeful, all
would be perfect.

They were not able to leave London. Wildford had spent a
guinea having Jess Ashcroft made comfortable, but even after she had been rubbed with salve and bandaged, she had
flinched from the motion of the carriage.

"You must rest a few days," Wildford said. "Emma is
very little hurt in comparison, but the journey could irk her
also. We'll stay in a hotel and I'll take my daughter to see
the sights while you are waited on in bed."

"Waited on? Who'd fetch and carry for the likes of me?
I'm a skivvy, sir."

"No longer. You are to be Emma's personal maid. She's
taken a liking to you. She has a gown in her baggage which
will do for now. Your training will commence once we get
back to Norwich. How does the notion strike you?"

"Very well, sir." The vivid blue eyes gleamed suddenly
with a curiously adult expression.

Wildford had not noticed. "Then that's settled, child."

And so it was. By sheer force of personality and the sight
of gold pieces, for the hour was late, the Wildfords and their
protégée were installed in separate rooms in a central part
of the city. Emma, sleepless with excitement and the raw
pain of the stroke from the cane, got up in the candlelight
and peered from the window. There were still vehicles traveling, the staccato clop of hooves, lit windows, shadowy
figures moving about on mysterious errands. Women spoke
to men who walked singly or in groups and before one knew

it, they were all in pairs and traveling in different directions, giggling and laughing, or invited into the darkness of a coach to vanish into silence.

It was all so different in the countryside beyond Staves. The house there lapsed into quiet after the evening meal and there were only the night sounds of nature, owls and foxes and the like.

Emma slept eventually and woke feeling stiff and sore. How much worse must Jess be feeling and all because of herself and her rebellion. She went into the girl's room and found her still asleep, her unbound hair thick and disordered on the pillow. There was a little crusted blood on her lip as though she had bitten it in the pain of the previous evening. Emma thought she looked beautiful, yet dangerous, like a vixen after a kill. She smiled at her own imagination.

Not wishing to waken Jess prematurely to face the burden of the weals on her back, Emma went to her father's bedchamber. Wildford was up and shaved and knotting his cravat, his face dark and unresponsive.

"What will we visit?" Emma inquired carefully, used to Wildford's unpredictable moods.

"The usual things. St. James's Palace, the Guildhall, Carlton House, the Serpentine, the House of Commons. The Bank of England—"

"Oh. Is it as large as your bank, Papa?"

He laughed then. "You are an innocent. Mine is very small fry compared with that of the nation. There's the British Museum too, of interest. They say Lord Elgin has acquired some famous marbles from Athens and the museum wishes to acquire them."

"Why should marbles excite such interest? A child's game—"

"Not those, Emma! Portions of a marble frieze and a woman's statue from a lesser temple. She was one of six, and the people of Athens swear that the night she was taken from her sisters, the remaining five wept until dawn. The Greeks are not, understandably, pleased."

"Why should they be? Was it not—stealing? Not much better than Elizabeth sending out her pirates in Tudor times."

"Can you be referring to Drake and Raleigh? I believe you are. You have such unconventional ideas. I cannot imagine where you got them."

"Can't you, Papa?" He was in a much better temper, she decided. That frowning arrogance was submerged in amusement. Wildford clapped his arm around her shoulder, reawakening the soreness, but he had not noticed her wince from the contact.

They breakfasted cheerfully, Emma enjoying Wildford's unaccustomed presence at the meal. Then he sent a message and another guinea to the doctor with instructions that the man visit Jess Ashcroft. After he asked Emma where she wanted to go, she chose the Tower with its bloodstained memories and its proximity to the Thames and its shipping. And, of course, the legendary ravens.

Her anticipation more than fulfilled, they left the Tower in brilliant sunshine, the white walls and turrets gleaming, the river dotted with sequins of light. Something about the bobbing craft and the billowing sails, tars in blue jackets and bell-bottomed trousers, boys in red stocking caps, the smell of timber, the old woman proffering sweets and oranges, filled Emma with delight at their suggestion of faraway places. She wanted suddenly to look different , be different.

"I wish I had not come in this old gown." She lifted a fold of the skirt in disgust.

"Old gown! It seems yesterday that I paid for it."

"Mama would always dress me as a child. I feel stupid in these clothes. Sham—"

"And you think yourself grown up?"

"More than she wished to believe. If I could be made to

appear younger, she would seem so to those she wanted to impress with her youth." She would not say Maybrick's name.

"So you adjudge yourself a woman." Wildford looked her up and down consideringly and said, "I do believe you are right. Thank God, you'll never be dull. Smallness of mind's the thing a man can least forgive. Remember that. You need not be a raving beauty to attract and retain a man's attention."

"I do not think I will ever want to."

Again that shaft of piercing sadness struck Wildford's eyes and Emma reached out to grasp his arm.

"I think I am to blame. My quarrels with Amelia. The mistakes I made—"

"I do not blame you—"

"And you must not think too harshly of your mother. I should have had the wits to see what lay under that tempting facade. I was blinded—but not for long. By that time I had fallen into the snare. There has been much time to repent of my folly."

"Sweetmeats—a toffee apple for the little lady," the old woman whined, her claws grubby on the tray, but neither heard in the stark moment of truth. The beldam grimaced.

"I still think I will not marry."

"Emma. Do not decide anything so irrevocable so soon. Just be —discerning."

The girl shook her head firmly. "I shall learn, and travel. That will be sufficient."

"Come," Wildford said, "we'll choose you some new gowns. There's a dress shop Amelia favored."

"I do not want the sort of thing she wore."

Once more, he studied her. "No. You are perfectly right. Frills and fal-lals are not for you. You take too much after me, I fear."

"That's what Grandmama says."

Wildford gave a smile that was half a snarl. "I'll not sully the morning with what I think of my charming mother-in-law."

"Was it true, what she said about Grandpapa's title helping to make the bank the success it is?"

He raised his head arrogantly. "Only up to a certain point. Hard work and certain gambles did the rest. I've a mind to see Grimaldi while I am here. The clown. He's at Sadler's Wells."

"Oh, let's! Will the bank be all right without you?"

"I have Tully for my right-hand man and the country is cast up on a wave of optimism after the drubbing of Boney. Wildford's will survive." His smile became real.

"Do you think we may see the duke?"

"Wellington? Who knows, but we should certainly see the Czar, who visits Britain, and most likely, the Regent. Not to mention the Marchioness of Hertford, his inamorata."

"Oh, Papa! Maybrick could not have abducted us at a more opportune time."

Wildford's face changed and Emma was filled with compunction. "I should not have said that. It's—just that such momentous things are happening. I think Mama really took me so that you'd be forced to come after her. Perhaps she wanted you to—notice?"

"Perhaps," Wildford said stiffly. "But she could have saved herself the trouble. She's made her bed and must lie on it. With or without Maybrick."

"How long it seems since breakfast," Emma remarked, not liking the trend of the conversation. "Are you not hungry?"

"Not very, but we'd best fortify ourselves for the rigors of the afternoon. I hope that child's all right. What's her name?"

"Jess Ashcroft."

"Ah, yes. Uncommonly pretty in her own fashion. Quite remarkable eyes, she has."

"I suppose so." Emma was instantly aware of her own lack of looks. A shadow fell over the day, but the clouds dissipated once they regained the services of the carriage and rattled past warehouses and wharves and up the rank cobbles of Fish Street where she held her nose and Wildford laughed at her, his teeth white against the dark skin. He did have a strongly foreign appearance, Emma thought, and she was counted like him, except that his hair waved crisply and hers was straight and black as an Indian's. Mama had done her best with curl papers and tongs but nothing made any impression. She would have to put it up like the woman in a picture she once saw, middle-parted and loops of braid around her ears or across the top of her head.

Father ate oysters and beef for luncheon and a big wedge of apple tart, while Emma had partridge and fruit and cheese. There was no time to have dresses specially made, but whatever Emma's deficiencies of feature, her figure was good, narrow and small-breasted, exactly right for the high-waisted, French-style gowns on display. She obtained a Swiss polka dot with velvet sash, and a subtle green with low, rounded neck, the only ornament, a gathered frill at the hem. There were shoes to match, and wrist-length gloves, a feather spray for her hair in case they went out in the evening, and a pelisse should it turn cold at night.

Wildford approved, obviously surprised by Emma's new sophistication. "How right you were about the childishness of your previous wardrobe. No one could have guessed. How old are you, Emma?"

"Nearly sixteen." It sounded better than fifteen and a half.

"I should have said seventeen. And you do not need prettiness, not with that aristocratic Spanish look. I'm well pleased you decided to wear the green this afternoon."

"Aristocratic! And Grandmama berating you for your crudity and coarseness, and I your living image!" Emma's finger smoothed the folds of the skirt.

"It was crudity of behavior she meant, though she but confused coarseness with any normal man's behavior in the marital bed." Wildford had taken drink with the meal and was uninhibited in his speech. "I was merely intended to put Amelia on a pedestal and worship her from afar, dress her in silver tissue and silk and never lay one grubby finger on her—"

"Look at the crowds!" Emma marveled a little desperately, not anxious to be let into Wildford's intimate secrets, but unable to push back the picture he evoked.

"They must be for the Czar," Wildford said, handing his daughter into the carriage and climbing up beside her. The pavements were, indeed, jampacked with men in tall hats and broadcloth coats and women in gaily colored gowns and straw bonnets, white-aproned bakers and apprentices. The road, partly blocked by wagons and hackney coaches and the occasional brewers' dray, was alive with cattle for Smithfield and barking dogs. Bosomy women hung over their windowsills, chattering, the dust cart bells clamored, urchins schreeched irrepressibly and threw tattered caps in the air. "The Czar! The Czar!" And then the bullocks were driven up a side street so that the Russian ruler could ride past in his green and gold uniform and padded tunic, his round, foreign face smiling at the noisy welcome. Following him was a horde of wild cossacks dripping with sheepskin, for all that it was June, and carrying lances long enough to pierce the sky.

The ragged boys went wild, turning cartwheels almost under the hooves of the mounted cossack soldiers and serving wenches blew kisses from poky attic windows. The Russian retinue was past too soon and Emma cried out in dismay.

"It was too thrilling. And I should so love to see them again!"

"They are sure to go to Kensington Palace or Hyde Park eventually. We will drive round the Ring and you will outshine all the grand, painted ladies. I'm sure we can circumvent the main route and meet the procession quite comfortably."

They left the packed road with difficulty, the postilion lashing about him with the whip to shift the urchins who tried to cling to the vehicle. Boys rolled away, their yelps of pain mingling with the cries of street vendors and grinding wheels. Emma was reminded of her own smarting shoulders and of Jess who had suffered so much more terribly. "I must buy something for Jess Ashcroft. I feel guilty enjoying myself while she lies abed because I encouraged her to disobey."

"You must not take everything onto your shoulders," Wildford commented. "You were not to know your grandfather would behave like a martinet or that that Ashcroft girl would be so careless as to be found out."

"Papa, why is it that moths allow themselves to be burnt?"

"They cannot help themselves."

"But that does not really answer the question." Somehow the thought of Jess had reminded Emma of the white moths that came swirling out of the dark to die inside the glass of the coach lamps.

"Only a moth could tell you. They are drawn by the incandescence and lose all caution, that's all I know. Thank God we are away from the crush at last. Now stop being so morbid, my girl. You look like some well-bred infanta, so put on an inscrutable smile and the populace may think *we* are visiting royalty. Raise your head. That's it! Splendid."

It was impossible not to be happy, with the new gown to give her confidence and her father putting himself out to please her. They stopped to buy Jess a basket of oranges and a blue ribbon the color of her extraordinary eyes, then continued toward Hyde Park past rows of ivory-colored, flat-fronted houses, glimpses of mews where the little dwellings were of brick, past doors with lion's-head knockers and windows that curved out like a bow and were glazed with bottle glass that Emma considered very beautiful in the same magical fashion as silhouetted chimney pots at night with the stars around them.

Hyde Park Ring was utterly splendid. The green grass and heavily foliaged trees made a perfect backcloth for the train of carriages and gleaming horses, the jewel colors of women's silk gowns and nodding plumes, the severe black and white of shirts and habits as mounts picked their way delicately or pounded down the Row to draw the attention of passersby. The Horse Guards' scarlet and gold vied with the Garter Knights and the cuirasses of the Russian Emperor's bodyguard.

Emma, her stomach muscles clamped tight with excitement, craned out to look the better into a carriage containing a woman with red hair and a green gown with white ribbons, her face shadowed with mystery under a jade parasol. A man on a horse drew alongside and leaned forward to speak to her. The woman looked in the direction of his pointing finger, and, incredibly quickly, his other hand dipped into her reticule and came out again palming a bulging purse which disappeared into his wide coat pocket. The woman turned back, laughing, just as the horseman became aware of Emma's horrified stare.

He had a longish face, bony and suntanned, and his hair was brown. His coat was well cut and a shade of dark green that complemented the woman's dress. Thin, well-shaped lips formed a guarded smile which Emma was unable to return.

Before the girl could decide what to do, both vehicles passed each other. Looking back she saw that the lean-faced man watched her over his shoulder, his eyes as cold as glass. She colored hotly, her mouth primmed with disapproval. He grinned engagingly, and she was both annoyed and distressed to find that the reflex awoke a response.

The red-haired woman called out, "Ringan! You're incorrigible. Women will be your downfall, but I suspect you know that." The rest of her badinage was lost in the wheels' rumble and the huzzahs of the crowds. Emma, unable to take her eyes from the man, watched the slim back until it was gone from sight. Relapsing into her seat she pinched herself to make sure it had not been a dream. But it was not. Her arm tingled. She had witnessed the smoothest robbery one could imagine. Her mind refused to forget the slender, surprisingly clean fingers, dipping, extracting, pocketing the plump purse while everyone's attention was on the display. All but hers.

"You're quiet, Emma," Wildford commented. "Does your back trouble you? We can go back to the hotel."

"No. If we go on we should meet all the people we have already passed, shouldn't we?"

"Yes."

"Let us have one more circuit then." Perhaps there might be some way in which she could tell the red-haired woman she'd been relieved of her money and valuables. She could inform her father but found she was disinclined to do so. They may never see the couple again, then the explanation would be useless.

A great train of horsemen had appeared from the direction of Kensington Palace, and Emma, seeing how close they passed by the carriages and the Emperor's entourage, was conscious of a premonition of danger.

People were crying out in the resulting crush. The Master of the Horse was unseated, his face white with shock and the proximity of dancing hooves. Horses backed toward the Wildfords' carriage, thrusting against the varnished panels, pushing it in juggernaut fashion to a dangerous tilt. Women were screaming, and carriages approaching on the other side of the Ring were driven out of the way of the approaching menace by sweating grooms and postilions.

Emma, who had been leaning out, half thrilled, half fearful of the power of the jostling equine bodies, was tossed onto the ground, sand flung into her mouth and eyes. She spat and rubbed away the fine grit, then stared in horror at the bulk of the vehicle which leaned at a drunken angle above her. There was a creaking that presaged disaster and she knew she must move but could not. Inside the carriage, her father dared not move in case the vehicle tilted in the wrong direction. She could well imagine his agony of mind.

A face she recognized looked down at her. It was the man called Ringan. His eyes surveyed her coolly as though he meant to make her wait for her previous disapproval. The coach seemed to tilt even farther and she wriggled frantically, her elbows scored with the painful grit, the shadow of the vehicle seeming to pursue her like some relentless ogre.

The man slid to the ground and smacked his mount's rump so that it cantered to safety. Then he came forward cautiously and took Emma by the armpits to pull her to a dubious safety, standing her on her feet to brush the sand from her gown. Incredibly, he went forward to the carriage, setting himself against the steeply slanting panels, pushing and cajoling until, with a startling abruptness, the conveyance shot upright, rocked crazily, then subsided to a normal position. But the horses still plunged and reared. She could have been under those hooves if Ringan had not dragged her clear.

"Are you well?" Ringan asked softly.

She nodded. "Why did you steal the purse?" she whispered, her back to Wildford. "Return it and I'll say nothing."

"Purse?"

She touched the pocket where she had seen him place it after the theft but it was empty.

"It was a game," Ringan said. "The lady's a friend. I need to keep my fingers supple for pistols and card play. Dipping pockets is good practice."

"You only put it back because I saw you." Emma discovered that she was shaking and that her shoulders hurt under the bandage. "That's the real answer, isn't it? Because you were found out?"

Ringan shook his head. Wildford appeared by her side, his arm sliding tightly around her waist. "I must thank you, sir. Had the carriage tipped any farther, Emma must surely be dead. I owe you a debt of gratitude impossible to repay. To whom do I owe so much?"

"My name's Ringan. Captain Ringan. She's a plucky miss. No tears. No vapors."

"That's not Emma's way. I must talk with you. Dine with us at our hotel. We must not lose touch—"

"I'm afraid I have an appointment—"

"Tomorrow, then?"

"Not even then. I'll be out of London for a time. But I was glad to be of service." His coat, Emma noticed, emerging from shock, was not only well cut but a little shabby.

"You must promise me then, that should you ever be in the vicinity of Norwich, you'll be sure to come to Wildford's Bank. Wildford's."

"You are Mr. Wildford?"

"I am. You will ask for me and say you are a friend who, under no circumstances, must be turned away."

"Very well," the captain murmured. "I should be pleased to call. Sometime."

"Are you not going to say your thanks, Emma?"

"Of course. Thank you." She could not believe a word the man said, yet he had saved her life. If it had not been the coach crushing her, it would have been death or mutilation by trampling. She put out her hand and Ringan gripped it briefly.

The lady with red hair opened her reticule and took out the purse, extracting a gold piece. "For your bravery, child."

"I really could not," Emma said. "It's your friend who was brave. Not I."

"As you please." The woman smiled and put away the coin. She had a satisfied look like a newly fed cat.

All the sounds of the day rushed back into Emma's hearing. The conveyances began to move again now that the excitement of the rescue was over. "Good luck to you, little miss!" a man shouted emotionally.

"Good-bye," Ringan said and cantered on his way.

"Come," Wildford ordered and lifted Emma carefully onto the carriage seat while the trees quivered in the breeze that had sprung up out of nowhere.

Jess Ashcroft was looking better when they returned. She thanked Emma for the fruit and the blue ribbon, then remarked on the new gown. "Suits you better than that babyish one, Miss Emma."

"Were you well looked after?" Emma was pleased with the compliment.

"Never 'ad so much attention. Piece of chicken for me dinner. That's a laugh!"

"And did the doctor call?"

Jess grimaced. "'Urt me proper, 'e did. But it's better now."

"We saw the Russian Emperor. The Czar."

"Did you now! What was he like?"

"Tall, with a round face and slanty eyes, and hundreds of cossacks, all with lances."

"Wish I'd seen that." Jess sat up, her breasts, astonishingly mature, straining against the white nightgown.

"Well, young lady," Wildford said from the doorway, "you seem somewhat recovered."

"Oh, I am, sir." Jess seemed unconscious of her provocative attitude. "It'd take more than a thrashing to lay me low. Me pa had a heavy hand. Had a rope wi' a knot in it, too. Glad to get away from home, I was."

"There'll be no rope at Norwich. But you must take great care of Miss Emma and do your work properly."

"I will, sir, I promise." Jess's eyes were suddenly luminous with tears, sparkling like jewels in the sunlight from the window. "Good to me, you've been."

"It's been an eventful trip," Wildford said. "Rescuing you from Amelia's. Then Emma delivered from an unpleasant mishap in the park. What else can happen?"

"I'm sure I don't know," Jess replied, in no sense awed by the fact that Wildford was her employer. Emma experienced a moment of anger. She did not understand herself. It was just that she was still shaken from the accident and Papa was obviously disinclined to leave Jess's bedside.

"Shall we not go to supper, Papa?" Emma asked sharply.

"What? Oh, supper. I daresay you're right. Good night, then, Jess Ashcroft."

"Good night, sir." Jess lay back, smiling. She really was going to be a beauty.

When they got downstairs to the dining room Wildford told his daughter, "I've a mind to go out this evening."

"Shall we go to the Sadler's Wells? Isn't that where Grimaldi is appearing? You did say—"

"Well—I think I may reserve Grimaldi for another night. I've a mind to look up a friend or two. The Frys at Mildred's Court, perhaps, though Joseph and Elizabeth will be at Plashet. You remember Mrs. Fry, my dear?"

"Yes, Father." Emma had a picture of a lady in a white Quaker cap with one or two small children in attendance. Mrs. Fry had been one of the Gurneys of Norwich, daughter of a well-known banking family, who had married into another. But the Frys were not Papa's cup of tea since he had no liking for Quakerism and it surprised her that with all the distractions London had to offer, he turned to acquaintances for diversion.

"And I think you should rest after the incident in the Ring. Combined with the blow from your grandpapa's cane, you've had sufficient to tire you."

She did not believe him any more than she'd trust Rin-

gan. Pushing away the remains of her pudding, she said,
"I'll go upstairs now, I think."

The relief in his eyes hurt her beyond measure but she returned his smile, then ran up to her room and looked down
into the street. A sedan chair disgorged a gentleman in
black, another, a lady with powdered hair and a beauty spot.
And then Wildford came down the steps and onto the pavement. There was a woman hanging onto his arm and laughing up into his face. Her laughter was too loud and she
showed too much bosom, but Wildford seemed well
pleased. He bent his head and kissed his doxy on the lips
then pushed a gold piece down the cleft between her
breasts. At least he would not have done that if she were
anyone who mattered. Emma jammed down the corner of
the curtain violently.

But her spirits lightened as she returned to Jess's room. A
woman of that type would be a transient figure in her father's life. And Mrs. Craven at Norwich would have plenty
to say if Wildford took her back with him. Wildford's mistress was reputed to be jealous according to Cook. If only he
had not lied to her about visiting the Frys. That was what
had upset her most.

Jess was pleased to see her. "It's been dull all day."

"Dull? Being waited on hand and foot?"

"I'm used to being busy. Time can hang heavy."

"It wouldn't for me. I'd lie in bed and think. Imagine
things."

"You been taught. Anyway, rather do things, I would.
Not much use dreaming for a girl like me. I tell you, Miss
Emma, I'm fair *itching* to be up and about."

"Father says you must stay there for the time being."

"Nice gentleman, your pa. Won't never forget how he
treated me like a lady."

"Ever," Emma corrected. "Won't ever."

"But I means never—"

"Then you must say *will* never."

"If you say so." Jess frowned.

"I do say so. If you're to be a lady's maid you must be grammatical. You'll have to address quite a number of strangers when I go visiting, as I shall now that I am older. And you'll have to accompany me to shops and when I go riding in the country lanes and to church."

"Oh. Your pa said you'd had something unpleasant happening to you in the park. What did he mean?"

"The Czar's entourage was crushed by a great troop of horse and people were flung off their mounts. Our carriage was all but overturned and I was thrown onto the ground." Emma shivered, disliking the remembrance. "The horses would have trampled me but for a man who rescued me just in time."

Jess's eyes gleamed. "Was he dark and handsome?" She clasped her hands around her knees, then made a face as the movement hurt her lacerated back. "Like your pa?"

"Not at all," Emma said sharply. "I should call him rather thin and nondescript."

"You sound as if you don't like the gent."

"I don't. But one always has obligations toward someone who saves one's life."

"Will I ever see him?"

"I daresay. Papa has told him to come anytime to Norwich. An open invitation."

"Why don't you like him?" Jess asked. "It's plain as a pikestaff you don't relish him turning up like a bad penny. It can't be 'cos he's thin and ordinary."

"Because he's a thief and a liar and I detest both."

"How come you know so much about him?" Jess queried shrewdly.

"I just do." Emma's tone was not forthcoming.

"I thought you'd be going out with your pa."

"He had—to see a friend."

"Then stay and help me eat these oranges."

"They were for you. Because you were not well."

"But I'd like to share them with you, Miss Emma. Really, I would."

"It's very generous of you, Jess."

"Can afford to be, can't I? Yesterday I couldn't have offered you a crust of bread. But you and your pa saved me from Sir Misery-Guts and Lady Bad-Smell and I got oranges and waited on in bed—"

"Sir Misery-Guts and Lady Bad-Smell!"

"She always looks as if there's one just under her nose, specially when I'm around."

"You are naughty," Emma said, then burst out laughing.

The girls looked at each other like conspirators.

She'll be fun, Emma thought and forgot Wildford and Captain Ringan and Maybrick's long, possessive arm. Her occasional doubts—

They seized an orange apiece and began to dig their fingers into the yielding skin. The fragance filled the room.

CHAPTER TWO

In the two years since the accident-fraught visit to London, both girls had developed, Jess physically, Emma mentally. Jess had grown like a succulent fruit, all curves and wide cheekbones, tantalizing lips and thickly curling hair. Added to a ready wit, an infectious laugh and wide blue eyes, she had the entire male staff in love with her in varying ways, not all of them brotherly or paternal.

This, naturally, did not endear her to the female servants who were jealous and backbiting, but Jess, secure in her position as Miss Emma's personal maid, did not care.

Mrs. Bott, the cook, was undoubtedly the most virulent. Strong and sharp-tongued, she aired her views openly and was copied by the maids who were both intimidated by the cook's position of strength and the inordinate length of her memory. No, Mrs. Bott was not one to forget a grudge and it paid to be on her good side.

And it was undoubtedly galling to see the footmen, Harrison and Jackson, vie for the favors of a nobody from London

thrust into the household. Jackson in particular, bull-necked and curly-haired, had a habit of seeming to undress Jess with a look. Emma did not care for the man. His loose, wet mouth repelled her, though she supposed it could appeal to someone else. More than once she had seen him reach out to slap Jess's rump on the stairs but the girl had always pushed him away. Harrison, though sly, was infinitely preferable even if he did talk suggestively of Miss Palsey who was shortly to visit the Wellings and was something of a mystery.

Emma, though drawn to the girl in one way, was irked in another by the fact that wherever she went, attention focused immediately on Jess. It was small-minded, she knew, and she fought against the emotion strenuously, being more than ever generous in some way to her maid after each twinge of resentment. And it was as though Jess knew the reason for the gift. She would smile a little guardedly and sound reluctant to take the discarded gown or the ribbons or strings of beads, though normally she accepted presents joyfully. It was difficult to recall the girl with the darned stockings and run-down heels, her back marked with the cane.

Of course, there were people who looked beyond Jess and found satisfaction in the narrow elegance of her mistress, the straight, gleaming hair with the tinge of blue, the determined mouth that was so like Wildford's with its touch of sensuality.

Emma saw less and less of her father. If he were not busy at the bank he might remain in Norwich to sup with Mrs. Craven, then he was either extremely late or did not bother to return home at all, depending on his mood.

She saw Mrs. Craven in town one morning as she and Jess did some shopping. Previously, all she had known of the woman was her name, spoken in whispers about the stair or in the kitchen. But, as she noted the passerby, a man called out, "Mrs. Craven, ma'am! A good day to you."

Instantly, Emma's idle regard became a sharp scrutiny. Her father's mistress bore no resemblance to the London doxy. She was small, brown-haired, inclined to plumpness. The girl was almost disappointed. Mrs. Craven looked more of a wife than a paramour. If anything, Amelia had more of the appearance of a kept woman, being fond of expensive gowns and jewelry and all those fair curls and ringlets.

It was when Mrs. Craven smiled dazzlingly at the salutation and the combination of lustrous teeth, clear skin and good grooming proved irresistible, that Emma saw what attracted her father. The woman was now aware of the passing carriage and of herself. It was obvious she knew Wildford's vehicle and also his daughter. How often, Emma wondered, had the woman noted her on her visits to Norwich? Ashamed and angry she stared straight ahead, her back straight as a ramrod, conscious that Jess was enjoying her discomfiture.

She nudged Emma once they were past. "Mrs. Craven, eh!"

"What of it?"

"I was thinking she's no one to be afraid of, Miss Emma. Anyone could take your pa away if they'd the mind. She'm plain, really."

"She's. She's plain." Yet Mrs. Craven was nothing of the sort. "You talk as though the entire county wished to entrap my father."

"Lots do, Miss Emma. I'm not blind."

"And I am?"

"Let's say I got me buttons sewn on where it comes to sizing up folks."

"My buttons," Emma said mechanically. What a silly expression it was.

"Wonder how your ma and those grandfolks of yours are?"

"My mother is having something called a divorce. It means she will no longer be married to Papa."

"Divorce! What next! Will he marry the Craven, d'you suppose?"

"Marry a woman like that?" The carriage bounced over a cobblestone.

"Men do marry their fancy pieces. And he's known her long enough."

"Papa will do no such thing," Emma said, disturbed in spite of her insistence.

"Just 'cos you tell yourself he won't, doesn't mean there's no chance."

"Mind your own business, Jess Ashcroft."

"What you want," Jess said, "is someone to take your pa's mind off her, just to be on the safe side. Someone who won't expect no marriage ring."

"Out of the frying pan, into the fire."

"She's reputed jealous, though," Jess went on. "I heard—"

"Kitchen gossip," Emma said crisply. "What do servants know?"

"More'n you think," Jess told her. "There's nothing abovestairs you can hide from the staff. They know the master's habits and all your secrets, Miss Emma. And it wasn't no surprise when your ma went off with Mr. Jeffrey Maybrick, neither."

"What do you mean, my secrets?"

"There's no call to look so put out. There's no one knows anything bad about you. But they all knows you read twelve pages of your book every night and uses a white leather bookmark; which drawer you keep your father's presents in; if there's fruit on the table that you'll take the pear first. How you like the orchard and the summerhouse and which side of the lake you prefer—"

"I seem to be quite transparent."

"And they know you don't forgive your ma for never writing—"

"Enough of my peccadilloes." Emma flushed.

"It's harmless, Miss Emma. 'Tis like being wed. You get to know folks' ways."

"I think it's like being on a dissecting table. I don't want to know their private thoughts and what they do, who they dislike."

"You try to find out about me, Miss Emma."

"Perhaps I do. But it's not prying, it's because I have a genuine interest."

The carriage had left the town and was rolling on between hedges and trees in full leaf. It had been a very wet summer and everything was brilliantly green.

There were small lakes in some of the meadows and the roadside grass was flattened under last night's downpour. The sky had grown perceptibly darker.

"Lucky we're inside." Jess peered from the open window then started back as a large drop of rain fell onto her up-turned nose. "The sky's black as that little nigger of Mrs. Crawley's."

"She treats him like a lapdog so long as it suits her. A different matter when he's past the age for coddling. She'll put him in the cupboard under the stair like that harpy friend of hers." The rain hissed as angrily as Emma's thoughts.

"They don't feel things like we do, Miss Emma. Not niggers. How could they?"

"Do *not* let me hear you say that again, Jess! Of course they have the same nervous system. Everything suffers under ill-treatment. It's only the pigment of the skin that differs."

"How angry you are!" Jess's face was shadowy in the new dimness. "Why?"

"I simply do not agree with spoiling someone while they are small and appealing and then casting them aside when they are older. Not only do they lose their favors but are punished for outgrowing the capacity to captivate without understanding why and how they have offended." The carriage turned into the sodden drive. "It's cruel."

"There's someone ahead. A horseman. He'll be soaked."

"It must be a caller for Papa. He did not mention that he expected anyone."

"And your father's not even at home. It's you will be expected to do the honors, Miss Emma. Don't frighten him off with all those long words you just used on me, will you! Nervous system! Pigment. Sounds like that should be something to do wi' farming. The farmer meant one thing but the pig meant another—"

"Very clever, Jess. Amazing, is it not, that someone so talented should still not have assimilated the simple facts of grammar?"

"It's dull. Anyway, having a pa who beat me so often made me stupid. Clouted me around the head whenever he felt like it and addled my brains for sure—"

"You're shrewd enough when it suits you," Emma retorted.

The carriage had drawn abreast the rider. He turned a pale face down which the steady stream of rain poured dispiritingly. His shoulders were hunched against the downpour. Emma leaned toward him. "Can I help you?"

"This is Mr. Wildford's house?" He indicated the building beyond the fringe of shrubbery. "Staves?"

"It is."

"He asked me to come. An interview."

"Interview?"

"For an opening in the bank. My uncle mentioned my name and Mr. Wildford wrote to me suggesting today. I am a little early but the rain drove me toward shelter." Jess was inclining forward the better to see the stranger and Emma shifted so that the girl's view was blocked. Jess must learn to outgrow her evident curiosity.

"It's true my father will not yet have returned but you must come inside and dry your coat and take tea with me, Mr. ———?"

"Critchley. Lewis Critchley."

"Mr. Critchley."

He looked nice, Emma decided. His features were well drawn without being effeminate and he was not made peevish by finding himself so wet as so many young men might have been under similar circumstances. She liked his mouth with its stubby good-humored corners and the cleanness of his hair. He appeared not to favor powder or a wig.

"Thank you, Miss Wildford."

Once inside, Emma dispatched Jess to the sewing room to finish a task begun earlier. It could do her no harm to learn her place, but it was difficult to be as firm as one could wish when they had met in so unorthodox a fashion. That had been unfortunate.

Lewis Critchley, coatless now, sat by the fire that was lit summer and winter in the east-facing sitting room. His clothes were plain to the point of severity but they suited the angular lines of his slim body.

Emma ordered tea and was pleased that she wore a gown that was in no way ornate. Mr. Critchley had, unconsciously, she was sure, the knack of showing up pretension by the nature of his own restraint. He seemed young to exert such a positive influence.

"How are you acquainted with my father?" she asked as she poured the China tea and handed the muffins and small cakes. "I've not heard him speak of you."

"I am nephew to Sir Peter Wymark."

"I do know Sir Peter, of course, and Lady Alicia. And Deborah."

"Ah, yes. Deborah." Young Mr. Critchley accepted a piece of muffin and said no more.

Emma was sure that the cryptic utterance meant something. Deborah Wymark had a reputation for having broken more hearts in the Norwich area than any other female. She had something of Amelia Wildford's fragile yet resilient blond good looks, a swan neck that always looked as if it would break under the weight of the silkstraw curls. She wore willow green and magnolia and Dresden blues, yet never looked anemic. Emma, noting Critchley's resolutely downbent gaze, decided that her diagnosis was correct.

"And you think you will like banking?"

Lewis Critchley raised his eyes again and wiped his fingers fastidiously on a spotless handkerchief. "I've a passion for figures and accounts."

"And what of the other side? The wooing of your clients, then keeping them."

"I recognize that the one depends on the other. Your father would have no complaints. I am not easily provoked."

"I did not think you would be. I wish I were as equable but at times my temper runs away with me. Indeed, I fear I may be shrewish, an unpleasant quality."

"Surely you exaggerate?" Critchley smiled charmingly and lifted his cup.

"Not at all." Emma was painfully honest. "But you cannot be interested in my faults."

"Why not? Faults can be more fascinating than virtues. I am always suspicious of those who seem not to have any."

Emma laughed. "I think Papa will like you. But you still have Mr. Tully to contend with. He's a perfectionist and I imagine that in an earlier life he must have been an eagle. He even looks like one. He may even bite like one."

"Thank you for warning me," Critchley said gravely, but he was amused, she knew, with a sudden, unexpected warmth of feeling that was like nothing she had ever known.

"Why are you not a young gentleman of leisure? Most with such connections would be."

"Because I cannot abide being idle."

He should get on with Jess Ashcroft, Emma thought. That was exactly what Jess had said when she was ordered to bed after her beating.

"That sounds like Papa now." Emma ran to the window.

Lewis Critchley rose. He was frowning slightly. "My coat—"

"I'll ring for Jackson."

The footman came almost immediately and was dispatched for the garment. He returned with it over his arm. "It is still slightly damp, sir, but it has been pressed. I will assist you to put it on."

"Thank you." Critchley had just shrugged himself into the coat, which now showed little sign of wear, when Wildford appeared, his cheeks glowing, dark eyes bright.

"Ah, Critchley. I apologize for my lateness."

"I had not noticed. Miss Emma has entertained me very well."

Wildford grimaced. "I'll indulge in something stronger than tea. Thank you, Emma. I'll take my visitor to the study."

"Very well." She tried to hide her disappointment.

"You've done well, child," her father said more encouragingly, and patted her shoulder.

"Oh, Papa! I'm not a child." She shrugged his hand away.

"Parents never notice the fact that one has grown up," Lewis Critchley said. "I experienced the same trouble. When I am fifty my mother will still be fussing over me. I expect you find—" He broke off suddenly as though he remembered Emma had no mother now to control her every action.

"Emma will not have that problem," Wildford said. "We go our own ways. But being open-minded does not mean one must never use an endearment. Some words I find sentimental, but child means what it says, my flesh and blood and therefore special. Come, Lewis."

Critchley bowed. "Again, Miss Emma, my thanks."

She nodded, smiling a little as they moved away. That parting glance had held just the right amount of interest. And Papa had said the most touching thing. Altogether, the past hour had been extremely pleasant. They'd be bound to meet again, she and Lewis Critchley, if he became part of her father's business. Perhaps she could suggest a dinner party sometime.

Emma found Jess biting off a thread on her best gloves. "Have I not impressed on you that threads should be cut off neatly with scissors?"

"Couldn't lay hands on them. But it don't really matter, Miss Emma. It's not going to poison you, my lips touching your gloves, is it?" The vivid eyes were laughing at her, though the mouth was demure.

"The scissors are there. Half under that piece of material. Finish it off properly, please. Really, Jess, I sometimes think—" Emma was struck dumb, partly by the strange look that Jess gave her and partly by the remembrance of that long-ago beating. It occurred to her that Jess had not really needed to be caught so blatantly with the chicken leg. Could she have done it so that the Wildfords would be under an obligation to her? Common sense told Emma that no one in her right mind would seek out such a punishment. But Jess did sometimes make capital out of the obligation and it seemed she understood that Emma was on the point of saying that if she could not learn to be a lady's maid that she must be replaced by someone more amenable. How she would hate to be relegated belowstairs. Emma knew she could not do it.

"Another time, find everything before you start."

"Very well, miss. A nice young gentleman, Mr. Critchley."

"He was."

"Should think he'd do well in the banking business. A real sharp eye to an advantage, that young man."

"Oh? What gave you that impression?" Emma knew she should not encourage the girl but Jess's assessment differed greatly from her own. It could be that she herself was a poor judge of character. She passed Jess the second glove for her attention.

"Keep me eyes open, miss. You weren't looking at him all the time, and he must have known it was your pa's house. It's the only one for miles 'cept for the farm. Then he said he was driven for shelter but he was at the foot of the drive before that sudden rain. Wanted to get you to himself, I should think, so's you'd put in a good word with Mr. Wildford. Expected you to be at home. Knew you'd take a fancy to 'im."

"Is there anything else?" Emma inquired with irony.

"Likes everything perfect, Jackson said. Real fussy about his coat."

"Naturally, he'd not want to be interviewed in his waistcoat and shirt-sleeves if he could help it."

"Beware of fussy gentlemen with a fondness for adding up figures. The figures will always win in the end."

"I thought you said he was nice!"

"Should be very gentlemanly in most ways but I think he'll know how to get his foot over the right doorstep."

"You make him sound like an opportunist."

"Most men are, Miss Emma."

"What a pity you must look forward to such a jaundiced future."

"There you go again!" Jess said irrepressibly and bit off another thread. "Them long words. Lucky I'm used to them."

Emma let herself out of the house. The world was the color of pigeons' wings and there was still the threat of rain in the air. All the newssheets printed stories of the wet summer. It had all been so different when the Czar was in London and people plucked the hairs from the tails of cossack mounts to keep for mementos of the visit. Wildford had taken Emma to the opera and all the women wore white satin and jewels and their escorts uniforms and gold lace. There had been a scandal when the Regent's estranged wife appeared and must be acknowledged by the Russian Emperor while the Prince regarded her with hate-filled eyes. It had been warm and sunny, the way summers were meant to be, not this strange, green dampness that went on until there seemed no other way of life.

As she hurried along the path, she thought of Waterloo and of Lady Caroline Lamb who had tried to engage the attentions of victorious Wellington with the aid of a riding habit the color of aubergines, and Highland soldiers who scandalized the Parisians by wearing kilts. The Peninsular War was long over, and now maimed survivors and soldiers of fortune from France thronged the highways. Miss Hannah More taught poor country children so they might better themselves and Mrs. Elizabeth Fry was engaged in reforming women prisoners in Newgate Jail.

The last seemed, to Emma, the most surprising. A banker's wife and mother of small children seemed the last person to venture into the terrors of prisons. Behind the deceptively quiet facade must live more strength of character than one suspected, seeing the woman in the plain colors and white Quaker cap.

She had been in Mrs. Fry's company on more than one occasion and oddly enough that strength did not seem to extend to the proper discipline of her offspring. She apologized for the failure, yet once away from them and faced by the harlots and thieves and murderesses of Newgate, she was reputed to become a female colossus, insisting upon this reform or that privilege and having her own way. It must be awe-inspiring to be so good and so determined.

Wildford was never intimidated by the benefactress of Newgate. Mrs. Fry always looked at him more in sorrow than anger, as though, he would say, "she regards me as more of a criminal than any she encounters in the debtors' jail." Emma knew that it was Mrs. Craven that Mrs. Fry remembered. But for all that, Wildford respected and liked her even though he always swore she made him feel like a recalcitrant child who must write out his penance every evening. Emma wondered how it must be to enter a room that was filled with women depraved and warped by crime, and fancied a lion's cage must seem safer.

The small lake was sullen under the lavender sky and a spiteful little wind whipped up cat's-paws from the surface. Emma pulled her cape the tighter and let herself into the summerhouse she used as a refuge. She stopped abruptly in the tiny entrance.

"This is my house," someone was saying. "Mine. Mine. All my own. This chair, this table, this book, this rug, these cups, this plate. Everything I can see from the windows. Mine."

There was a sound of feet dancing lightly over the yielding boards and a bubble of laughter, a breathless whisper. "I must have you. They don't need you. That great house to themselves— It's greed to want you as well."

Jess came into view, her arms bent ballerina fashion, a neat ankle showing under the gray skirt and white edge of petticoat. The light died out of her eyes as she saw Emma. Her face became expressionless and she dropped her arms to her sides, but there was no confusion.

"I thought you were pressing my gown for the Wymarks' party," Emma said.

"Didn't mean to be more than a minute. Thought I saw a strange dog and I knew Mr. Welling's sheep were over the fence there."

Her hair was unbound. The dark waves that framed the vital face were soft and lustrous. Emma's heart beat fast as it did whenever her feelings concerning Jess were divided. "I think you came here to meet someone."

"Didn't, miss. It's as I said. I saw the dog. Yellow sort o' creature—"

"Where is it, then?"

"Ran off into the trees."

"Why is your hair loose?"

"Lost me ribbon on the way, but it feels so nice. Why is it only ladies must feel pleasure in their hair and their bodies?" Jess drew her fingers through the silky strands. "Don't rightly seem fair, does it?" A queer little smile touched her lips.

"You said this was your house. That we didn't need it because we had so much."

"It's true, though, and you can't deny it." Jess stared at her boldly, seeing Emma's hesitation. "Didn't mean no harm, Miss Emma. We all have our own dreams—"

"You knew this was a private place for me. You said so, remember? Said all the servants knew. You are allowed more freedom than any of the others, Jess, but you must not abuse the privilege or there will be an end to discipline. The boot boy will think he can ride my father's horse and the cook will want to take afternoon tea in the parlor. Now do up your hair and go back to your duties. I cannot turn you into a lady because you once did me a favor that cost you dear. You make it hard for me, Jess."

"Do I, miss?"

"You know you do. Now do as I say."

There was a long silence, then Jess said, "I hear someone coming. Listen."

Somebody was riding by the lakeside. Emma's heart leaped. If it was not so early, so impossible, she might imagine it was Lewis Critchley. But he would be at Wildford's Bank, sitting at the great ebony desk, oblivious to everything but his calculations.

Emma went to the door. Jess followed, standing behind her shoulder, the cruel, unseasonal wind whipping up her long hair.

The horseman's face was taut and there was a wide scar wandering under the right cheekbone so she did not at first recognize him. When she did she bit her lips with shock.

"Captain Ringan."

He inclined his head. "I went to the farm in error so came across the park to shorten the ride."

"Have you been to the bank?" Emma was aware of Jess's interest and the fact that Ringan included the girl in that close scrutiny.

"I thought I should not interrupt at your father's place of business."

"But he will not be back for hours—if at all," she added, thinking of Mrs. Craven.

"I'd not bother you, but I'm newly returned from France and homeless, and I remembered your father's generous invitation. It's not that I'd want recompense for pulling you out of the way of that carriage. Had I wished to presume, I could have done that long ago—"

"So you're the gentleman who saved Miss Emma!" Jess exclaimed.

He smiled wearily.

"Jess. You are supposed to be pressing my gown for the Wymarks' rout," Emma reminded her. "I suggest you start immediately."

"Very well," Jess said unwillingly and stepped down onto the path in a flurry of tossed skirts and windblown hair. And a backward look that was presumption.

"And tell Cook that some refreshment is needed for myself and Captain Ringan."

"Yes, Miss Emma."

Ringan dismounted. His boots were dusty and his coat shabby. Emma, conscious of his scar, was sorry for him.

"Don't be too sorry," he told her, reading her thoughts. "You did not approve of my sleight of hand two years ago."

"Perhaps I was ungrateful. But, in any case, I would not wish any disfigurement on a human being, however much I disliked what he did."

"It was harmless, Miss Emma. Harmless and stupid. I tried to explain—"

"I think you need restoring. You look tired and hungry."

"To think that probably my only selfless impulse should result in this." He touched the long scar with his fingertips. "I'd rather it had been my leg."

"Impulse?" She closed the door of the summerhouse with a final bang.

"I had been long free of the army. But I was swayed by the tales of poor men to whom the campaign meant something better than their customary ill-use, and the peasants from Ireland who were brave as lions with a dram inside them, so I reenlisted."

"As a mercenary?" Emma did not think it was for the King's shilling.

"An astute young miss, as I recall from the incident in the Ring. Aye, as a mercenary."

"Then—it was not quite so—"

"Selfless?" He laughed without humor. "You would make a good advocate, Miss Emma. There's a piercing direction about your questions and your ability to have them answered."

"I always like to know the truth."

"I should have remembered that. You were most condemnatory of my filching—"

"That's in the past."

"Along with my arm. Not that I'm quite defenseless."

"True, Captain Ringan. I'll have your horse tended. We pass the stable."

He bowed. "At your service." They began to walk back toward the larger building.

The mount removed to a stall, they entered the house and found the fire burning brightly in the morning room. Emma dispatched a maid for the victuals and wine for the captain and motioned him to sit by the blaze.

"The worst of this weather is that the bones are never warmed," Ringan complained, holding his thin fingers to the flames. The scar became a thin, rose-colored river meandering below the dark-ringed eye. And Emma noticed something odd about his eyes. One was darker than the other though both were blue. The pale eye transfixed her.

"How—?" She motioned toward his face. "Or do you prefer not to talk of it?"

He shrugged, and for a moment his mouth was bitter. "What difference, now?"

"I should not have asked."

"You thought, maybe, that there was some tale of valor?"

"I thought that if I knew, I should not say the wrong thing at some future date."

"Have you always been so correct?" He looked more at peace now that he was warmed and relaxed in the warmth of the cosy room, yet there was still a hint of abrasion.

It was not like the time she had entertained Lewis Critchley in Wildford's absence. Then, there had been a feeling of ease; now there was a tension that was all too evident. The thought of Lewis reminded Emma of the Wymarks. Critchley would be at the rout and she looked forward to the renewal of their acquaintance more than she'd admit.

"What do you know of the campaign?" Ringan asked, and drew a finger down the dust on his boot.

"Little. Just that Blücher carried the day at Waterloo. Napoleon had made up his mind that the general was still licking his wounds after La Hay Sainte but that was his great mistake."

"You make it sound so clear-cut, my dear Miss Emma. Whereas it was all so messy. If you can imagine the incessant reek of burnt cartridges and gunpowder, the dead and dying. The dead were luckiest. I saw a rifleman minus legs and arms yet still with life in him, and the woods were full of mist and rain and bullets. There was not a tree trunk left unscarred. And I can never forget the sight of the Guards' bearskins suddenly rising, like a row of animals, from a dusky cornfield. They frightened me, never mind the enemy—"

Emma let him talk on, recognizing his necessity to speak, and Anna brought in the food and drink so that Ringan could satisfy his all too evident hunger between the snatches of reminiscence.

"It was at La Belle Alliance that I saw that the French were dropping their arms and running, and I lost my caution. There must always be a last shot and it seems I had it. A great thud across the side of my face, a feeling of surprise, my senses reeling, then waking to a searing pain from the hot iron. So now you have the whole sorry tale, Miss Emma, and it don't matter if you ever make a gaffe. Nothing else could ever matter, you see."

Emma could see. The day at the Ring returned with all its color and excitement. Once more, the redheaded woman's carriage bowled along in the sunshine, the reticule lying in the shadow of the green parasol. And Ringan's hand snaked down with incredible swiftness to snatch away the fat purse. Only, now the sunshine was gone and Ringan was tired and the darting hand was buried in his lap.

"I'm sorry," Emma said huskily.

"Too late. The milk's split. But I can still ride and still shoot. There must be some work I'm fit for. Eh, Miss Emma?" His grin was a travesty.

"I'm sure there must be something." So long as it had nothing to do with money or valuables!

"I'm exhausted," he said and now his lips were white.

"It's a long time since Waterloo," Emma pointed out, rising to tug the bellpull. "What have you done since then?"

"I took a fever after being shot and was looked after by a French widow. She—didn't want to part with me, but I had this feeling of nostalgia after a time—"

"I see. Oh, Anna, could you have a bed made ready for the captain? The Gray Room, I think. It's quiet there."

"Do you not think it's taking a risk to entertain a complete stranger? I could have come to murder you," Ringan said when Anna had gone.

"Do you take me for a complete fool? If you look outside you will find at least two footmen in the corridor. My father made that a condition of my so-called emancipation. I did not care for the idea originally but came to see that it was necessary in a world that is full of cutthroats and footpads. The usual aftermath of a war, I am told."

"And returned mercenaries?"

"Those, too."

He groaned suddenly. "Oh, God! I'm so tired."

"Then you must sleep. You'll find soap and water in your room. Jackson will clean your clothes if you wish. I'll send him to you."

"I warn you. I may snore round the clock."

"It will not matter. The room's not required."

"You've been kind, Miss Emma. I hope your father will not send me back with a flea in my ear."

"Why should he when it was he invited you? He's often said our meeting was too short to express his real gratitude and how he wished things had been different."

"But you did not feel the same."

"No."

"Your honesty hurts like the point of a knife."

"I may retract if you give my father good service."

"Then I am on trial."

"As far as I am concerned, yes."

"I see I must be on my best behavior. Old soldiers have a habit of ending up on muck heaps, begging in alleys—"

"I hope that does not happen to you. By the way, Captain Ringan, what became of the lady with red hair? The one who offered me money from her purse."

"That lady. Oh, she married someone else a year since."

"When she thought, perhaps, that you lay dead in France?"

He inclined his head.

"And all the time you were with a Frenchwoman who would not let you go. You must tell me, sometime, the secret of your success." As soon as she had spoken, Emma was ashamed of her mockery. It was enough that he had been scarred. Surely she should not grudge him some little comfort? Sometimes she did not like herself.

"The captain's bed is ready," Anna announced in the ensuing silence.

"I'll sleep like the dead," Ringan said, and his smile was like Jess's in the summerhouse, queer and sensual and oddly disturbing. "And don't worry, Miss Emma. I'll tell you my secret, never fear. One of these days—"

His laughter stayed with her long after he had gone.

Ringan had not awakened when Wildford returned. He was still asleep when the household retired. Emma and her father had stood just inside the door of the Gray Room with a lighted candle, but the captain's pallid, unshaven face remained oblivious against the pillow.

Emma lay for a long time, sleepless, then was impelled to go to her father's room to ask what he meant to do for the man. She thought she should advise caution. It was not enough to take Ringan on trust because he happened to be on the spot when she had fallen in the path of a tilting coach and stamping horses. She must tell Wildford about the stealing of the purse and of its surreptitious return. All during supper she had tried to broach the subject, but her sense of obligation and the fact of Ringan's disfigurement had stood in the way like giant rocks.

Putting on her robe, for the cutting wind still mourned around the windows and out of chimney openings, she crossed the room in moonlight, startled briefly by the pale outline of the gown she was to wear at the Wymarks tomorrow night. Jess had hung it up to air properly after the pressing and it moved slightly in the night air.

All the way to her father's bedchamber, Emma cursed herself for a fool. If there were any repercussions from Ringan's appearance, they were Wildford's business and he'd not thank her for waking him from sleep.

But Wildford was not asleep. Her hand was on the door-knob when she heard him say, "I think we should not advertise the fact that you've at last found your way here."

"Don't worry. I shan't say a word."

"Then keep your voice down, wench. Why did you come?"

The girl's voice, softer now, "I thought it was a pity you'd to go as far as Norwich on a night like this. Cold enough to freeze—" Her voice dropped at the end of the sentence, but whatever she whispered amused Wildford, for he chuckled.

There was a silence, then he said in a different voice, "I never imagined— Where did you learn such things? So you'll keep it to yourself. Well, discretion never hurt. If I find you've let this out to Emma, I'll kill you, girl. So long as you know that's taboo." The rest of his murmurings were lost in the thumping of blood in Emma's eardrums.

The quality of the girl's tones had been partially lost through the thickness of the door but Emma could not help thinking about Jess. What was it she had said that afternoon, when Lewis Critchley came riding in the rain? "Mrs. Craven's no one to be afraid of. Anyone could take away your pa if they'd the mind. What you want is someone to take his mind off her, someone who won't expect no marriage ring—"

Emma became aware that her fingers were pressed hurtfully into her thighs. It wouldn't be Jess. Jess Ashcroft was eighteen and Wildford was forty. He'd never take a girl young enough to be his daughter. It could be someone from Welling's Farm. Only there was no one there who was not lumpy and plain, a stout wife and three daughters who were replicas of their mother. Jess had lovely hair, startlingly blue eyes and made no secret of the fact that she thought Wildford attractive. She had unconventional ideas—ideas beyond her station.

Emma blundered away in the direction of her room, all thoughts of Ringan vanished. Once back in bed, she was cold and more than ever wide awake. Desperately, she told herself she must compose herself for sleep, for there would be little tomorrow. Routs had a habit of going on until the small hours, and the Wymarks' were always successful and immensely enjoyable with the cream of the country society there and good food, fine wines and the setting of their beautiful house in its acres of parkland. But the spurious anticipation turned back to gall and wormwood. Why had she expressed her dismay at the thought of Wildford marrying Mrs. Craven? If it was Jess who now shared her father's bed, it was she who had triggered off the event.

She slept eventually, but it was a haunted sleep from which she rose white and drawn and late for breakfast. Wildford had already gone and the dining room was empty. Lewis, Emma thought. She must concentrate on the party and on him. Spirits of pleasure lit the gloom that shrouded her spirits.

Jess was in her bedchamber when she returned. "You didn't ring for me, Miss Emma. I'd have heard."

Emma stared at the girl. She looked much as usual; if anything, more restrained. Certainly not triumphant or arrogant. "I did not feel like company," she replied coolly.

"I hope I've done nothing wrong? The gown is properly done?"

"The gown seems well pressed. Only you can know if you've done wrong. Have you, Jess?" Directness seemed the best tactic.

The blue eyes met Emma's with nothing in their depths but surprise and a little hurt.

"I don't know what you mean, Miss Emma. Truly I don't."

"Did you visit anyone's room last night?"

Jess flushed. "Miss Emma, if Jackson has said anything, it's only wishful thinking. He has tried to make Harrison jealous by—insin—insin—"

"Insinuations?"

"Yes, those. But I'd never misbehave so. You understand me better than that. Don't you?"

"I sometimes feel I know nothing about you at all."

"You know me better than anyone."

Something in Jess's secretive smile infuriated Emma. "I think," she said deliberately, "that you bore me a grudge for what I said in the summerhouse and that, in revenge—"

"Yes?" Jess inquired. "In revenge, I did what?"

The words stuck in Emma's gullet as they were intended to do. "Talking of it will not make it better. But I can mention to my father that I know and hint that you told me."

Jess had turned pale. "Don't know what you're talking about, miss, I'm sure."

"I think you do. I was not spying on my father. It was chance that took me to his door. There was a problem I had to discuss."

"You needn't make excuses to me, Miss Emma. I'm only your maid, remember?"

"It's you, seem to forget."

"I—always thought we were friends."

"I cannot pretend to like you if what I suspect is true. And I am sure it is. I've not forgotten what you said in Norwich."

"I said lots of things in Norwich. How am I expected to remember the one thing you now hold against me?"

"It was the day we met Mrs. Craven."

"All I said was that she was plain! For a fancy woman, that is."

"And that anyone who'd a mind could take him away from her."

"Mr. Wildford, you mean? Whatever should he see in me?" Jess was smiling openly now, everything about her proclaiming that she was beautiful and desirable. A little maggot of envy stirred in Emma's heart. That unbecoming jealousy had not been subdued by all her self-detestation, her only too transparent overtures of appeasement.

"Whatever it was, it was something he'd go to any lengths to keep quiet. As though he were ashamed," Emma pointed out clearly and coldly. "I clearly recall his insistence on secrecy."

The blue eyes blazed. Jess, sheet-white, compressed her lips.

"Then I *was* right. Please go and busy yourself elsewhere. I must have time to think." For a moment Emma was terribly aware of Jess's clenched hands and a suggestion of danger as though the girl would use physical violence against her, then there was only the open door, the diminishing clatter of feet on the servants' stair. She felt a little sick. It would be awkward broaching the subject of Jess Ashcroft's dismissal with Wildford, but it must be done. She could no longer bear to have the girl in the house. Tiredly, she went into the passage.

"Difficulties?" Ringan asked and she started. She had heard nothing of his approach.

Ignoring the question that revealed that he knew perfectly well what had transpired, she said, "So you're awake at last."

"I warned you I'd sleep the clock round."

"Papa could not wait for you to rise. An important client was to come to the bank this morning. He said he'd come back afterward."

"Then I've time to make myself presentable?"

"All you need do is to pull the bell rope in your room. Someone will come."

"Then that's what I shall do." He rubbed his unshaven chin.

"I see Jackson has attended to your clothes."

"And polished my boots to mirrors."

"There's something I must do," Emma told him. "Please excuse me."

"I'm sure you are busy. You are young to be mistress of so large a house."

"If you are wondering why, my mother ran off with another man."

Ringan laughed with genuine amusement. "Your honesty is the kind that kills."

As it had destroyed the bond there once was between herself and Jess.

"I must tell my father about the incident of the purse. You know that."

"Indeed, I see that it is imperative." He bowed formally, amusement lost in gravity.

"It's best you should know."

"The knowledge will hang over my head like Damocles' sword," he murmured.

"He may make light of it once he hears your explanation."

"Perhaps. You're a harsh mistress for a girl of eighteen."

"That's really no business of yours, Captain."

"True. But there's gray between the black and white. So much gray—if you could but see it."

"Excuse me, but as I said, I've much to do."

"Beg pardon for keeping you, Miss Emma." He showed his teeth in the gloom, like a battle-scarred wolf, then walked away, shoulders erect.

I should have been nicer to him, Emma thought uselessly, then went toward the side door that led to the lake and the summerhouse. The threat of rain still oppressed the sky.

She was halfway along the path when she saw the dog at the edge of the wood, a tough, wild-haired creature with yellow fur and a snarling grin that put her in mind of the captain. Emma stopped, irresolute. Jess had been telling the truth, and if she had told it then, could she not now be trusted? I should have been nicer, Emma thought again, knowing it was too late.

The dog seemed to melt into the wood's shadows like the essence of Ringan.

"How quiet you are, Emma," Wildford said, his dark face

thoughtful. His white shirts always looked whiter than anyone else's, she reflected.

"I did not sleep well last night."

"Any particular reason?"

"Captain Ringan," she began.

"Oh, you need not worry any further. We've come to an agreement. I did not tell you that Tom Hunt wanted to go back to Cornwall, did I?"

"No."

"He lost heart after Ellen died and his lass wed a cousin close by Polperro and has a bed for her father and a place in her husband's pilchard boat. He wants to be near, and there's a grandchild on the way. There's Tom's cottage and Tom's job and the captain can cope with the best of them it seems."

"And will that content him? He seems well-educated—" Emma was doubtful.

"He'd no mind for any indoor post and I'll make sure he's well paid for his factoring. He's no family left and no money. Told me he'd gambled it away and damn me if I wasn't struck by his honesty! Almost admitted he'd a shady past but that's none of my affair. He's paid for that with his wound and with rescuing you. Can't forget an obligation like that."

"We know nothing about him—" So Ringan had forestalled her!

"What's there to know more than he's already said? The man's a rogue, doubtless, but he's not concealed that. Can't help liking the fellow. There's little he can steal but rabbits and birds and he's welcome to those if he keeps trespassers off the estate. He's useful with that pistol of his. Should strike terror to the hearts of the local poachers and, more to the point, the riffraff that pass by now the war's finished."

"You've made up your mind, then?"

"I have. Where's your sense of gratitude?"

"I think he will not always be satisfied with the woods and that poky house."

Wildford yawned. "We must let time decide. Anyway, enough of Ringan. I wish the Wymarks' rout had been any night but this. I'm weary."

"Did you not sleep well?" Emma asked and watched for his reaction.

Wildford laughed and his mouth took on a curve of satisfaction. "Well enough. Once I got to sleep."

There was no way to ask him what she wanted to know.

"You'd best go and pretty yourself, child. I daresay I can put on a show of enjoyment for your benefit. Can't disappoint you now."

"Will Mr. Critchley be there?"

"So I believe. Wymark told me Lewis was taken with Deborah. He was not often down in these parts, for his parents lived mostly in London, but on those few occasions he must have made some headway with the girl. She's not encouraged a beau for some weeks now."

Emma's heart beat faster. "But that need not mean that he loves her. It could be a cousinly affection." She thought she disliked the Wymarks' daughter.

"Can you imagine any man having a cousinly affection for Deborah Wymark?"

"No," she answered ruefully.

"Of course, Wymark could be wrong. Lewis never mentions the wench. But I suspect he's secretive. Tully abhors him."

"Because he does not work well? That amazes me."

"Because he works too well. Tully wants never to retire but now he sees a finger writing on the wall, telling him his days are surely numbered. Critchley's made for advancement."

"A man can be too long in the same place. It cannot be right to bar the way for younger men."

"Someone should say this in Parliament," Wildford growled.

"You say it," Emma smiled suddenly.

"You should smile more often," her father told her. "Now go and get Jess to fasten you into that gown of yours."

"There was something I had to mention about Jess," Emma forced herself to say. "And now I do not want to."

Wildford leaned back in his chair. "Well? What is it?" His gaze refused to meet hers.

"We do not get on as we used to. She—presumes upon our friendship and I fear it may undermine discipline. I think we should provide her with a reference and let her find another position. I know people myself who would be glad to employ a girl from this household."

"You make it sound a cold-blooded business."

"A truthful one. I can no longer even like her and I fear in case I do her some injustice because of it. She needs someone older who will not put up with her nonsense."

"A sudden decision." Wildford got up abruptly and prowled around the room.

"Only to you. I have tried to say this for some time and only today found the courage."

"Courage? You've never lacked that."

"Opportunity, then."

"Or whim. You've had some tiff and tomorrow you'll be round each other's necks again."

"*No*, Father! Not this time."

"That's decided enough. And the only reason is that she's grown high-handed?"

"The only reason. What other should there be?" Her surprise was convincing.

Wildford shrugged. "None that I know of. The servants are your business."

"Then let me do as I suggest."

"Another post, then, in the house?"

"It would not be fair to Jess to turn her into a chamber-maid or to the parlor. She's learnt her own job well."

"I think you'll regret it in a week."

Emma shook her head.

"Perhaps you should put the matter from your mind for a day or two."

"Only till the weekend, then, but I know my own mind. As you usually do."

"You're an arrogant hussy, Emma, and heaven help the man who gets you."

She flushed then, thinking of Lewis, and hoped Wildford had not noticed. He had not, being too absorbed in thoughts of Jess Ashcroft.

Upstairs, she rang for the girl and Jess came silently. It seemed strange that once they had laughed and chatted and teased. Emma experienced a sensation of loss but she could not change her mind. Some could live lies and pretend friendship but she was not one of these. Hardly a word passed between them and all were necessary. If the strokes of the silver-backed brush hurt her scalp, they must be her penance for her jealousies and for passing judgment.

"Is it true," Jess asked once the awkward toilette was finished, "that the captain is to take Tom's place and live in his cottage?"

"Quite true."

"That's what they said downstairs."

"Someone has been listening at doors," Emma said.

"We all do that at some time or other," Jess pointed out sulkily. "Even you."

Sharp words rose to Emma's lips and were forced back. She would not have to tolerate Jess for much longer and she'd not let the girl provoke her into an unseemly quarrel.

"That will do, Jess," she said calmly. "I shall not need you again this evening."

"Am I not to go with you to the Wymarks?"

"There's no need. I can manage perfectly well."

"I was looking forward to it. Meeting all the other maids and footmen—"

"I'm sure you were. But you should have thought of that earlier, shouldn't you?"

"Mr. Wildford will expect me to go with you. It's custom."

"I don't think he will. I told him I'd not need your services for much longer and he agrees that it's best. You will receive a reference, of course—"

"Damn your reference!" Jess was panting with rage.

Her voice must be heard all over the house, Emma thought uneasily.

"All right," Jess said, and now she was dangerously quiet. "All right, Miss Wildford. You'll be sorry. Really sorry—" And she ran from the room.

The house was unquiet. Footfalls, the wind around the gables, rain on the windows and a mutter of thunder. Emma was trembling.

"Emma! Emma? Aren't you ready yet?" Wildford sounded impatient.

"Coming, Father." She took one swift look in the mirror to see herself strange and bridal in the pale dress, her black hair braided into a coronet, then she snatched up her velvet cloak. The worst was over. Wildford knew and Jess knew that her time was running out. Emma began to descend the wide staircase.

CHAPTER THREE

Every window in the Wymarks' house blazed with light. The rain that streamed down the carriage glass distorted the yellow oblongs into shifting shapes and the crouched trees were sinister. Emma, consumed by a feeling of wickedness, found that her anticipation had turned to Dead Sea fruit. Jess's face kept appearing in the shadows inside the coach, first angry then reproachful.

Wildford sat beside Emma, saying little, the proximity of his large body less comforting than usual. She knew that he was not pleased that she intended to discard the Ashcroft girl after two years of apparent closeness. It was circumstantial evidence, after all. The thickness of a door altered voices. It was only because Papa and his night visitor had been standing close to it that she had heard the gist of the conversation that had petered out into whispers and murmurings.

It was Jess, Emma told herself, and the cold lump in her chest became still heavier.

Footmen appeared with large umbrellas and they were es-

corted inside the hall that was floored in white marble and
paneled halfway to the intricate plaster ceiling. In spite of
the rain and wind, the house was warm enough. Emma's
cloak was removed and she and Wildford, splendid in dark
coat and embroidered waistcoat, were announced at the
fine double door that led to the ballroom. There were candles in gilt sconces shedding their uneven light onto powdered shoulders and shining materials, taut bosoms and
piled wigs, crossed legs and tapping feet, buckled shoes.

Lady Rayleigh was there, her harsh, high-cheekboned
face raddled, hair impossibly red, brows drawn in thick and
black so that she looked clownish. She was holding court
near the fire, and Lewis Critchley and Deborah Wymark
were in the small gathering. Deborah was dressed in mis-
tletoe green and her hair had a silvery fairness that should
have been overshadowed by so much positive color and vi-
tality, yet was not. The curls reminded Emma of new wood
shavings. If one pulled them out they would spring back
into shape immediately. Everything about Deborah echoed
this resilience. She was a strong girl who gave an impression of fragility and this seemed to be what drew men to her
side, for they fought for a place like dogs shut out from a
hearth on a cold night.

She smiled prettily at Emma and more intimately at
Wildford. She must learn to be more subtle, Emma thought,
even as she returned the smile.

Emma, noting the afterthought, turned her attention toward Critchley. He was plainly dressed, as usual, though
his clothes were of good quality and well cut. His hair
shone and was cut fashionably short so that it framed his
face. She still hankered after the good-humored, stubby
mouth. But he did not look at her, only went on with his
chat to Lady Rayleigh. Perhaps he was not aware that they
had arrived, yet how could that be when they had not only
been announced, but saluted by Deborah?

She took Wildford's arm and they joined the fringe of the group around Lady Rayleigh.

"What a pretty dress," Deborah said. "White is so virginal." Her purring voice grated.

Emma, who was not feeling virginal, said, "I notice you never wear it."

Deborah's eyes widened. "I always think it is so unenterprising. Every young girl favors it."

"I cannot agree with you that it is unenterprising. Color can be overdone. Is that champagne? I should love a glass, Papa."

"Shall I come back with a brace of swords?" he asked.

"That will not be necessary," Deborah said, laughing. "A friendly spar, is that not so?"

"Very friendly," Emma agreed without amusement. "Please fetch the champagne. I think I need it."

"You'd never think that this girl had been looking forward to this evening for days," Wildford said. "What's wrong, Emma?"

"Nothing is wrong. I didn't sleep well. I suppose I'm bad-tempered."

"You suppose! Champagne for you, Deborah?"

"Yes, please."

Wildford strode away and Deborah asked, "Have you a bad conscience, Emma?" Her eyes were curious.

"I don't think so," Emma replied with an effort, repressing a desire to tweak one of those immaculate curls. "Do not feel you must talk to me out of politeness. I will quite understand if you wish to welcome someone else."

"Really!" Deborah retorted. "You are very odd tonight. I can't imagine why you bothered to come."

"Neither can I." Emma, aware of her intolerable rudeness, felt a coldness in the pit of her stomach. She'd never be asked here again and then she might seldom set eyes on Lewis Critchley. So far, Papa had not risen to her bait concerning a dinner party at Staves. Swallowing her pride, she muttered, "I'm sorry, Deborah. I really do feel out of sorts and it's an effort to make small talk. Forgive me?"

"Of course." Deborah could afford to be magnanimous. She turned away to speak to a new arrival.

Wildford returned and Emma seized her glass thankfully.

"You'd best be careful," her father warned. "That stuff has a kick to it. Where's that Wymark girl? Ah, well, I can always drink it myself. Is it because of Jess, this attack of black dog? I told you you'd not do it when it came to the moment—"

"I've not changed my mind." The champagne was doing pleasurable things to her senses and Lewis Critchley was coming toward her. Though his nose was a trifle long it did not detract from his looks. Rather, it gave him a look of breeding. Yes, he was like a thoroughbred horse, she decided, caught on a pendulum between happiness and regret.

"Emma—" Wildford began, then Critchley was there, bowing, seemingly well pleased to see her.

"Miss Wildford."

"Mr. Critchley."

"Will you dance with me? With your permission, sir."

"With pleasure." Emma drained her glass and gave it to her father who took it silently. She saw his face as they moved off, remote and scowling, and the misery came bubbling up through the content she felt with Lewis, spoiling that gladness. Damn Jess Ashcroft and her temerity! How dare she set her cap at Wildford, whatever her motive? She had put a wedge between them that might never be removed.

"You look sad," Lewis told her.

"No, I'm not."

"You said that most defensively."

"If you say so. Tell me, what was so interesting about Lady Rayleigh? You seemed so engrossed."

"Her money is what held me spellbound."

"You are not—contemplating—marrying her?"

Lady Rayleigh's overbearing voice, which could be heard so readily above everyone else's, was, people said, the cause of her husband's early demise. Emma almost forgot the next step in the dance.

Lewis laughed. "My dear Miss Emma! If I were to marry every rich widow with whom I came into contact in the course of your father's business, I'd commit bigamy ten times over."

"But she's with Gurney's Bank and has been from time immemorial."

"I have reason to think she contemplates a change."

"You mean, you have given her reason to think she wishes to turn to Wildford's. How did you do it?"

"Principally, because I do think Wildford's has the most stability. I'd not invite rats onto a sinking ship! Rather, I'd follow them to safety. I have come to know Lady Rayleigh from my visits here—"

"And not only her." The champagne had made Emma bold.

"And what is that supposed to mean?"

The sensation of drifting over the marble floor of a palazzo had taken hold of her quite strongly. Staring down, Emma could see parquet flooring but her feet did not seem to touch the ground. If this was what champagne did for you, she would simply have to have more. "Deborah is what I mean."

His face changed. If it were not so ridiculous she could imagine she read contempt in its boyish smoothness. "She's my cousin and I'm fond of her. Naturally."

"Naturally."

"Miss Wildford—" He was looking pleasant again and his mouth was tempting.

"Emma."

"Emma. Do I understand that you are—?"

"Jealous? I suppose I am. I'd not be saying this but for the champagne. It makes me feel that I am flying—" She'd regret her candor tomorrow! Emma laughed unheeding.

"You are very light on your feet. And your eyes are brilliant."

"And those sconces are swimming by like—yellow jellyfish."

"I hate to say this but your father looks quite murderous."

"Let him!" They were dancing past Lady Rayleigh who had assumed the aspect of a large, red rocking horse. Lewis looked more than ever like a thoroughbred. Emma was proud of him.

"Another girl to break in, I suppose," Lady Rayleigh boomed. "It takes time to train a lady's maid."

"Why not someone older?" another woman suggested, fanning herself against the heat.

"Older women are usually satisfied with their position. Anyway, they are inclined to be set in their ways—" The loud voice receded as Lewis guided Emma toward the far side of the room.

"Do I understand Lady Rayleigh seeks a lady's maid?"

"I believe she did say something of the sort earlier. With much talk of ingratitude."

"Perhaps you will introduce me later?"

"I should not have thought you'd have a great deal in common with her ladyship?"

"It's not that. I know a girl who could fit the bill."

"Indeed?"

"My own maid. Jess Ashcroft."

"That pretty girl with the blue eyes? I should not have thought you the kind of person to relinquish servants without good cause, and Lady R will lead her a dog's life."

"This valse is quite agreeable, is it not? As you say, Mr. Critchley, I could not do it if it were not necessary."

"Then—if you have cause for complaint—should you recommend her to another?"

"I've no grumbles about her work. But she takes advantage because we are of an age and the rest of the servants follow her example." It was not true about the rest of the staff, yet, but she could not bear to be diminished in his eyes. She had never knowingly lied to anyone before.

"And you think an older, more forceful woman would cure her of the fault?"

"I'm sure of it." How horrid guilt felt. But it was not all falsehood—

"And that is why you looked so upset when I first saw you this evening?"

"Yes. My feelings were divided."

The strains of music were unbearably captivating. Emma closed her eyes so that all that existed was the sensuous sound and the feel of his arms around her.

She felt ill in the carriage going home. Groaning, she put her head out of the window and let the cool night air lick her face. Now that the rain had dried, the white moths had come, to fry in the deadly candle flame. Dimly she perceived a connection between herself and Lewis Critchley, he the candle, she the moth.

"I told you you should not have taken the second glass," Wildford said bad-temperedly. "Insidious stuff, champagne, especially on top of that buffet."

"Oh, Father! Don't—"

"And what possessed you, to deliver Jess Ashcroft to that dreadful woman?"

"That woman is to become your client, thanks to Lewis Critchley. You'll enjoy having all that money gathering interest, will you not?" She could not resist the dig.

Wildford grunted and pulled out a cigar.

"Please! Not tobacco smoke," Emma pleaded. "I'm wretched enough."

"You are far too headstrong for your own good," he grumbled.

"Then we are two of a kind."

"I'm tempted to put you over my knee. Perhaps I should have done it years ago."

Emma put her head out of the window again. The nausea receded. But her present misery could not totally obliterate the raptures of the earlier evening. The music was echoed in the tossing trees. The buttoned interior of the carriage enclosed her like Lewis's arms. She had imagined that fleeting expression of contempt or it was there for some reason far removed from her own behavior. It could not have been for her.

She wished she had not been told that the Wellings had that smart second cousin from Peterborough paying a visit. Vera Palsey continued to come two or three times a year though no one had been able to fathom why. The Wellings were dull folk and the farm was not overcomfortable. Miss Palsey was slim, pretty and dressed attractively in lilacs and mauves and poke bonnets with ribbons around the crown. Father liked his ride round the estate and he must have noticed the girl, spoken to her. Knowing Wildford, Emma was all too aware that he enjoyed feminine society more than most. What if his visitor had not, after all, been Jess, but Vera? The Wellings retired early and slept heavily. The opportunity was there. Wildford could have admitted her into the house by assignation.

If she had not had a bad conscience when Deborah asked her, Emma had one now. But she had already arranged for Jess to go to the Rayleigh household before Vera Palsey was mentioned, and her ladyship would brook no change of mind. She had told Emma that her coach would arrive at precisely ten o'clock the following day to pick up both Jess Ashcroft and her belongings. Emma could not antagonize a rich client.

I shall have to find someone new, Emma thought, but the reflection had no reality. It was as though it happened to a stranger. The worst of the affair was that she would never know if her suspicions of Jess were correct or if she had misjudged her, and for Emma that was punishment enough.

"I have not been pleased with your behavior tonight," Wildford told her. "First, you are unkind to Jess. Then rude to Deborah. And much too familiar with Critchley—"

"I was enjoying myself! It is not for you to judge familiarity, Father! They say something about glass houses and stones, do they not?"

Wildford reached out and slapped her face. "You presume too much," he said icily. "I have been weak with you because you are my only child and I liked your spirit. But I cannot like you as you are, or, rather, I cannot admire what you do, or fathom why you are behaving so."

Emma, sobered, sat stiff with shock and resentment.

"I do not feel inclined to let that girl go to that beldam—"

"Then you'll lose her business," Emma said flatly.

"I suppose so. And Lewis worked hard for that." Wildford relapsed into a dark silence that lasted till they reached home.

As soon as they entered the house, Emma ran upstairs, her eyes hot with unshed tears. The bedchamber was chill and uninviting and the bed unwelcoming. Normally, Jess would chivy someone into having a fire ready but tonight it had been forgotten and Emma did not feel inclined to rouse anyone from bed.

She sat for a long time, still in her white dress and the velvet cloak, staring out of the window and over the hunched outline of the wood. Shame warmed her. Miss Hannah More worked miracles of goodness in her schools for the poor. Elizabeth Fry redeemed the fallen and the wicked in prisons. All over the country people gave of their time and their resources to set up soup kitchens and the like, while she, Emma Wildford, was irredeemably selfish and bad and could not think how to mend matters.

Someone was tapping on the door.

"Emma? Emma—" Wildford's voice was kept studiously low.

She did not reply.

"Emma?"

Still she did not speak and after a time he went away.

The dog howled from the wood, accentuating her self-inflicted loneliness. She knew suddenly that she could not wait until morning before telling Jess that she was to go to Lady Rayleigh. The girl deserved some warning.

Emma went upstairs slowly. Her head ached abominably. There was only one comfort. Jess had her own room so she'd not need to wake up another girl. She tapped on the door.

"Who is it?"

Jess had not been asleep. She'd answered immediately. Emma entered the bedchamber. There was a piece of candle burning in the stand and the place was faintly warm. Clothes were flung anywhere as though Jess had undressed in a rage. Even the white nightgown could not conceal her splendid shape, the beauty of her breasts. Emma found herself wondering if Jackson had ever found his way here, and, if so, what kind of reception he'd had.

"It's you, miss." Jess sat up, perfectly composed, her eyes dark-ringed. "Have you come to complain of the fire? Didn't think it was my business anymore."

"No, it was not the lack of the fire that brought me."

"Did you think I might have your pa under the bed? You're welcome to look."

Emma shook her head. "Nor that."

Jess sprang from the bed and dragged up the valance to display the chamber pot. "There you are, miss. Best to be sure."

Emma pulled the cloak closer around her. It was going to be more difficult than she'd imagined. "I would have taken your word."

"Not you, Miss Emma! Filled with suspicions, you are."

"I came to tell you that you need not worry about your future."

"Then—I can stay?"

"I have found a good place for you."

Jess's expression changed from hope to resignation. "Quick off your mark, weren't you? Couldn't you abide me one more month?"

"Actually, it was one more day," Emma replied, stung. "You will be called for at ten tomorrow so you must have your box packed in readiness."

Jess took a deep breath. "And who—"

"Lady Rayleigh happened to mention she required a lady's maid—at the rout."

"Just happened!"

"That's how it was, Jess. But you can have no complaints—"

"Oh, but I can, miss. The tales I've heard from her other servants! She's a tyrant."

"All servants' gossip. You told me so yourself. They are prone to exaggeration."

"I shall hate it!" Jess said desperately. "She's a face as hard as a cliff and a heart to match. I saw her own maid with an eye like a plum—"

"You can't know that Lady Rayleigh gave it to her."

"Who else?"

"It is all arranged, Jess. I cannot change it. I did not want you taken unawares in the morning—"

"You're so considerate when everything's cut and dried!"

All of a sudden, Emma was bone tired. For the last twenty-four hours she had been at loggerheads with the world and his cousin. "See that you don't keep her ladyship's coachman waiting, that's all."

"I've little enough to pack. You could have left it till breakfast and it'd have made no difference."

"I thought it only right—"

Jess flung herself across the room and sank onto the edge of the bed. "You want to know, don't you, Miss Emma!" Haggard though she was, it did not detract from her looks.

"Know?"

"About Mr. Wildford and me. But I won't tell you. I'll go to her ladyship and you'll lie wondering of nights, never able to make up your mind. I hope you suffer!"

"I expect I shall. Good night, Jess."

The girl did not answer. Emma, in a daze of weariness, found herself in the attic passage, then halfway down the stair, without realizing how she had got there. Back in her room, she began to undress. The yellow dog howled eerily from the direction of the lake and she was reminded of Ringan. He'd be tucked up in bed at Thomas's cottage, waiting for the old man's departure tomorrow. Or maybe, sleepless, he'd be riding the wood, his pistol at the ready. She could almost see him, the moonlight on his face and breast. The scar had not deterred the Frenchwoman from wanting him. The red-haired lady had not wed until she thought him in his grave.

Emma crept between the cold sheets and tried to think of Lewis but all she saw was the white scar that wound like a river from Ringan's temple to the hollow of his cheek.

"You really mean to open a bank in London, Father?"

"Another branch of the same bank, my dear Emma."

"Well, it's another building, a new staff. What made you think of it?"

"Critchley has brought a number of prospective clients into my orbit. I told you he'd lived most of his life in London and has good connections, did I not?"

Emma poured out a cup of China tea and handed it to Wildford. "You did."

"Clients who'd not want the trouble of coming to Norwich."

"So the mountain will go to Mahomet."

"It's certainly worth the trouble. The introductions have been eminently satisfactory. But I'd not want to close the Norwich bank as Tully is so set against going and he's so good at his work. The man would be miserable without motive. I must keep the original business."

"But you said he and Lewis Critchley were anathema to each other."

"I've a mind to let Lewis take over the London branch. After all, they're his cronies. Why give someone else the benefit of his endeavors?"

"But he'd have to leave Norwich. He could not travel so far."

"Naturally. But I'd keep two good men and enlarge the business profitably. It's been in my mind in the past but did not seem feasible, part money reasons, part wartime uncertainty, and lack of a responsible man at the helm. Taking Critchley on chance was one of my more inspired gambles—"

"But he was recommended—"

"By his relatives. That makes a difference. Not that I did not trust Wymark—"

"Only there is such a thing as nepotism."

"My dear Emma, you breakfast on dictionary pie."

"I like words."

"As Lewis likes figures. You'd be oil and water. Lucky he has other ideas."

"Has he?" Emma was cold.

"I told you. The evening of the rout. Yet still you persisted—"

"He asked me to dance and take supper. It was not I pursued him."

"You are my daughter. Mark my words, it's politeness only. Expediency—"

"You do not want me to become involved with a man, do you, Father? Any man. You used to say things like, 'Heaven help the man that gets you' or 'never be too obvious, for men like subtlety,' but that was when I was sixteen. Now you put up barriers against anyone in breeches."

The truth was in his eyes.

"I'm like any other girl. I want happiness, children one day." She was disturbed.

"You are too young, Emma. Precocious, but overyoung, and I'd not have you make the same mistake I did."

"I've done nothing but dance a time or two with your own protégé and take supper with him. Why is there one rule for men and another for women?"

"Because women are vulnerable in ways that men are not. You must be aware of—the physical differences."

"You mean you are afraid I'll bear someone a bastard?"

"Since you are already aware of the dangers, I need not elaborate. But apart from those pitfalls, there is also the sad likelihood that what you may take to be a lasting affection may prove to be all too transient." Wildford frowned over the dainty cup. "I know."

"I still think you would raise objections, whoever the man. You'd rather have me an old maid in the chimney corner, crocheting lace and wearing mittens against the cold? Set in prim ways—? Tied to your apron strings?"

"Do not be ridiculous!" Wildford snapped and slammed down the cup so that it cracked.

He was sending Lewis Critchley away because she had betrayed her interest in him, not because he wanted another bank to make him still more money. He was rich enough.

"You are allowed your indulgences," Emma could not forbear saying and was rewarded by a look of such anger that she flinched.

"I'd not have you a whore."

"All because I like a man for the first time!"

"That is the operative word. First. It's a calf love. Baying for the moon. And he ready to take advantage."

Emma's face whitened. This was a scene that would be

repeated often, and Wildford would see that he had his own way. She stared out of the window almost blindly. It was still damp, green weather. Everything unhealthily moist.

"I saw Lady Rayleigh driving in Norwich yesterday," Wildford went on.

"Oh?" She pretended disinterest.

"Jess Ashcroft did not look well."

"I'm sorry."

"I still think it was a mistake."

"And I cannot agree. I like Miss Fallon. She is quite amenable." And dull, Emma thought a little hopelessly. Nothing on which to sharpen her wits. Jess had been stimulating.

"I'd hardly have known Jess for the girl we knew."

"It's not our fault she's unwell."

"It was no physical ailment, I'll be bound. Sick at heart, that's my diagnosis."

"More tea, Papa?" She tried to change the subject.

"Do not humor me. I think I may go into Norwich tonight so you'd better inform Cook not to expect me for dinner."

To Mrs. Craven who was the indirect cause of her present situation! Emma bit back the words that would have worsened relations between herself and Wildford. But she had no intention of losing Lewis Critchley who liked her for herself and not just because she was the daughter of his employer. Wildford was wrong.

She could not analyze Critchley's attraction for her. Nothing about him was remarkable. His plumage, in contrast to so many splendid popinjays, was restrained. His looks were not obvious. She had no love of figures; rather she detested them. Yet there remained this disconcerting need to mean something to Lewis.

Anna took away the tea things after Wildford's chilly departure. Emma, disinclined to seek out Miss Fallon who was distressingly sycophantic and who would be diligently occupied anyway in sewing or pressing, was on her way to the garden door when a coach crunched over the gravel and came to a stop just outside the window.

Intrigued, Emma returned to the sitting room and almost immediately heard Lady Rayleigh's stentorian tones booming in the hallway. It was too late for flight. There was only a moment in which to gather her courage, then the big, red-faced figure was there, straddling the fireplace, her expression monstrously accusing.

"A fine maid *she* turned out to be!"

Emma, taken aback, said, "Maid? You mean Jess Ashcroft?"

"What other maid should I mean? How many did you send me?" Lady Rayleigh looked apoplectic.

"What has Jess done to make you so angry?"

"What has she done!"

Emma waited for the woman to control herself.

"She's run away. That's the reward I get for giving the minx a chance."

"Run away?"

"Must you repeat everything I say? I expect you found the girl troublesome yourself and those rosy references were sham."

"Not at all," Emma said stiffly. "Jess never wanted to leave us. And she worked well."

"She did not do so for me. I had nothing but complaints about her deportment and her ability. She did not suit me!"

"Then you must be relieved that she is gone," Emma murmured and braced herself for the tirade that was not long in coming.

"Relieved? When I am put to such inconvenience? Where shall I turn?"

"I'm afraid I cannot help you, Lady Rayleigh. I have no other maids to send."

"I thought she might have come back here."

"She has not."

"Are you sure, Miss Wildford?"

Just in time Emma remembered that this woman was her father's client and that Lewis had worked hard to bring her custom to the bank. "I am perfectly sure."

The woman's face was suffused with angry color. "The ungrateful wretch must be somewhere—"

"But *not* in my father's house. Would you take a dish of tea and we can talk over the matter calmly? It concerns me that Ashcroft has now no permanent home."

"And whose fault is that! Not mine." Only slightly mollified, Lady Rayleigh accepted the olive branch with ill grace, while Emma elicited the information that Jess had, according to her mistress, been forward, had been slapped to bring her to her senses, had sworn like a blacksmith, burst into tears and run from the Rayleigh boudoir. Another servant had seen her leave the house carrying a carpetbag and while she was reporting the matter to the housekeeper, Jess had disappeared. Grooms had been sent out to search a radius of the estate but none had set eyes on the hussy.

"Perhaps you are better off without her," Emma said as the bigoted recital ended.

Lady Rayleigh drank tea and ate a large quantity of sticky cakes before she sallied forth, still full of righteous indignation, to vent her spleen upon another victim.

Emma watched her go with a dislike that grew by the minute. How horrible the woman was even when one was not under her thumb. And how clever Lewis must have been in bending that inflexible will to his own ends. A warning bell in her mind told her that Critchley was doubly astute in that he did not appear to influence those with whom he came into contact.

Belatedly, she set out to walk around the lake but the usual peace did not come.

It was two days later, while wandering through the main shop in Norwich, that she encountered Mrs. Fry, unaccustomedly alone. Emma, remembering that it was only a few months since Elizabeth Fry had lost a child, a little girl of four and a half, was half afraid to mention her family, but she, her eyes shining, told Emma that she now had another son, only a few weeks old, a beautiful baby.

"If you are in London," she suggested, "you might call on us at Mildred's Court. Not," and here her face changed, "that you will see any but the youngest of my brood. The older children are scattered, some with relatives or at school."

Emma recalled, too, that the Frys had fallen on hard times. Wildford's Bank might flourish but Fry's did not. This knowledge that she was comfortable while the Frys, who were so worthy and had so many mouths to feed, were in straitened circumstances made the girl acutely uncomfortable. It must hurt to have others bring up one's family.

"I should like that," she said sincerely, for the stories circulating about Mrs. Fry's prison reforms had fired her spirit of adventure and she was in a mood for penance. "Perhaps—perhaps I might accompany you sometime, to Newgate? I know you take other ladies with you."

"You'd really go there?" Mrs. Fry raised her brows and stared at Emma as though she had never seen her before. "I've never taken anyone so young."

"I wish to," Emma assured her, although half an hour ago it had been the last thing in her mind. Now, she knew that she must compensate in some way for her own good fortune, and this seemed part of the answer. "I think I have to."

"Your father will allow you to come to London?"

"I'm sure he will, if he knows the reason why." And, Emma could not help reflecting, Lewis was going to be there and it would be natural to want to see the new bank premises. She experienced a moment of warm happiness when everything in the world seemed in tune.

"I should not count too much on it," Mrs. Fry said and smiled very kindly. "It's no place for a girl and I suspect Mr. Wildford knows that. I could not recount some of the things I see. But there are often those of your age or even younger and they could respond more easily to youth."

"Is it necessary to be a Quaker?" Not even as a penance could she adopt that plain dress and faith.

"No. Only to be a Christian."

I am not good enough, Emma thought instantly, and knew that Mrs. Fry understood. She pressed Emma's hand and a great current of strength seemed to flow from one to the other.

"I will come," the girl promised, "when I am able."

"I think you will, my dear." Mrs. Fry was gone in a rustle of gray skirts, her head held proudly in its white cap. Emma was profoundly moved. She had come with the intention of buying some ribbons and lace, and velvet to make an indispensable, but she no longer wanted the trifles.

"Have you not forgotten what you came for?" Miss Fallon prompted a little nervously. She was not entirely at ease with her unpredictable young mistress.

"I do not really need the things. I'll wait until I do."

"Then you have had a wasted journey?"

"Not at all," Emma replied. "The opposite if you want to know. Come, let us walk in the sunshine. Like as not it will rain tomorrow. It's a summer of mildew and soddenness. The crops will go bad and Farmer Welling will be bankrupt. Only I will prevail upon Papa not to foreclose." Or Vera Palsey will, Emma reflected, and wondered why she no longer detested the slight figure in the lavender gowns.

The image of Jess came back to haunt her, vibrant and mocking. The branches of the trees in the square almost swept the ground, so heavy were they. Where was the girl? She'd have it on her conscience forever if she'd fallen into the wrong hands.

Emma was halted by the sight of Mr. Critchley stepping onto the cobbles of the square. The swaying branches cast green shadows over his face and hands so that he appeared mysterious, like a being from another world. At the same moment he became aware of herself and her companion. Just for a second his expression was blank, then he flashed his disarming smile and came toward them as though they were his dearest friends. How white and shining his teeth were, and very well shaped.

"Miss Emma. How pleasant to see you. And so unexpectedly."

"This is Miss Fallon, my new maid."

Miss Fallon colored under the level gaze. She always became flustered in male company, fiddling with her reticule or the knuckles of her hand if she should not be carrying anything. Sometimes her knuckles cracked and then her discomfiture was painful to watch. Jess would have smiled and flirted a little.

Critchley bowed politely then turned his attention back to Emma. The ribbon on her bonnet fluttered in the breeze and the trees' foliage moved like a woman's green skirts.

"I have to visit a client who is bedridden," he told her, "but there is no immediate hurry. Which way were you going, Miss Emma?"

"Only for a walk in the sun. I was tired of being confined."

"Then perhaps we can walk together? I go this way."

The sun was suddenly too bright to be real. The caverns between the trees were emerald and malachite and dark reseda. Yet only a short time ago they had been moist and unhealthy, breeding disease. When had a summer been so wet? And now so wonderful.

Miss Fallon slowed discreetly to a few paces behind. Emma and Lewis—she could not help but think of him so intimately—walked very close, the warmth on their faces, the light bringing out the blue shadows in her hair. She was calm and self-possessed. Intuitively, she had known this moment would come, that it was preordained.

"Miss Fallon is the replacement for that pretty young girl?"

Emma was conscious of a swift anger. "I told you. She took liberties."

"As all pretty young women will."

She wished, futilely, that he would not go on about prettiness. It made her feel inadequate.

"I suppose so. Has my father said anything—?" She stopped abruptly, knowing that it would be indiscreet to divulge Wildford's plans for the London branch prematurely.

"You mean London?" His face assumed a guarded look. "The new premises?"

"Yes. I was not quite sure if I anticipated—"

"Mr. Wildford told me yesterday that this was in his mind. There are accounts I could put in his way."

"And you would go back home?"

"Either that or to rooms close by the bank. That could be more convenient."

"Because your mother fusses over you?" She smiled at the remembrance.

"She will. You can count on it." His hand tightened, as if by accident, on her forearm as he guided her over the uneven pavement. Emma was conscious of a treacherous pleasure, as though his touch had traveled her body from end to end, leaving a permanent imprint. The winding street, the black outlines of the cathedral, the shape of the medieval gateway were like signposts to some magical place that she would find only with him. The smell of wallflowers crept out of a walled garden and Miss Fallon's footsteps were almost inaudible.

"I've drunk no champagne today," Emma said recklessly, "but I *was* jealous of Deborah. Do you think me horribly immodest for saying so?"

She had never heard him laugh before, but he did so now.

"I cannot imagine why you'd be envious!" Then his face changed and he was grasping her by both arms and staring at her. "Unless—"

Miss Fallon had stopped to look into a bow-fronted shop window with bottle-glass panes that reflected the white sun so sharply that it hurt the eyes.

"Unless you are fond of me?" he asked so low that it was almost a whisper.

"Fond is not the word I would use. I feel I must tell you, before you go away—"

"But why? Why me?"

"I cannot explain. I only know that you fill my thoughts. And that my father knows and that is why he is sending you away." She was being terribly indiscreet but she could not help herself.

"I never met anyone with such honesty." His voice was gentle.

"But you must take no notice if I have embarrassed you. If you have no such feelings where I am concerned." The words poured from her lips. "Please—"

"You have opened my eyes. I confess that I had not previously thought of you as anything but your father's daughter, but now, in the strangest way, you have touched me—"

"Have I?" Miss Fallon was still standing by the bottle-glass panes through which the goods displayed must appear misshapen. She obviously sensed she played gooseberry but she was very tactful. Jess would not have stayed so, in the background. Always, she must thrust herself forward, hating to remain unnoticed. Elation drained away with the return of misgiving.

"I'd not say so if I did not mean it. And your father, you say, wishes me out of your reach? He gave no inkling—"

"I'm sure he admires you for your contribution to Wildford's and would detest seeing you go to anyone else. But he's become possessive where I am concerned. It is nothing he has against you as a person, just a mistrust of men in general as related to my—well-being. My future."

"He may alter—"

"I fear not."

"Then what are we to do about it?"

"I have an excuse to go to London." She told him of the meeting with Mrs. Fry and of her genuine desire to go with her to Newgate.

Lewis seemed doubtful. "Such women would think nothing of attacking a girl once the door was closed on the turnkey. I do not care for the thought."

"They say Mrs. Fry is a good influence. They quiet themselves when she goes."

"I still think there is a risk attached to it. They cannot all be won over."

"But I can think of no other way to be allowed to visit London from time to time."

"No. I can see you must have a reason."

"And you'd be pleased to see me?"

"You know I would."

"And—Deborah?"

"Is my cousin and has the affection one normally gives to one's family."

"Nothing—nothing more?"

He shook his head, and the short, smooth hair splayed out against the light. If he looked a little tight about the lips it was because the sun was in his eyes.

Emma took a deep breath. Miss Fallon could not pretend to be oblivious forever.

"I could write to you at the new premises."

"Oh, no! A clerk may open the letters first. To separate the sheep from the goats."

"Even if I wrote private above the seal?"

"Perhaps. If your father had an inkling, I'd be out, neck and crop, and I will have worked for nothing."

"Would it matter so much?"

"You cannot know me if you can ask such a question."
He had become a little remote and it was as though the sun
had been obscured by cloud.

Miss Fallon half turned, then wandered alongside the
window as though attracted by some article she had newly
noticed. Emma realized she could not be sure that the
woman would not tell Wildford of the meeting with Lewis.
And she would be expected to take Miss Fallon with her on
any trip to London. It was not going to be easy to deceive
her father. Perhaps the woman had some relative in the city
she'd not be averse to visiting. Where was her own much-
vaunted honesty now? She'd lie only for him.

"I must go," Emma told Critchley.

He cast a quick look at Fallon who was apparently absorbed in the window's contents, then picked up her hand
and bent his head over it. The brief kiss burned like fire.

"Where shall I write?" she asked.

"To my home. That would be best."

"Won't your mother pry?"

"She may wish to but she knows she'd forfeit my good-
will."

"Then that's what I'll do." The day was brilliant again
with raised hopes and a delicious warmth that stole the
length of all her bones.

Critchley bowed and moved on, his slender figure con-
trasting with those of portly men in wigs and overbright
clothing and plump, bosomy women whose gowns left little to the imagination. The ladies chattered like parakeets.
Emma knew that she admired Lewis for his elegance, his
understatement, his reserve. She wondered how he would
behave in the intimacy of marriage but, somehow, the
thought had no reality.

Wildford was expansive after the recent estrangement.

He unbuttoned his embroidered waistcoat and poured out claret. "I heard a piece of news today."

"Oh?" Emma, who had been going to excuse herself, sat still, surveying the pyramid of fruit in the center of the table.

"Our friends, the Wymarks—"

"What about them?" She forgot the apples and grapes, the yellowing pears.

"That evening was their swan song. Wymark has speculated but not wisely. The house will have to go, and all the extravagances. No portion now for Miss Deborah, I fear. It was not Wymark who told me, not that one can keep such matters hidden. The war's created major problems for many." He tipped back his head and emptied the glass.

"But not for you."

"You needn't worry your pretty head on that score." Wildford reached across the table and patted her hand. "We are all right."

"But not the Wymarks or the Frys." She drew away from him unsmilingly.

"Emma! You cannot lay their misfortunes at my door!"

"No. But it does seem wrong. And Mrs. Fry is separated from her children because she and her husband cannot afford to bring them up. Some with aunts and uncles—scattered piecemeal."

"I am sorry."

"I told Mrs. Fry I would visit Newgate with her. She says there are girls there who'd welcome someone young—"

"You cannot mean it!"

"I do. I have promised."

He scowled darkly. "You'll catch some illness or be rapped over the head for the buttons off your gown, or some trinket from your finger."

"I'll go dressed as plainly as Mrs. Fry. I've been selfish, Fa-

ther, and I want to do something for persons less fortu-
nate."

"You sound priggish, young Emma."

"I do not feel it. You might have had cause for complaint
had I wanted to indulge in a course of riotous living!"

"I confess I'd find it more natural," Wildford grumbled,
stretching out his long legs and tilting back in his chair. "I
don't know that I want you cavorting about in London."

"Can you imagine me cavorting with Miss Fallon!"

Wildford grinned. "She's straitlaced as you'd find 'em."

"And you'd trust Mrs. Fry, would you not?"

"Like the woman," he confessed, "though she makes me
feel a reprobate."

"Then may I go now and again? To appease my conscience."

"I'd not thought of you as a crusader, I confess. You're
full of surprises, young miss. I'll sleep on it."

"You won't forget?"

"You'll not allow me. Isn't that true?"

"Quite true. Thank you for not damping the idea without
consideration."

"And thank you for not bearing me ill will over our last
clash."

Emma was silent for a moment. "I hoped we'd find some
common meeting ground in future to talk over such matters. When you have had time to think."

"You won't expect complete capitulation, I hope?"

"No." She was suddenly reminded of Wildford's revelations about the Wymarks. Deborah was without dowry and
her only hope of a good marriage was to a man so rich that
her lack of portion was of no account. If Critchley had entertained any hopes in that direction, they must have been
dashed. But he hadn't, Emma told herself stoutly. They
were cousins and had only a family affection. He'd assured
her on that count. He had singled Emma out at the rout,
danced with her and fetched her delicious food from the

laden tables. Yet the Wymarks must have known of the impending disaster, and so, presumably, must Lewis. That was the worst of being well off. It made one suspicious.

"Has your sudden urge to turn sober and industrious anything to do with Jess?" her father asked disconcertingly, and now the well-fed complacency was gone.

It was on the tip of her tongue to repudiate the suggestion, but honesty won. "I confess I do find her plight affects me. But we should never have been friends again. I cannot pretend. She had to go to someone—"

"I said you should wait. A more suitable post would have presented itself."

"Well, it's spilt milk now. I only hope she's safe."

"And if she comes here?" Wildford poured more wine. "It's not impossible."

"It will be as before. If I am not firm and place her elsewhere, she'd turn the house upside down, oversetting my orders." Going to your room, Papa. It will not do. The thought disturbed her afresh so that she almost hated the man she had loved and championed so long. Only now, that love had been eroded by Wildford's unwillingness to allow her the normal relationships that were part of maturity, his proposed banishment of Lewis. Lewis. A glow that was unconnected with the wine pervaded her body, making her restless.

"There's something of your grandmama in you after all," Wildford observed. "An almost relentless obstinacy in the pursuit of despotism—"

"That's unfair! Anyway, that sounds much more like you."

"Emma!" he said, warningly. "However you conceal it, it's there, and I fear you'll founder on its rocks more than once. That particular blend of honesty and self-righteousness can destroy."

"You mean I should begin to tell lies, make evasions?"

"Sometimes white lies are less damaging."

"But lies, nevertheless."

"Do not glare at me like some medusa! If I thought that, only once, you'd tried to wrap up some bitter pill, I'd have hope for your future."

I have lied, she thought, to Lewis, but it would be useless to tell this to Wildford. He had his own prejudices and obduracy, and the sound of Critchley's name at this point would be showing a red rag to a bull.

"You should be glad you'd always get the truth from me. At least you can trust what I tell you. Is dependence not important?"

"It's rigidity I abhor."

"It can hurt to be deceived. You told me once, during the Czar's visit, that you were visiting the Frys, but I saw you leave the hotel with a loud woman to whom you paid money."

Wildford became very still. Even the wine in the glass he held did not shiver.

"I came to your room one night not long ago and there was a girl with you. I believe it was Jess Ashcroft."

"Don't be a fool!" Wildford exploded into action, banging the glass down onto the table, the contents flying, getting to his feet, apparently unaware that the red liquid made bloody patches on the white shirt. "I need not explain my actions to a child. Nor name the women who alleviate my—" Not finding a suitable word, he glared angrily at Emma, his face paler than usual. But he had not denied outright that his visitor was Jess. Emma felt a little sick. Her father looked not like someone who was guiltless, but rather like a man found out.

"If I am wrong then I am sorry," she said stiffly.

"Only you are so certain you are not that any denial would be useless," Wildford answered bitterly.

She could not answer. It came to her like a blow that the quarrel would not help to soften her father's attitude toward Lewis Critchley. Her sharp tongue had dug a pit in which her hopes could be lost.

Wildford slammed out of the room and she realized that she'd sent him into the arms of Mrs. Craven or someone like her. For the first time she knew something of what he felt. Since the recent meeting with Lewis she was aware of bodily needs and sensations, of the strength of physical desire. It was this last of which Wildford was afraid on her behalf.

Emma fetched her cloak, it being dull again, and took her usual way toward the summerhouse. She'd stayed away from it after the strange episode with Jess but now she thought of it gratefully. It was a haven where no one else would intrude.

Something moved on the edge of the wood just as she reached the lakeside, and she thought of the yellow dog that skulked there. Welling had already complained of a lamb savaged and part eaten, but, as yet, no one had got near the beast. It was Ringan's job to find it. Passing the familiar shape of the folly, she began to approach the hummock upon which much of the wood rested.

Small spots of rain struck her face and a warm dampness seemed to exude from the earth. There was fungus under the trees, brown and shiny, bitter-scented. Grape-blue shadows were turning that sinister gray that heralded twilight, but Emma was made brave with wine and with thoughts of Critchley. Her hair blew across her cheek and she remembered Jess saying, ". . . it feels so nice. Why is it only ladies must feel pleasure in their hair and their bodies?" She hurried for shelter into the obscurity.

The sensation of being close to Jess was so strong that Emma stared around her in every direction. There were fir cones underfoot and a smell of resin that she liked, but no suggestion of movement. It was the memory of her quarrel with Wildford that conjured up the ghost of Jess Ashcroft, nothing else.

Rain dropped between the branches, the soft sound making queer, sibilant music that drew her on like the pipes of Pan. What little touched her skin felt fresh and sensuous as though she pulled silk over her head. It was much darker now and only the occasional glimmer of pearl showed her the way out of the maze of trees.

There was something in the wood. Emma stood still, listening. Leaves rustled. A stick cracked, then there was a silence tangible as sound. With appalling suddenness, an arm came around her throat, pinning her captive. Half-choking, she fought against it, thrashing and kicking. "Let me go. Let me go!" Her accompanying scream pulsed, echoing down the shadowy aisles to be lost in distance.

The arm was removed as quickly as it had come, and she turned, stumbling in her haste, to make out Ringan's thin, mocking face as he leaned back against the nearest trunk.

"How dare you!"

"How could I know? You'd your back to me and the hood pulled up."

Emma hated the hungry smile.

"I saw the dog that attacked the lamb."

"Indeed? You're certain?"

"Not absolutely. But there was something. Or someone."

"We have, I fear, stalked each other."

Something in the rueful way in which he said it made Emma laugh, and her laughter, as well as the earlier scream, reverberated through the reaches of the copse. Relief, wine or amusement? She was never sure why she had laughed.

"Well, that's better, Miss Emma."

"It—it seemed so silly."

Her eyes, accustomed to the gloom, saw the white scar. He spoke so well that he must once have been a gentleman. What was he now?

"I'm a ruffian, as well you know," Ringan said. "You are so delightfully open, Miss Emma. Your eyes mirror your thoughts."

"Father says I am too much so for my own good."

"I like a spirited girl."

"Was your Frenchwoman courageous?"

"Aye. A little like you. Dark. Outspoken. Bedworthy—"

"I did not ask for such intimate details." Emma was instantly aware that she was inviting familiarities by lingering here in the murky wood, the thin patter of the rain the only sound.

"You wanted to know. You asked for the secret of my success. Remember?" His body was, inexplicably, between her and safety.

"It was a stupid joke."

"I promised to let you know." Without seeming to move, he was close beside her, blotting out the watery gray that marked the boundary of the copse. "I always keep my promises."

"I don't want to know."

He took no more notice than he did of the suddenly quickened rain. Pressing her against the tree at her back, his arms went around her and his mouth came down on her own, stifling breath and protest. His knee separated her thighs and for one brief, shocking moment, his body was thrust against hers, arousing a burning necessity to know what would happen next. Then he stood back, smiling a pale smile that did not reach his eyes, saluted with one hand and was gone.

Emma thought of all the things she should have said. The rain was pelting down now, plastering her hair to her scalp, but she stood, not bothering to shelter, as if there was some dark spot that must be washed away.

Chapter Four

Wildford had bought the premises he required in Clarges Street and was to spend a week or so in London in order to supervise the fitting out of the rooms and to interview prospective clerks.

Emma, fluctuating between frustration and the novelty of her physical awakening, wanted to go with him. The thought of meeting Ringan on his solitary patrols, having to shrug off, or condemn him, for his crude familiarity, intimidated her in spite of the fact that he had been in the wrong. She had not invited nor participated in his embrace that was like nothing she had ever encountered, and she felt shame that she had experienced a vicarious excitement as a result.

Several times she had intended to inform her father of Captain Ringan's behavior but found at the last moment that she could not.

A picture would flash into her mind of Wildford similarly engaged with a variety of women, Amelia, Mrs. Craven, Vera—even Jess Ashcroft, and the strange, wild fluttering in her breast would catch at her breath, making her mute, almost hating him. He looked larger, stronger, grosser, and the love that was once between them was reduced to the occasional shaft of its former self, and that always unexpectedly aroused by a momentary look of helplessness or inadequacy, even of bluster. Wildford had developed feet of clay and the knowledge saddened her.

Yet she must not entertain too much pity, for he was her stumbling block over Lewis, and Critchley was what she wanted, and he wanted her. Somehow, they must be married. But how, in the face of her father's opposition and her own youth?

"Shall I come to London with you?" she asked and wondered where she had left the book of Scott's poems. It might be safer to send one to Lewis than a letter. He would know who it was from.

"But what would you do? I shall be busy."

"Miss Fallon and I would see the sights—those that I previously missed, and I should call on Mrs. Fry."

Wildford gave her a calculating look and she knew that he was thinking that she would be unable to encounter Critchley if she went with him. Lewis was not to go to the new branch until the premises were ready for occupation and the staff chosen.

"I suppose that means another visit to the dressmaker?" he grumbled without too much conviction.

He was so generous in other ways. Why couldn't he see that he could not keep her with him permanently, a possession like his fine furniture, silver and paintings, his horses and the family jewelry? "Of course! You know you like me to appear at my best." She feigned gaiety. "And last time I was not too demanding, was I?"

"No." He seemed faintly surprised by the fact, as though all other women constantly cheated him. "I shall give you carte blanche this time, knowing that you'll not overstep the mark."

A thrill ran through her body. She could order a trousseau and demand that Lewis run away with her. Surely he had some other relative who'd find a post for him? Or there were other banks— But Emma knew that Critchley wanted the London bank above all else and wondered, a little bitterly, at that certainty. Anywhere else, he'd be young Mr. Critchley; there he'd be Mr. Critchley, the head manager. Her father would be forced to take him into partnership if he proved himself. As he would. Wildford could not refuse to wed her to his partner. But he could make her wait until he was ready to accept the inevitable and he had all of her own obstinacy.

"How good you are," she replied with an irony he did not perceive.

"Then get yourselves ready." He returned to his brandy and the morning's newssheets, neglected until supper, and Emma went to ask Fallon to pack for them both, then went to stare from the window at the burnished mirror of the lake. There was a sound of hooves beyond the rain, which had never really stopped for months, and she knew it would be Ringan with his humorless smile and his way with all women except herself.

She thought, as she stood there, that something crossed the lawn below the window and the rhododendron bushes moved and rustled, though that could have been the persistent wind that helped to alleviate the closeness and mugginess of the damp, warm weather. The noises faded after a time and she decided it must have been a fox or a badger, or even the homely hedgehog which was more nocturnal in its wanderings than the rabbits and hares.

As she prepared for bed, she recognized, afresh, the problems that faced her, none of which seemed easily solved. Once asleep, she dreamed of Lewis, of his smooth skin and perfect teeth, then his face changed to the scarred aspect of Ringan. She saw his pale arms held aloft on a battlefield where a man with no arms or legs lay staring into his bleak future. I'd as soon be a cabbage, Emma felt herself thinking and woke with her eyes full of scalding tears that brought no release.

She saw Ringan as the carriage left next day, the rain beating on his coat, and knew that he lived a very different life because of that last shot of Napoleon's war. But the poor rifleman had so much less and she could not bear it. Her eyes burned afresh as she thought of his total dependence—if he still lived. Ringan had never finished the story but perhaps he'd never known the end of it.

"You look sad," Wildford said.

"I'm saying good-bye to youth," she replied. "I feel I shall never be young again."

"And who has wrought this transformation?"

Miss Fallon cracked her knuckles very loudly in the silence inside the carriage. She would be remembering Norwich and the green, burdened trees, the prolonged survey of a shop window with bottle-glass panes, herself and Lewis in a conversation that was too long to be trivial.

"No one in particular. Captain Ringan—"

"What of him?" Wildford asked sharply. Jealousy— Then it was true. It was not only Lewis he feared.

"Told me of the last days of the war. What happened to those poor men—"

"It's a bad thing," he said soberly. "But he should not have imposed those atrocities on you."

"But I ought to know! Everyone should know so that the situation can be avoided another time."

"My dear child! Life has been one continuous battle since the first dawn."

"Is that any reason to accept that it must always be so? An eye for an eye?"

"Turning the other cheek may not be the answer, either. There's an element of scorn creeps in. Accusations of cowardice."

"Only by ignoramuses!"

"How different you are." He hesitated, and she knew he had been going to say "child" and had thought better of it. It was a small step she thought, but an important one. Soon he would say "woman," and with that might come the implications that the word aroused. It would be natural for a woman to need a man. Even Wildford's daughter.

"We are like each other," she told him while she had the advantage. "We can see with adult eyes. So many cannot."

"You little egotist!" he roared, delighted, and slapped his thighs.

Miss Fallon averted her eyes and turned quite pale. Heavens, Emma thought, I hope she is not going to fall hopelessly in love with Papa! But the telltale knuckles cracked again and she decided that this was a sign of disapproval. Fallon would need someone much more negative if she were to give up her virginity. Someone quiet and gentle. Only, and the knowledge lacerated her, no one was ever likely to need Miss Fallon.

London was unendingly exciting. From the milk sellers in St. James's Park to the horehound and coltsfoot stalls in the streets, the new, packed life was satisfying. The streets were, indeed, so much more fascinating than the rather cold, museum-type buildings, Emma decided. She loved the costermongers crying out their wares. Mackerel and sole, plaice and crab, oysters and mussels in their raised black shells, that, with the blue mark in the "hump" that looked like an eye, were her favorites; Yarmouth bloaters and live salmon flashing their blue-silver scales—she could not see enough of them. Then there were eels and herrings, cherries and oranges, and rabbits caught on Hampstead Heath and looking so quiet and sad in their immobility.

It seemed worse that animals hung dead than the fish that looked so bright and glorious, though some people went by muttering "Kennetseeno," that meant stinking for some peculiar reason, and "a regular trosseno," that indicated the market was bad and led to men going off for a top o reeb. At this point Emma realized that the latter slang was merely the three words said backward, but that did not help with the others that remained a mystery. Miss Fallon was always uneasy about these excursions, and the sharp "snap" of her bones was a never-failing background to their peregrinations.

She was happier about standing outside Buck House and Carlton House where the Prince Regent held court, but Emma reveled in the common streak she had so belatedly discovered and made sure that the day held as much study of everyday human beings as of princes and nobility.

It was in the Strand that she was elbowed aside roughly and turned to see the angry face of Maybrick. The shock was so great that she could only stare at him without speaking.

"Bitch!" he snarled, and she knew that he was much the worse for drink.

Miss Fallon, not recognizing him, tried to pull her away, her thin hands like claws, but Emma stayed her ground, waiting until the bloodshot eyes focused and became filled with recognition. "Amelia's brat!"

"It is Emma. And you are, more than ever, the gentleman I remember."

"What I am is no business of yours."

"No, I'm thankful to say."

For a moment, he raised his cane and she remembered the beating of Jess. Then the arm was lowered and he smiled. "I always wondered how best to get back at Wildford. Now I think I know."

"Get back at Papa? Why?"

He presented his other cheek, and she could see the mark of the cane still there, an ugly red accentuated by the heat.

"You should see that girl's back! That's nothing in comparison."

"It's a lot to me!" he snarled, voice slurred. "A lot—to—me."

"Let me past, please."

"Why? Because you are his spawn? Why should I?"

Miss Fallon gave a distressed cough, and the man ran his eyes over her gray-clad figure, the fluttering hands that betrayed her fear.

"Where's that wench you took away? Ashcroft."

"Gone to another mistress."

"You should have known she'd be no good. A thief—"

"She was a million times better than you."

Again the drunken eyes threatened her. "I'll get the better of him one day, now that I recall his Achilles' heel."

"You're wrong—"

"Oh, no! No. I remember that day in Amelia's house. Your championship of him and his of you. You'd best look out, Miss Wildford. Amelia never liked this mark and now she likes it less than ever and it's your father's doing. And cease your fussing, you old sheep! Looking at me as though I were dirt. I'm kin to the girl and her mother, I'll have you know, you old fossil—"

The sun was suddenly obscured by a man's shape. An authoritative voice asked, "Is this man annoying you, young lady?"

"Yes," Emma said. "He has insulted my maid and threatens me."

"Perhaps I should escort you to your house."

"Hotel. But I'd rather he did not see which one it is."

Maybrick swayed, his face set in evil lines that frightened Emma more than she would admit. "Bitch!" he whispered. "You cannot hide at Staves. Remember that."

A stalwart arm seized his and propelled him to a safe distance. Boot heels rang on the narrow pavement. Emma had a last sight of Jeffrey Maybrick leaning against the wall, then the purposeful figure interposed itself between her and her enemy.

She took a deep breath. "I must thank you, Mr. ——?"

"John Old."

"Mr. Old. But for you, I fear there might have been violence. I'm Emma Wildford."

"Are you acquainted with the person?" The gray eyes were curious.

"He is a distant relative. One I have not seen for some time. I'd almost forgotten him."

"He bears you some grudge?"

"It's my father he dislikes."

"I've a carriage nearby. Would you and your companion care to share it as far as your destination?"

"I'd be grateful. We wanted to walk. One gets closer to everything—"

"Including relatives the worse for drink. I think we should go. He's still watching you, Miss Wildford. Is your father, by any chance, Luke Wildford?"

"Why yes!" Emma exclaimed, surprised. "How did you know?" They were, all three, walking very quickly in an effort to put some distance between themselves and Maybrick. Miss Fallon was trembling a little and there was perspiration on her upper lip. But Mr. Old was reassuringly sturdy and looked dependable.

"You resemble him and the name is uncommon. One of my friends is to become a client of the projected bank through the offices of Lewis Critchley who's a connection of my wife's. You see, London is not such a large place."

"No." Emma forgot Maybrick and his sour, wine-laden breath. "I suppose you see Lewis from time to time?"

"We do."

"He is—a very able young man." The fleeting sunshine grew dimmer as though the ubiquitous rain were not far away.

"We think highly of his unusual abilities."

"My father, too. You'll probably see a good deal of him once he returns?"

Mr. Old had stopped in front of a handsome carriage drawn by four blacks. He was obviously a man of substance, and since he knew both Wildford and Lewis, Emma had no compunction about entering the vehicle though she recognized symptoms in Miss Fallon that pointed out certain reservations. "Come, Miss Fallon," she whispered, "it's all right."

"We intend to make it our business to invite Lewis frequently. And poor Deborah, of course. You must know Miss Wymark, since she lives so close to Norwich?"

Emma, with a quick memory-picture of wood-shaving curls and determined blue eyes, felt a thrust of pain that almost, but not quite, struck her dumb. Was this business of Critchley and Deborah not so moribund as she thought?

"They shared a boy-and-girl love affair. But you must be acquainted with that? Deborah's our goddaughter and we've no children of our own so Mrs. Old and I intend to make it our business to see she makes a proper marriage now that adversity has entered all their lives. Apart from Lewis, who has good prospects, you'll agree."

Emma nodded, stiff-lipped. "He has indeed." She arranged her skirts, seeing nothing of the busy street which only quarter of an hour ago was so entrancing. Lewis had said so definitely that his feelings toward Deborah were merely those of an affectionate cousin. But he might not have known then that the prosperous-seeming Olds were to sponsor Deborah. How horrible suspicions were. The unpleasantness of the scene with Maybrick became intensified.

Mr. Old continued to speak kindly and sensibly and she could not help but like him. But she was glad when the conveyance came to a stop outside the hotel and she and Miss Fallon were handed out, their rescuer bowing while they thanked him. They hurried inside out of the spiteful lances of rain that struck them out of a suddenly colorless sky.

Wildford commented on Emma's tight silence that evening on his return from the new bank. "Tired of London already, my dear?"

"Not of London."

"Then of what?"

"I don't know."

"I see we must have some final fling. Some unique happening. What shall it be?"

"I can think of nothing I wish to do. Except visit Mrs. Fry tomorrow."

"I do not know that I like you so grim and determined." Wildford, uncharacteristically, pushed away the decanter as though he recognized the need for a clear head.

"You describe me so unattractively."

"You do not look like the daughter I thought I knew."

Miss Fallon, who had been hovering close by the door, said, "Miss Wildford had a great shock today—"

"I wish you had not told him!" Emma burst out, for the first time angry with the woman.

"What's this?" Wildford sat up straight, his brows drawn together.

Miss Fallon was silent in the face of Emma's outburst, but the damage was done.

"I insist upon knowing," her father said firmly. "What was this shock?"

"We went for a walk. I thought it perfectly safe since I was accompanied. But I was jostled by a man the worse for drink who turned out to be Jeffrey Maybrick—"

"Maybrick! The swine."

"He—threatened me."

"Threatened you!" Wildford was choleric. "That whippersnapper. Wife stealer—"

"A Mr. Old was passing by and he intervened and brought us back here so that we could get away from him. He was really kind." And cruel, Emma thought, painfully. He had shown her that Lewis might not be within her reach for all Wildford's money and authority.

"Old? I do know someone of that name."

"He said he knew you. And the Wymarks."

"Aye. The same man. I'm grateful to him. But that Maybrick should intimidate you! That I'll not tolerate."

"He was tipsy. I think he hardly knew what he said."

"I'll leave him in no doubt as to what *I'll* say."

"You don't mean to seek him out? Please, Father, I wish you would not." Emma looked at Wildford, the broad darkness against which his shirt looked white as snow, the handsome, sensual profile.

"He was very alarming," Miss Fallon was constrained to say. "I feel he intended some harm to Miss Emma in order to punish you, Mr. Wildford. He said as much—"

Wildford sprang out of his chair in a fury. "The presumption of the man to waylay my daughter! I thought I'd seen the last of him. It's Amelia's put him up to it—"

"No," Emma said. "It seems he's fallen out of favor with her and he blames that cut you gave him on the face. Not that it will be that, for he's had it for two years and more. But he must blame something, and he's chosen your treatment of him the night we rescued Jess."

"Ah, yes. Jess." He was quiet now and his face had turned secretive.

"It's only petulance because Mama no longer wants him."

"Perhaps," Wildford agreed, deceptively quiet. "But he could have harmed you—"

"But did not!" Emma retorted quickly, afraid of the consequences of his wrath. "I think I will not need you again this evening, Miss Fallon."

The woman hesitated, then, noting the flash of Emma's eyes, gave up the brief attempt at renewing her need to register disquiet. After she had gone, Wildford sat wrapped in his own thoughts while Emma finished her wine and wiped her lips on the linen napkin, all the time conscious of the tick of the strange clock, of the furnishings that were alien. She had a compelling need to be reassured, about Lewis, about her future, that Wildford did not contemplate any move that could harm him. There was nothing that could be done about her pessimism about Critchley. Only time would unravel those uneasy strands.

"I'm sorry," her father said after a time, "that your holiday has been spoiled, and by such an upstart."

Only it was not Maybrick who had ruined the happy interlude, but, ironically, that nice man, John Old.

Though Emma had expected Wildford to go out that evening, he did not. They sat together until bedtime, like prisoner and jailer. It was plain that her father took the threat seriously and was not inclined to let her out of his sight. She was afraid that she'd not be allowed to visit Elizabeth Fry, but Wildford drove her there himself and watched her admitted to the house, promising to return in a few hours to take her for a drive or to some entertainment of her choosing.

Emma, who had discovered that the Norwich mail coach left from The Swan with Two Necks in Lad Lane, had been tormented by a desire to send a letter to Lewis, only she could never deliver it without Miss Fallon, at least, knowing about it. She could, of course, insist that her maid promise not to say anything, but that would make the poor woman acutely miserable. She was not the stuff of dissemblers.

Mrs. Fry greeted Emma quietly but with a sincere pleasure. She had with her Anna Buxton, who was her sister-in-law, sister Hannah having married Fowell Buxton some years ago, he being a member of Parliament with an interest in Elizabeth's doings at Newgate.

"I do not usually," Mrs. Fry said over the dishes of tea, "take very young persons with me to Newgate. But you seem so grown up and level-headed, Emma. And quite without ingenuousness, though with Mr. Wildford as your father, you could not be less than sophisticated." She still did not approve of Papa, Emma noted almost with amusement.

"I know that I may see things that could revolt me but that would be as little compared with the need to help." Emma hoped this did not sound as sycophantic as she feared but the honesty of her tones seemed to weigh more with the lady of Newgate.

"You have nothing about you that would attract the attentions of pilferers?"

"I have no jewelry or ribbons and I should leave my reticule here, if I may."

The calm eyes surveyed her. The effect was of being scrutinized by a Greek statue come suddenly to life, Emma thought, and smiled involuntarily.

"You should make use of that smile," Elizabeth told the girl. "It could soften the hardest heart."

"Could it?" Emma's surprise was transparent.

"Did no one tell you that?"

"Only my father."

"Then he has more sense than I imagined."

Emma smiled again and asked after the welfare of her son Samuel and of his brothers and sisters, enjoying the pleasure in Mrs. Fry's serene, yet determined face. Anna Buxton seemed an intelligent, energetic woman, and the three soon began to feel a comradeship that boded well for their future relationship. It began to dawn upon Emma that she was in the presence of, not merely another acquaintance from Norwich in Mrs. Fry, but a woman who would leave an imprint upon world affairs. Already Mrs. Fry was discussed and quoted and flexed her humanitarian muscles, and this was only the beginning of her endeavors. All great women were taken as a matter of course until they had lit some fire, made some stand against brutality or injustice. It would be so with this Quaker fallen on such impoverished times that she must part with the children she so obviously adored.

The first sight of Newgate was reassuring. It could be rated quite beautiful, Emma reflected, with its niches harboring statues of Plenty and Liberty. Then the Horn of Plenty seemed needlessly cruel because it did not echo what lay inside those windowless walls. According to Elizabeth Fry there was only poverty and frustration, deep wells of deprivation.

"Some of the windows are blocked for tax reasons," Mrs. Fry told her, noticing the direction of her gaze, "but Dance, the architect, arranged for what windows there are to face the inner courts."

"It cannot be very light," Emma said as they were let inside.

"No, my dear. It's the darkest place I ever saw. I still do not think I should have brought you."

"Don't send me back just as I've got here. I promise I'll remember all you told me."

"And to forget what you should see," Mrs. Fry warned. "And not only see—"

The force of this last remark was clear when they arrived at the women's quarters after an echoing walk filled with the sound of chains and bestial cries through which could be heard the occasional cultured voice that spoke of its despair and seemed more terrible than the fusillade of oaths and threats. Through one of the dingy windows Emma spied a tap in the yard below, with a man measuring out what looked like ale. Gaslight illuminated the vaulted passages only poorly and the smell was even worse than the babel of noise.

The bars in front of her were suddenly filled with hands and arms, the fingers like gray talons, the arms thin and whipcorded, not like those of any women she had seen. They would be pulled back, and after much shrieking and whining for money, other hands and arms would appear, some covered with sores or scratches, the occasional one white and soft. These disappeared more quickly than the skinny ones. Women yelled to others to come away so that they might have their turn, and yanked at one another's hair and throats when they could not get their way. She caught brief glimpses of a gypsylike creature dancing grotesquely, while a cross-legged audience grinned at her with rotted teeth and made gestures she realized were obscene though she had never before witnessed them. The bundles she and the two other women carried could not contain a fraction of what would be needed here, and how would they pacify those who received nothing?

Wails of children rose above the screeches of these harridans. The smells made her stomach rise, but Emma forced the nausea back as best she could. It was not that she'd been unprepared. She had thought Mrs. Fry exaggerated, but she had not. This place was worse than her vilest dreams.

"Get back, you bitches!" the turnkey shouted, then, more apologetically to Mrs. Fry, "I got to be firm, ain't I, or you'd never get near? Is the young lady going inside too?" He leered at Emma as he spoke and she thought she'd be in more danger if she remained outside.

"Of course I am."

He grimaced at the sharpness of her voice. "Only arsking," he muttered, and bellowed again for the poor wretches to leave the bars at once. They were disinclined to take any notice until one of them caught sight of Elizabeth Fry's face, then she pulled at the woman next to her, mouthing and pointing, and snatched at the pallid shrew who knelt before her, muttering something Emma could not make out in the general bedlam, but it had a magical effect.

Anna Buxton had paled but it was not to be wondered at. Emma's eardrums felt battered as though she'd been hit with some weapon, and her gorge still rose and must be dealt with firmly if she were not to disgrace herself. Even through her misery she was aware that Elizabeth Fry's lips moved silently in prayer.

There was a dreadful moment when the huge key grated in the lock and the door swung open. Mrs. Fry passed firmly inside the gap, to be followed by Anna Buxton. The jailer said, "'Urry along there, miss. It's as much as my life's worth to keep this open, and you did say as you weren't staying outside."

Emma, clutching her bundle as a drowning man might cling to an improvised raft, closed her eyes and allowed herself to be swallowed in a vortex of smells, sounds, jeering and touch. Her skirts were pulled by numerous fingers so that she had an instant's horror of being dragged to the odorous straw on the floor and trampled.

"Don't!" she said sharply. "Don't touch me or I'll go."

" 'Oo cares!"

"You will care," she replied with spurious bravery, "if I take away all I brought."

An old woman cackled as though this were a great joke, the stumps of her teeth exposed like rocks rising from a fetid sea. "Bibles," she mumbled. "What should we want with Bibles and psalm singing? Won't be much good when we're transported."

"How can you know that?" Emma asked. "None of you can know what Australia's like."

"We 'eard tales. It's all soldiers and heat, and 'ard work. Nothing but that. And if it ain't the soldiers it's men 'oo won't leave you peace to look at no Bible. Not that we'm great readers. Look around you, my clean, pretty miss. For Christ's sake, look! Where'd we learn lettering?"

"I'd teach you if you'd listen. If I'd time—"

"You ain't going to make time! Your no need. Your little charity's finished now. You'll open your parcels and go back home and think now and again that you must be good. And scrub all your clothes 'cos we touched 'em, and bathe ten times to wash us out of your mind."

"You're wrong."

"No, little missy. What could you do for us? Me, f'rinstance. 'Ow old d'you take me for?"

The dull eyes in the withered, dirty face brightened as though the woman relished the exchange.

"Sixty?" Emma thought she erred on the side of generosity.

"Thirty-two."

The girl stared. Stared again, and still was not really convinced. Another tug to her skirts by someone behind her and the material tearing to reveal the lace-trimmed petticoat.

"Don't believe me, do you?" the woman said, quiet now and resigned. "Leave 'er alone," she went on in a quite different voice, "just leave 'er be, you bitches!"

Mrs. Fry was beside Emma now, murmuring over the torn garment.

"It's of no account," Emma told her, pulling the gown over the rent. "It is an old thing." She had let go of the bundle in order to tidy herself, and in a moment, a dozen women were crouched over the contents, snatching frantically at the combs and secondhand clothing, the shawls and pattens that were revealed. Bibles were tossed aside in favor of stockings and shifts, and the woman who had danced so suggestively, her raddled face painted, was posturing, the drawers she had filched held over her pelvis and thighs, her audience hooting and crying out expressions hitherto unknown to Emma, yet contriving to be disgustingly understandable. Her skin crept.

Mrs. Fry was speaking very clearly, not overloudly, yet heard above the din which gradually reduced, then miraculously stopped. There were one or two mutters of "Lady Bountiful" and " 'Oo do she think she is?" but the perpetrators were slapped and cuffed into silence. Predatory eyes fixed themselves on the bundles still held by Elizabeth Fry and Anna Buxton, but no one as yet made a move to take them. Expressions varied from curiosity and cupidity to downright lust or a dreadful blankness, as though the spirit had withdrawn forever, leaving only a shell of flesh and bone and wasting muscle. The regiments of emaciated limbs, the dirt-ingrained skin, the dead eyes of the autistic, worked strongly upon Emma's previous discrimination, shocking her into, first, a state of revulsion, and then into a blinding anger against the forces that had made these creatures what they were.

Incongruously, Elizabeth was praying. Someone tittered and was clouted by a white-faced woman who made Emma think of the crawling things one saw when one lifted a large stone in a damp place. "Shut up, you bugger! We can 'ear you anytime. Let 'er say 'er piece, such as it is." But the apparent deference was belied by the ugly twist to the gray lips that passed for a smile. Mrs. Fry affected not to notice and went on with a clear-toned reading from the Bible that was disturbed by a growing tendency among her listeners to fidget and scratch their heads. Some captured lice and clapped their hands together sharply to kill the insects. A bug crept across a striped mattress cover where someone had urinated not once, but countless times, to leave a brown stain that smelled rank and caught in the throat like acid.

By the time Elizabeth Fry had finished, and the miracle was that the women had waited so long, there was a rush to surround the three visitors, and the remaining bundles were only kept intact by the reappearance of the turnkey with reinforcements, alerted by the upsurge of bedlam.

"I must keep some things for the infirmary," Elizabeth told the pathetic riffraff, here and there interspersed with a more thoughtful or intelligent face that showed suffering many degrees deeper than that of her more down-to-earth fellows who could accustom themselves to the indignities and lack of privacy that must make the lives of the few with sensibilities a hell worse than Emma, for all her efforts, could imagine.

Some prisoners turned ugly and were beaten off by the jailer and his cronies who seemed to enjoy their work. The visitors were hastened out and the door clanged shut to the harsh rattle of bolts and keys and the renewed onslaught of the gray tentacles of entreating arms and calls for pennies for ale from the prison tap. Already the contents of the parcels were fought over, hidden inside the nauseous and unwashed clothes and found again, to be removed amid searing scratches from sharp and broken nails.

The sound of the catcalls and sobbing died to a sullen murmur. Mrs. Fry was dreadfully pale and Emma could think of nothing to say. She trailed upstairs after the two ladies, conscious of her empty arms and of their bulging bundles. Somehow, it would have been an impertinence to take them from them. A man appeared behind Emma with a great armful of clean straw and Mrs. Fry smiled at him and looked less haunted. "There will still not be enough," she said. "There will never be enough of anything."

Then there was no time to suggest relieving either Anna Buxton or Elizabeth of their burdens because they had reached the infirmary. It was a dreadful place, Emma thought, flinching from the smells of suppurating flesh and the filthy rags many of the younger women wore because they were menstruating and had not the means to change themselves. There were children crying, too, their small voices almost lost among the tiers of dirty rushes and slung hammocks that gave the place the atmosphere of the hold of some evil-smelling slave ship. Here, too, there were brutal and depraved faces, glimpses of sly mockery and brazen impudence. Oddly shocking were the newcomers in clean garments and with presentable hair, for Emma knew that in the space of days they would resemble the rest. The lice would be passed from one to another, the bugs would feast on the white arms and legs, the still pretty necks, the clothes be torn from them and fripperies be commandeered by the more terrifying of the old hands.

"How dreadful," Anna Buxton confided, whispering, "that the jailers and the male prisoners are let in here. Better to be old and ugly and left alone."

Emma thought of the woman downstairs, who was thirty-two and looked at least twice her age. Nothing, however degrading, seemed worse than to have one's youth stolen, never to be replaced. A woman could retain her inner self in spite of violation, or Emma thought she could if she were strong enough mentally to shut that part of herself away from physical force. Then she realized her own arrogance. How could she know what it was like to be made to submit to a man in some furtive corner of a crowded room inhabited by the gutter scrapings of a city?

Mrs. Fry produced cleaning materials to efface the worst of the filth, and Emma was violently grateful for the outlet of using the soap and water herself and enlisting the aid of one or two decent women who did not mind the coarse abuse showered on them by the degenerate.

The turnkey who brought the straw was followed by two others, and the worst of the sick were made comfortable and placed on the fresh litter. Emma helped dress some of the puny babies in clean, new clothes made by Elizabeth and her friends, and piles of napkins were left with the, by now, tearful mothers, most of whom sobbed out their gratitude though others were unnatural in their animosity, seeming to hate the children they had borne.

" 'Is father was a pig and so will he be," a very young girl said, not moving a finger to wash and change her infant, leaving everything to Mrs. Fry and an older prisoner. " 'Ates him, I do."

A small girl, bruised and vacant, bore the marks of frequent beatings. Emma's heart ached for the little creature who seemed, by process of being struck about the head, to have been reduced to near idiocy. She spoke to the child softly and took her close to brush out the tangled yellow hair and was anguished to perceive a swift look of naked misery that vanished immediately in studied imbecility. Appalled, Emma stared at the mother, a dark, thickset woman with more than a trace of mustache, who intercepted the unspoken anger and broke into a shrill vindication of her cruelty.

"Went orf and left me, 'e did, the swine! Like a millstone she's been—"

The yellow head drooped. The small shoulders hunched defensively. A great, salty lump lodged in Emma's throat.

"You must not be overinvolved," Mrs. Fry said quietly from a far-off place where ordinary human decency had retreated. "There are others, Emma, who need us. You cannot choose one, and that one impossible to remove. Do you think I have never wished to take away a child from this place? But one can't. You must try not even to recall the person who affects you. You must promise."

Emma closed her eyes. The hanging head with the pale-marigold hair still filled her vision. That terrible shaft of awareness. How could she promise?

She opened her eyes again and the child had gone and the woman with her. Agonized, she tried to see her again between the hanging hammocks, in the shadows between the patients on the straw, but there was no sign of her.

"Come," Elizabeth said gently, "we've done all we can for today."

"But we'll come again! We will come again?" She could not understand her own insistence.

"If you wish."

"Yes. I do."

"Very well."

It was much darker when they went back down the echoing stairs. The cries beat upon Emma's ears but they seemed muted since she entered the place. She knew she would never again feel as she had before this afternoon.

It was raining as they ran across the cobbles to the hackney carriage. Emma stared out of the window, seeing nothing.

She had time to change her clothes and make herself presentable before Wildford appeared to take her back to the hotel suite. He bowed formally to Mrs. Fry and asked after her husband, Joseph, then inquired about the prison visit and what was needed.

"They need soup in the infirmary. Many things, but soup most and straw."

"I should like to contribute to these things."

For the briefest instant Mrs. Fry looked as though she would like to refuse, then, remembering the scenes of the afternoon, she thanked him quietly.

"How much do you need?"

"There is no end to what is required."

He named the sum he was prepared to donate and Mrs. Fry's eyes widened and became curiously predatory. She would never have looked so on her own behalf, Emma realized, then determined that she'd work on Wildford to make his offer even more impressive.

"And there are lots of children's clothes needed," Emma said as they were leaving and Mrs. Fry waved from her doorstep, face fatigued. "Dear God, those children—"

"Are you sorry you went?"

Emma turned her head away. "No—"

"It *was* worse than you thought. I knew it would be."

"Other people can endure it. And I'm strong as a horse."

"There's no need for you to endure anything. I can send money to Mrs. Fry and you need never set foot in the place again."

"It would not be the same as making the effort. I'm not sorry at all. I intend to do it again."

"Oh, well, flagellate yourself if you must!"

"And where did you go," Emma asked, "while I was with Mrs. Fry?"

"Nowhere in particular."

"That sounds very evasive."

"Well, if you must know, I went to your grandfather's. He saw me—unwillingly."

"Was Mama there? And Maybrick?"

"Neither. Amelia is holidaying at Brighton with her mother. Maybrick is no longer a welcome visitor. Even someone with impeccable breeding can have coarse impulses." He laughed humorlessly. "Apparently he's taken a liking for drink and has offended Amelia by his gross behavior, the very thing she found distasteful in me."

"When do we return home?" Emma recalled, uneasily, Maybrick's parting threat.

"The day after tomorrow."

"So soon?"

"We must, I fear. Business matters that cannot wait. So make the most of what's left of the week, for we'll not be here again in a hurry."

"But I can go to Newgate again if I have Miss Fallon as chaperone during the stay?"

"We'll discuss that later."

"Are you glad Mama wasn't there?"

"Why should I want to see Amelia?" Wildford countered.

"Why indeed?"

"Do you mind, then, that she has never wanted to see either of us again?"

"I used to, not because I loved her but because it rankled that I was such a disappointment to Mama. She'd have loved a pretty doll to dress but she thought me plain and hoydenish. A sense of failure more than a sorrow."

"You have not disappointed me, Emma, always remember that."

"Oh, Papa!" The tiredness and grief were sloughed off in a rush of tenderness. She put her arms around him, feeling the strong beat of his heart. He was indestructible, a rock to cling to after emotional buffeting, and anything he did was for her good. Remembering Lewis, she drew away again, the spontaneity gone, then was surprised to realize that Critchley had not entered her mind for some hours.

"Papa, are you as rich as Mr. John Old?"

"Why ever should you ask that? What's Old to you?"

"He seemed a man of substance."

"He is; an East Indian company official, also having private means, so he's no need to worry about banks failing because of the country's politics."

"Then he is more stable than a banker?"

"I should say he was. But I have so much faith in my bank that I seek to expand."

"So everything comes back to personalities."

"I think so. You're not setting your cap at Old are you? He has a wife already."

"He told me himself."

"You can be devious when you wish. You never used to be. What's afoot?"

"I'm grown up, Papa. I know you've set your face against the idea, but I'm a woman and I feel—" She choked a little, recalling the afternoon, the gray plucking fingers, the dancer with the obscene gestures, the baby girl who knew what hatred was and defended herself against it by pretending to be an idiot. "So—old," she whispered.

He looked at her sharply. "It's since you employed Fallon. She's no spark of humor. Probably stifles you."

"It's nothing to do with her, poor old thing."

"You should have kept—"

"Jess? We'll not get her back. Oh, there's the hotel. I think I could eat an ox. It seems a lifetime since I ate." But she was anything but hungry. That child. When did she last eat? And would her hair be a mass of tangles by tomorrow? And what was her name? She would never know and the thought hurt her far more than the fact that she'd never be sure that Wildford and Jess had shared the same bed. Her sense of values had altered quite radically and she was not even disturbed that it was so.

"Damn that woman Fry. You're crying, aren't you?"

"A little."

"Now that concerns me! That you do not even argue. What has she done to you?"

"It is not what *she* has done. It—it's a little girl, little more than two or three years old who turns herself into a—thing, to avoid being noticed. And by her own mother."

"You must learn to treat them in a more detached fashion, my dear Emma. Only, I doubt you'll succeed, being the person you are. Don't tear yourself apart—"

"I'm of an age where I'm most likely to. I can no longer

cushion myself in childhood and I've not yet applied the usual adult veneer. I'm—vulnerable, Papa."

She did not usually put her feelings on display. Being a woman was the most uncomfortable process, Emma decided, allowing herself the luxury of being helped into the hotel and up to their suite which was furnished in the French style and had a delicious lightness of gilt and pale satin, and delicately wrought chairs and sofas. She had not appreciated its beauty or the fragile grace of the chandeliers until today when she had looked upon filth and want. Mrs. Fry had made a start in Newgate but there was a long road yet to travel.

It was with an effort that she brought her mind back to Lewis.

Miss Fallon appeared, quite flustered under the sardonic gaze of Wildford and wringing her hands like Lady Macbeth. "Mr. Old called while you were out—"

"And?" Wildford barked.

She started visibly, as he had no doubt intended. "He wished you and Miss Emma to take supper at his home this evening. He has a surprise for you."

Wildford laughed unkindly. "There's nothing will surprise me any longer. I've lived to the full, you might say."

Miss Fallon averted her eyes. "Er, yes. The hotel will send a messenger. I did inquire."

"How very astute of you."

The woman flushed. Even her neck was red and Emma was angry with her father.

"Thank you," she said. "Would you press the blue gown, please? I should like to go."

After the woman had left, Emma told Wildford, "I think you were extremely rude to Miss Fallon."

"She's making you dull like herself," Wildford grumbled.

"Are you going to the Olds'?"

"I have no choice, have I, since you've made up your mind?"

"He did me a great service," she reminded him.

"Aye. He did. Of course we must both go."

"Wear your most handsome coat."

"Why?"

"Because I want you to look more affluent than he does."

"I can't make you out, girl." But he laughed.

"Women do not give away everything. It's always policy to keep some mystery in reserve. You should know that, with your vast experience. Oh, and you'd best cancel supper, had you not?"

Wildford grinned and went off to dispatch an acceptance and make himself presentable.

Emma had Fallon send for hot water which seemed the most essential thing in the world and only when she was seated in the hip bath, the air fragrant with rose essence, did she hear the hateful voice of the young-old woman of Newgate, saying, "You'll scrub all your clothes 'cos we touched 'em, and bath ten times to wash us out of your mind."

The blue gown did not give her the usual pleasure, nor the jewelry her father urged her to wear in order to point out his supposed affluence. When she said she'd half a mind to take it all off again, he clapped his hands to his head in mock despair.

"You find out for the first time how it is to live on the other side of the coin and you imagine you must take on sackcloth and ashes. My dear Emma, it's not practical. I've mortgaged my interest to pay for soup and bales of straw for Mrs. Fry, but I've no intention of bankrupting myself. You're not consistent! How do we impress John Old in a couple of potato sacks?"

And because winning Lewis seemed to depend on success, she left the necklace of sapphires and diamonds where it was, though it did feel unaccountably cold, like some snake that had crept there to lie in wait.

The carriage arrived punctually and a little crowd gathered to watch them come down the imposing steps where the new gaslight shone yellowly on Emma's trinkets and brought forth gasps from some of the poorer folks in the alfresco audience.

"Coo! Ain't she grand?"

"Good luck, little lady."

"Spare a penny, for the love of Gawd."

"For the love of ale, more like," Wildford said, sotto voce, but threw the contents of his pocket into the gutter. The urchins and at least half of the adults were on their knees in a flash, poking about in the muck, the light of the gas lamp picking out the shapes of metal that could mean so much when one had so little. For all her bathing Emma felt dirty.

Even when the carriage rolled away, the golden glow on the polished panels, boys still ran after it, faces black-streaked. "Pretty as a princess! You'll give us rhino, won't yer, miss!"

She emptied the contents of her purse out of the window and the faces vanished like magic. A few scattered cries and oaths followed them, then were lost in distance and the sullen rumble of the wheels.

"That was gilding the lily, my dear, but I suppose, in your newfound zeal—"

"Oh, do be quiet, Papa!" she almost shouted.

Wildford looked at her, startled, and relapsed into silence. Emma could not recall ever having got the better of him and felt a flicker of satisfaction that was quickly lost in the grinding pain of wondering how that child was, what would become of her. She'd not grown dark and hirsute like her mother? She must not become brutalized!

The Olds' house was of yellow stone, black ironwork shaped into fleurs-de-lis and much white paint work, all fresh and sparkling. The curtains were not drawn because of the warmth of the evening and Emma could see pleasant things, vases and flowers, glimpses of expensive crystal and lit candles, the splendor of livery and tied wig as a footman passed across the window space framed by silken curtains.

"I could not compete with him," Wildford observed. "Are you disappointed?"

"No," Emma replied, meaning yes. Old could give Deborah Wymark the earth and she'd know how to twist him around her little finger, scheming baggage!

"What think you of gas lighting?" Wildford asked. "They say it will be in all our homes by the middle of the century."

"I prefer candles."

"And so do I. It seems that for once we are in agreement. Would you have preferred bringing that drowned cat of yours?"

"No, Father! I felt Miss Fallon had had enough of you for one day."

"I wish she would not wear gray. Allow me to hand you down, my dear. And do not *glare* at me so!" he whispered mischievously. "It will give a bad impression and you are so very anxious to make a good one."

Once inside, her irritation vanished. It was a beautiful house and perfectly cared for, a mixture of well-known and Oriental treasures that charmed her exacting eye. They were shown into a large room whose parquet floor shone mellowly and was filled with large plants on stands and pictures and very little else but chaise longues and an enormous mirror that ran the length of the marble mantelpiece.

Mrs. Old hurried across the room to greet them. "John!" she called over her shoulder. "John! Your guests have arrived." She was as pleasant looking as her husband, tall and attractively gray-haired, her eyes blue in a round, fair-skinned face. "Sit down, please. It is Emma, is it not? And Mr. Wildford, I've heard my husband speak of you so often, I feel I know you already."

Wildford favored Emma with a conspiratorial smile that he swiftly subdued into a deference that was unnatural. It was as though he tried to show her that he'd pander to her every wish, however foolish he thought it. He smiled very fetchingly at his hostess and engaged her in what promised to be a scintillating appraisal of the Rothschilds, who had started business modestly, trading in old coins and acting as advisers to the Elector of Hesse and had since set themselves up in every important European capital.

"What is their chief source of profit?" Mrs. Old wanted to know.

"Subsidies and loans for our allies."

"They often seem to me to be more a kind of enormous spiderweb than a family."

"Aha!" John Old hurried across the room, his eyes twinkling. "I see you are unable, Luke, to leave your work behind. Miss Emma. None the worse for the scare that rascal gave you, I hope?"

"I'd almost forgotten that."

"I had not. He was a very unpleasant man."

"More to be pitied than feared," Wildford interposed. "I think it was all bluster now I can view the matter objectively."

"I can only hope you are right. So you've brought the Rothschilds into our drawing room. It's Nathan I know. They say he made his money taking bullion through France to Wellington's armies. And it was his courier brought the first news of Waterloo. Galling for Wellington's own messenger to be outdistanced by a moneylender."

"I think one *could* call Nathan a banker," Wildford smiled wryly. "Would I and my compatriots held their secrets, the whole Rothschild fraternity, I'd eat off gold plate."

"But you didn't come here to talk of a family of usurers. I told you I had a surprise for you—well, it's for Miss Emma, really. You may come in now, my dear."

He had left the door ajar and for a nerve-tingling moment Emma expected to see Lewis walk into the room. She half rose from her chair, then subsided again as she saw Deborah enter, wearing what was surely a brand-new chartreuse silk gown, very high-waisted and deceptively simple, her corkscrew curls glistening.

"Deborah."

Miss Wymark looked wickedly demure. Emma had a strong desire to shake her but made herself appear welcoming since it was expected of her and she liked the Olds.

"I knew you'd be flabbergasted."

"I am. I meet Mr. Old for the first time and quite by accident, and then, there you are."

"Would you like to see my new clothes?"

"Er—yes." She could not force enthusiasm.

"Do not be longer than a quarter of an hour," Mrs. Old warned. "The food will not be edible otherwise."

"She's a dear person but fusses," Deborah whispered conspiratorially as they went in search of her room.

"I should rather enjoy being cosseted from time to time," Emma responded coolly.

"Of course, you have nobody. But you seem always so self-reliant."

Deborah flung open a door and ran across a fine Chinese carpet to the bed where gowns and gloves, stockings and underwear lay stretched across the counterpane.

"You have been extravagant."

"Oh, come, Emma, there's no need to sound so grudging. I've nothing costlier than that blue thing you are wearing and certainly nothing better than those stones round your neck."

"But I thought—"

"That I must dress like a milkmaid because Papa has lost all his money?"

"Under the circumstances—"

"I don't need to. Uncle John is to take me off his hands, make me his daughter in a manner of speaking. I'm to live here and will certainly lack for nothing. Oh, it will be so glorious to be in London all the time! Norwich is so very provincial. And it is especially gratifying that Lewis is to come so soon—"

"Lewis? You've seen him recently?"

"Why should I not?"

"Of course. He's a cousin. More like a brother, I imagine."

Deborah laughed meaningfully. "Then you imagine wrongly. I admit there was a period when we lost interest—he was rarely in Norwich and I had so many beaux but none quite like him. Then he came after a long interval and it was all as it had been—"

"I see." Emma's hands were cold. She rubbed them together and tried to visualize the cobbled square at home, the skirts of the green trees sweeping the ground and Lewis with leaf shadows on his face and hands. "And how was it in those halcyon days?"

"I've never had anyone to talk to about Lewis. How kind of you to be interested." Deborah pushed back a wood-shaving curl languidly and smiled secretly. "It would be pleasing to have a confidante."

"I'd be quite the wrong person," Emma objected quickly. "I don't approve of divulging what's private—or should be."

"Oh, I'd hoped—I never had a girl with whom to be close. But it was you who asked—"

"I'm no good at intimacy. I shouldn't have pried."

"You seemed to have no trouble with that former maid of yours. I've seen you chattering twenty to the dozen with her in the carriage on trips to Norwich."

"Indeed?"

"But, you don't know the latest news of—what was her name?—Ashcroft?"

"What about her?"

"One of Papa's gamekeepers was visiting at the Wellings and saw someone who looked very like her talking to—who's that picturesque rogue who factors the estate?"

"Captain Ringan?"

"The very man. I wonder if Lady Rayleigh knows? She'd be quite interested in tracking down her elusive maid if only for the pleasure of beating her."

"And that would give you a vicarious satisfaction?" Emma failed to control her tongue.

"My dear, what long words you do use. I always thought one had to keep servants in their place. Do I take it you do not? Wasn't that the reason you let the girl go? Because she was unbiddable?" Deborah lifted a fold of white satin and held it against her.

"I suspect I was wrong and that much of the fault was on my side."

The white satin fell back and slithered over the side of the bed. Deborah hooted. "May the skies fall! Emma Wildford confessing to a fault! My dear, what has altered you?"

"Nothing I care to speak about."

"Well!"

"When—when did you see Lewis last?"

The blue eyes became sharper. "Two days since. That was when we both discovered we were to come to London with our separate fortunes changed beyond measure. I told him about Uncle John's generosity and he told me of the new bank. He means to delve back into the methods used by the Rothschilds your father and Aunt Jenny were discussing. It seems he admires those who start from small beginnings and raise themselves by their own efforts."

"But the Rothschilds were a large family and aided one another."

"Lewis seems to think he does not need more than the proper contacts."

"He said nothing—else?"

"Not that I can remember." The eyes widened warningly. "Should there be something he ought to have told me?"

"I merely wondered."

"Then you can set your mind at rest. He did not mention you at all."

"Deborah! Deborah? You are wanted at table." Mrs. Old's voice traveled from the stair foot, firm yet pleasant.

"Drat the woman!" Deborah murmured. "I can see I'm to be treated as a child if I do not have a word with Uncle John." Then in tones as sweet as honey she called, "Coming, Aunt Jenny! Now, Emma, I suppose we must be good little girls."

Emma could not speak for vexation.

Chapter Five

The first evening back at home was one of the worst Emma had spent. The thought of Lewis tormented her. Deborah's divulgence about the girl who might be Jess was, if anything, even more disturbing. Not that it would be Ashcroft. The Wymarks' gamekeeper could have been fuddled with gin or too far away to receive more than a general impression.

She tried to tell herself that it was she who had done what wooing there was that day in Norwich and that Lewis had no recourse but to save her face by indulging in some diluted flirting. After all, what had he said but that it would be indiscreet to write to him at the bank and finally kissed the back of her ungloved hand? Captain Ringan's approach had been so much more positive if offensively crude.

Emma went to the window to look in the direction of the wood. No yellow dog tonight, only a deathly silence. There was not even the ubiquitous rain. Then, she saw in the distance a pale gleam flickering in the heart of the trees and knew that it was issuing from old Tom's cottage window. Miss Fallon had retired to bed and Papa was involved in papers appertaining to the new branch that Lewis was to manage. And turn himself into a Rothschild in the process if Deborah was to be believed!

She went to the press and fetched her cloak then let herself out by the side door. The night was dark and the air warm. Only the sullen gleam of the lake and the occasional peep of light between the trees showed her the way.

The night air oppressed her. She did not really need the cloak but did not want the trouble of carrying it. Emma was perspiring by the time she reached the cottage and began to make her way to the door. The window was uncurtained and she could see straight into the room. A small fire burned in the grate and a kettle was suspended over it, steam issuing from the blackened spout. A bench, a table, a bread shovel, two shelves holding plates, a hold net for fish suspended from the roof beam, the shadow of the small gallery at the other side of the room where Tom had slept; it looked much as it always had. Another shadow joined that of the bed rail, then became Jess, her hair tumbled, her shoulders covered with a shawl. She reached up and took down a plate, then fetched bread and cheese from the cupboard in the corner.

A mouse ran over the flagstones and the girl gave a little cry, then lifted the broom and swept the creature toward the door. Her gaze rested on the window as she did so, and her jaw dropped. "Miss Emma!"

By the time Emma had gone inside, the mouse had scuttled to shelter and Jess, a little pale, the remnants of a bruise yellowing on one cheek, faced her with some of her old defiance. "He said I could stay here. I wouldn't of if he hadn't said so."

"That was very kind of Captain Ringan," Emma said dryly.

Jess pushed forward one of two rickety chairs. "You'd best sit."

Emma accepted the grudging invitation. "Do not let me keep you from supper."

"Don't know that I can stomach it and you there, Miss Wildford."

Ignoring the insolence, Emma asked, "Where is Ringan?"

"Out on his rounds. Where he should be."

"And when he returns?"

"He eats and sleeps."

"Sleeps?"

Jess's lip curled. "Yes'm. Sleeps. Up there on the loft. Ain't you going to ask me where I do?"

"No." Emma shrugged and let the cloak slip from her shoulders. "So Deborah Wymark's gossip was founded on fact."

"Was it?"

"Her gamekeeper saw you with Ringan."

"Careless of us."

"Did Lady Rayleigh give you that bruise?"

"She did, the old bitch, and others you can't see."

"I'm sorry, Jess. Truly I am—"

"Are you, Miss Emma? Weren't you just the smallest bit glad that she beat some of the sauce out of me?"

"How am I supposed to answer that? Perhaps it was true in the beginning but I was concerned when she stormed up to the house to say you'd run away. How did you live?"

"Rough. Wore out my slippers and tore all my stockings."

Her bare feet and legs were well shaped like the rest of her. Even the bruise did not detract greatly from her undeniable good looks. How different she and Deborah were, yet both possessed the quality that drew men. I repel them, Emma thought, except for Papa's money—but for the promise of that. Pain came with the knowledge.

"But—you were not ill-treated by anyone other than Lady Rayleigh?"

"Depends what you mean by ill-treated. Men consider it natural behavior but you know all about that."

"Do I, Jess?" How angry she'd have been only a short time ago. Now it seemed unimportant.

"Having Wildford for your pa."

"You know you cannot stay here."

Jess shrugged. "Where else?"

"It's not suitable. Only the room and the loft uncurtained. Papa would never countenance the idea."

"And you'd not want me in the house again."

"I confess I'd not welcome the notion. You're too much for me, Jess."

"Funny, most people say that."

"We should not have taken you from Grandpapa's in the first place."

"Or taught me to ape my betters. It does unsettle a person." Jess picked up a crumb of cheese and chewed it with enjoyment. "Hungry, Miss Emma? No? But then you've already supped in your grand room on beef and oysters and raspberry tart. Cream from Welling's Farm. Stupid of me to ask."

"Oh, Jess. You are your own worst enemy."

"That makes two of us, then." The girl seized a crust from the loaf and began to gnaw the crisp exterior.

"You see why we cannot be together? Your tongue runs away with you. I'm sorry I did not take time to see you properly placed but any mistress would object to your frank speaking. You cannot be an equal, however much you wish it."

"Not with a gin-drunk pa who'd beg for everything we had. And did other things besides beat us with a knotted rope when the urge was on him. Had a little 'un once, I did."

Emma stared at her in horror. "You mean, a baby?"

"Course I do; it was his—my pa's. Suffered something cruel I did and not likely have no more which is a good thing. Don't matter so much when you're taken advantage of. Happens to lots o' girls, but that's nothing to do with you. Nice, clean, tidy sort of life you ladies must have. Pretty things next to your skin, new gowns when the fancy takes you—scents and soap. Trinkets. A husband with plenty o' money. Bought if need be—"

"When? When did you—? The infant—"

"Afore I ran off and went to your grandpapa's. It died."

"But they'd want a reference—"

"Took some money of Pa's and got a clerk to write one for me. Pa'd be mad when he found it gone. And me. I'd to give the clerk more than the money. It wasn't enough."

"What are we to do with you? A pity you'd not wed one of the servants. They all had a penchant for you. Jackson particularly."

Jess flung back her head, two little candle flames reflected in her eyes. "Nice and tidy for you, but no! Pawing beast! Told lies about me. I hates him if you want to know. Once get the ring on my finger and it would be a beating every Saturday or whenever it came over him. Cruel he could be with a girl, not that you'd understand. You'll moon about thinking you're in love with Mr. Lewis Critchley, when all he cares about is money and being master."

"You're wrong."

"You'll see. We don't all go about wi' blinkers on, Miss Emma. I was thinking, there would be one answer to my problem."

"Oh. What's that?"

"The captain. Poor sort o' life in the middle of a wood and only bread and cheese in the larder. Very taking ways, Captain Ringan."

"I'm sure he has." Emma got up suddenly and went to the

fire, holding out her fingers to the blaze. She did not know why Jess's suggestion was so repugnant to her and yet it was. "But perhaps he has his own ideas on the subject."

"You think he'd be marrying beneath him? A girl who was had by her pa?"

"Do not put words into my mouth."

"Maybe he was a gentleman once. Can't afford to be too particular now, though."

"Is marrying really only a matter of a roof over one's head? Is there nothing more?"

"A bed, miss, begging your pardon." Jess finished the last of the crust and flicked crumbs off her bodice. "There's always that whether it's Ringan or Mr. Lewis." She smiled. "You'd like to know what that was like, wouldn't you, Miss Emma. Irks you not to know. It can mean all sorts o' things, good and bad. Depending—"

Emma took a deep breath. "Does anyone else know you are here?"

"Not that I knows of." Jess had gone to lift the lid of the kettle. "Like to make him a rabbit stew, I would. Not that the captain worries about food. Drink, maybe—"

"I'll fetch you some shoes and stockings and a cloak."

"Thanks. It's hard walking in the wood without."

"But we must also have a serious talk about what's to become of you. What's the matter, Jess?"

The girl was looking fixedly at the window. "Thought I saw the captain, but if it was him he'd have been inside by now. Must have been mistaken."

"The shadow of a branch. A bird?"

Jess gave a little shudder. "Goose over me grave, Miss Emma." She was pale.

"I must go. Will you be all right?"

"Right as a trivet."

"By rights you should come back with me. I should insist."

"Only you know it's no use. And what could I lose that

ain't been lost already, eh ? Locking the stable, that would be."

Emma was aware of a pity she had never before felt for Jess Ashcroft. Hers was a terrible story and it was no wonder her head had been turned by the change in her fortunes. It was equally certain that Jess had known how desirable she had looked in bed in that London hotel during the visit of the Czar, despite her affectation of innocence.

"I'll come back tomorrow with the things I promised you."

"Very well, Miss Emma."

Emma had decided she must go to Norwich in an attempt to see Lewis in the morning. She wondered whether she should postpone the projected trip in view of Jess's situation, but the girl had been here for some days now and if the captain had seduced her there was nothing that could be done to reverse the position. Knowing Jess, the seduction could well have been of her volition. It still surprised Emma that the thought angered her where Jess's insolence had not.

Emma tried to analyze her own feelings about Ringan. Try as she would, she could never erase the memory of that meeting in the rainswept copse, the strength of his body against her own. It no longer shocked her that he had left such a ruthless imprint of his personality because, since then, she had seen it tempered in different ways. He had his own brand of charm. His eyes, in spite of their imperfection, had a habit of lighting up with a kind of wit and amusement to which one could, perhaps too readily, respond.

She could never like him, but he did feel for others—that dying rifleman, Jess.

She looked back when she had gone a few paces into the wood, seeing Jess's silhouetted head against the pane. What problems Mama had introduced when she left Wildford. There seemed no end to them.

The shock of the girl's disclosures had not worn off and Emma stumbled more than once on the rough downward path. It was cold for the time of year and the wind blew away her need for sleep. If Jess had not falsified that reference, she could have been one of Mrs. Fry's lame dogs at Newgate.

Emma saw that if she were wholehearted in her wish to alleviate misery, she had a ready-made subject for her generosity on her own doorstep. Somehow, and without prejudice, she must help the girl.

She was wide awake when she reached the side door by which she had left earlier. A shadow detached itself from a penumbra of glooming rhododendrons.

"Miss Emma," Ringan said softly, "I must speak to you."

"Yes. I can see we have things to discuss. I've just come from the cottage." Her heart returned to its ordered beat. It seemed that the captain had, after all, a sense of responsibility.

"Why did you go there?" There was a queer, mocking note in his voice that had the power to disturb her afresh.

"Someone told me they had seen you and Jess."

Though it was dim, she saw his lips twist in distorted amusement. "Even the trees have eyes, it seems."

"No. It was the Wymarks' gamekeeper taking a shortcut from the farm."

He laughed mirthlessly. "There's no harm to the arrangement. The girl was in a state of exhaustion and hunger when I found her in the wood, and you were not here. I could hardly leave her to starve in the rain."

"Why did you not call on Papa? He was downstairs when I left."

"It seemed more a matter for yourself."

Emma shivered in spite of the cloak.

"Could we not talk inside?" Ringan urged softly.

"It's late and the servants in bed."

"And you cannot forget our last encounter."

"No."

"You should not have asked for the secret."

"And is that all? A crude embrace. A kiss?"

"You did not think that at the time. I fancied you'd have let me go further—"

It was in her mind to strike him but that would have been to admit the truth of his words. "I can't think what you mean." She yawned elaborately while admitting to herself that she found him stimulating. He never, she noticed, played on others' sympathies because of his disfigurement, and this she could admire.

He treated his spoiled looks as though they did not exist, never tried to shield his scar from curious glances. Just stared one in the face with those curiously fascinating eyes that were seldom without humor even if it sometimes bordered on irony.

"Then you won't invite me into your parlor? I'd play fly to your spider."

"I will not."

"But you'll give the business your attention?"

"I will, though I cannot imagine what would be best. She seems against marriage, though there were plenty on the staff who admired her." It had been on the tip of her tongue to say "against marriage except for you," but stopped herself in time. No use in putting ideas into his head; not that they might not already have been there. All this nonsense of spiders and flies was to conceal something else.

"I'd not force the girl into some loveless match with a butler," he said bluntly. "In fact, she needs careful handling altogether—"

"Well, you must know all about that," she retorted.

"How hard you sound. Terrible things have shaped Jess Ashcroft."

"She has told me. But only tonight. It would have been better if she'd been honest from the start." Emma laid her hand upon the doorknob.

"Would it? You'd have kept away from her as you'd avoid a tar barrel. You were too self-righteous for comfort a few years back."

"I'm surprised you remember. All those women in between," she taunted.

"Two. Geraldine, whom you met, and Jeanne."

"No one since the Frenchwoman?"

"No one. And only one kiss, though I could have had them from most of the female staff, all of the Welling girls and Miss Palsey."

"I applaud your modesty. You've not mentioned Jess."

"You've not listened. There were things that happened to her after leaving the Rayleigh woman and hiding in the wood. Things that shouldn't happen to an animal. She's in a dangerous mood—"

Ringan shifted and disturbed a trickle of gravel. "She's best left where she is. She seems content to look after me. I confess it's a pleasant change."

Still no mention of his scar, no self-pity. Emma wanted to tell him that he should be taken care of, but could not think where to start without inviting unwanted intimacy.

"If it comes out, there will be gossip. It's only because the Wymarks' gamekeeper has not been back that you've kept her presence secret."

Ringan shrugged and came closer. "What's gossip? I think nothing of it."

"What have you to lose?"

"As you so rightly say, what?"

She drew away from him, turning the knob. The door creaked protestingly.

"Running away?" he suggested.

"I have learnt caution."

"We must discuss the business," he said again firmly, "out of Jess's hearing."

She hesitated. "I'm tired—"

"There's always tomorrow."

"Tomorrow, I'll be in Norwich."

"In the evening?"

"No. But Papa— No, I remember now, he's to be out. Perhaps you'd dine with me?"

He smiled. "And start gossip?"

"We will be discussing the matter of the yellow dog and of a suspected entering of the summerhouse."

"That's where Jess intended to hide but I told her she'd be found very quickly. It's so close to the house. No one comes to the cottage."

"Do people—shun you?"

"Rather, it's I shun them."

"You could have done so much better for yourself."

"Tomorrow, then," he broke in abruptly. "Eight of the clock?"

"Eight will be perfectly suitable. Good night, Captain."

"Ringan. Everyone always calls me Ringan."

"Good night."

Emma let herself into the house and fastened the bolt. He had not moved. She leaned against the glossy panel and listened. There was still no sound of footsteps on the gravel. Something touched the door as though he had slid a hand or arm across it. Her pulse quickened. She wished he would go away. It was altogether too disturbing to know that he lingered. But it was Emma who went first.

She dreamed of dark things. Of Jess and her father, of the woman in Newgate and of the yellow-haired child with the tortured eyes. Emma thought of them all during breakfast and while she saw the housekeeper about the day's menus. Mrs. Bott looked at her strangely, a hint of strong curiosity behind the usual complacency.

Miss Fallon was nervous for some reason and Emma elicited the information that her maid had seen a man prowling around the house the previous night.

"I would have come to you, Miss Emma, but I did not want to disturb you."

"Papa, then , or the butler?"

Miss Fallon flushed. She'd not approach Wildford if her throat were being cut and she did not like the butler. Mr. Perry was so very masculine, all hair and bulging thighs, and he laughed at Miss Fallon and her old-maidish ways.

"I may have been mistaken. But I fancied I heard voices."

"Anyone with bad intentions would have kept quiet," Emma said. "Did you hear anything of the conversation?"

"Nothing. Unless—"

"Unless?"

"I imagined that some business was to be discussed. That was all."

"Perhaps it was Papa and Captain Ringan. They usually have much to talk about."

The woman's face cleared. "Quite possibly. It was just that they seemed to be at the side door. Your papa—"

"Papa might have been letting the captain out and the side door was more convenient for the cottage." Strangely, the lie did not disturb Emma.

"I wish I had your gift of clear thinking."

"I like you as you are." Emma meant it.

Miss Fallon colored again, this time with pleasure. "Thank you, Miss Emma. Now I must look at your gloves. It is the green outfit you are wearing?"

"Please— Oh, and the object of our visit to Norwich is to order a large supply of baby clothes."

"B-baby clothes?"

"For those poor mites whose mothers are in prison."

"Very laudable, Miss Emma."

"Papa is to send large quantities of soup and straw for the invalid beds."

"Indeed? That is very good of Mr. Wildford."

Miss Fallon took herself off thoughtfully. Emma, still smiling inwardly at her maid's expression when the baby clothes were mentioned, sobered immediately when she remembered. Jess. What had happened to Jess Ashcroft was far from amusing and it might prove almost impossible to rehabilitate the girl. Emma's good humor evaporated. Fitter by far that she sought a solution there than went off to Norwich on a wild-goose chase. The clothes could be ordered anytime. Lewis might not go out at all.

She still worried over Jess as the carriage passed under the black pool of shadow that was cast by the city gate. The light was dull so that everything was dark and clearly etched, the church spire, the houses with their timbered fronts, the chimney pots and the nests in the elms. Even the bishop's garden, normally a green jewel in the setting of narrow streets, was dark and a little sinister, a place for beast as well as beauty. The tiny hills with their winding paths were uncannily solid, lumps of semiluminous stone. The castle watched, blind-eyed.

Emma went first to the shop to place her order for the children's garments which were to be sent straight to Mrs. Fry at Mildred's Court. "They must be warm and strongly made," she stipulated, wishing that they could also have been gay and beautiful. But if they had been, the children would not have been allowed to keep them. They'd have been sold for ale from the yard tap.

When the matter was settled to her satisfaction, she bought a dress and shoes and stockings for Jess, and a bonnet and reticule for Miss Fallon, who was overcome with pleased surprise.

"Nothing for yourself, Miss Emma?"

"I already have too much."

Miss Fallon made a deprecating noise and hugged the box containing her new possessions. "Then are we to go home?"

It occurred to Emma for the first time that people like Miss Fallon had no home but their place of work. Often it was only a badly situated room which was furnished with the leavings of the household, not planned or cared about. And there was little social coming and going for ladies' maids, for they fitted in nowhere. Too grand for downstairs, too inferior for their employers. Jess had been different from the start. They had spoiled her because she was pretty and had suffered on Emma's behalf.

"We will take a little drive," she said. "There's no saying who we will meet."

They passed Mrs. Craven, who looked pale and plain and who no longer cared about her appearance. Her clothes were quite neglected and her hair dull. She has been discarded by Papa, Emma thought, and was sorry. She wondered what had happened to sever the long relationship. Whose fault had it been? And as she pondered, Mrs. Craven looked straight at her and her eyes were those of the yellow-haired child.

For a long, terrible moment, Emma thought the woman was going to grasp at the bridle of the nearest horse but the limp hand fell away. She turned an ashen profile and continued to walk slowly on, her shoulders hunched.

She should not take it so hard, Emma told herself. No one is worth such defeat. Then she made herself find some piece of architecture to admire to avoid thinking of her father's mistress, but the pale, desperate face was reflected in every window. She had always known Mrs. Craven to be jealous, for the servants had gossiped endlessly, forgetting that children have ears. Mrs. Craven was removed from the immediate, a glamorized being, sought after by a master they respected, endlessly interesting. Cook would know by now that Wildford's lengthy interest had waned. Who, she would be asking, would be the new paramour? Who indeed?

There were not many folk abroad because of the dullness of the weather and no sign of Lewis. Emma could not reasonably have expected to arrive on the day he would be visiting another bedridden client. It would have been too opportune.

Green-caped and bonneted, she sat back in the carriage and thought out her next move. She would have to call at

the bank on some pretext and risk annoying Wildford.
There was no help for it.

She directed the driver and completed the journey with
ill-concealed impatience. It was disconcerting to find that
she had almost forgotten what Lewis looked like. Not that
he could have changed, but not remembering was like coming upon a high wall set across a familiar thoroughfare.

The bank was all gray stone and olive-green paint with
glints of brass, the door black and glossy and bearing the nu-
merals 11 in bold relief. It was so much more striking than
the London premises.

"Shall I wait in the carriage?" Miss Fallon asked, her thin
hands linking across her precious parcel twitched in a prelude to knuckle-cracking.

"It is intended to be a brief visit. Papa is sure to scowl and
fuss so I don't see why you should endure that as well as I."
Emma's smile was reassuring.

Descending, she entered the bank, aware of several pairs
of surprised eyes as the clerks lifted their gaze from the big
ledgers on the high desks. The books were intimidating
enough, the inkpots and quills a reminder of disliked lessons, but the appearance of Mr. Tully, skeletal lean and tal-
low-skinned, gave Emma a well-remembered grue. Tully
looked at the world darkly. His present mistrust of paper
currency caused a good deal of strain, as Wildford maintained that it was a necessary evil of war but Tully insisted
that greater efforts were required to bring about the re-
sumption of cash payments. Gold, he maintained, was always gold and could only appreciate in value. Paper notes
never realized their supposed figure when used in exchange.
Then Wildford would remind him of Napoleon's "poisoned
dart," the increase of the National Debt to well over £860
millions, and that would keep Tully quiet for a week or
two, but today he looked as though set for another eruption
in the near future.

"I know I should not intrude," Emma said quickly. "But it was a matter of urgency."

"We do not have the pleasure of seeing you often enough," Tully said surprisingly. "Mrs. Tully was only asking yesterday how you were and I had to tell her I did not know."

"How kind of her. You look troubled, Mr. Tully."

"I was thinking that we'll pay dearly for Napoleon's belligerence, Miss Emma. This system of financing war by borrowing in order to keep faith with investors, it can only lead to a crash. Some banks have already fallen."

"Mr. Tully, I feel sure you may trust my father." But Emma recalled the Frys.

"It's not your father I mistrust. It's young Critchley and his ideas. I think he sees himself as —"

"A Rothschild?" Emma prompted mischievously.

Tully looked at her as though she'd been a witch.

"Wouldn't it be splendid if he were?" she went on. "We'd all make our fortunes and need not call the King our cousin."

"Emma!" Wildford's door was open and he beckoned imperiously.

Inside the handsome room, she forced herself to penitence. "I seem to have spent all the money I had with me, Papa, and I still have one or two articles to buy. I thought you'd overlook the intrusion. Indeed, Mr. Tully was delighted to see me—"

"Stop chattering. I know you have some ulterior motive." His face was grim.

"It's not true. I bought a great number of children's clothes, for Mrs. Fry's charity. And a gift for Miss Fallon, who seems never to receive any, not to mention a gown and shoes for Jess."

Too late Emma realized her indiscretion.

Wildford frowned. "What do you mean? A gown and shoes for Jess. Have you seen the girl?"

"She made me promise to say nothing."

"Where the devil is she?"

"At—Ringan's cottage. It appears she collapsed in the wood and he found her."

"Why did he not report the matter?" Wildford's dark eyes were angry.

"She told some dreadful story of what had happened after leaving Lady Rayleigh. Captain Ringan was afraid of making matters worse. She wished only to be left alone."

"I should have been informed. The matter will certainly be resolved tomorrow. To think that all three of you conspired to keep it from me."

"You make us sound like criminals."

"Do not be pert. Must you have money?" How forbidding he was, but she could not go without one more attempt at seeing Lewis. "Please, Papa."

"Very well. Wait here."

She felt cold after he had gone. It was lucky he was invited out this evening and would not get back until too late to go to the cottage.

Someone knocked at the door. "Come in," she said automatically, then grew still as Lewis entered the room. It seemed years since she had seen him but his high-cheekboned, long-nosed face still pleased her. And then it occurred to her that he looked like Ringan before the scar, before the process of dissipation. Even their physique had a similarity, a narrow elegance.

"Miss Emma. I had not thought to see you here."

She looked in vain for warmth, for the interest he had shown at the Wymarks', but his expression showed only a smooth impassivity.

"I did not manage to write—"

"Write?"

"From London. You know I was there. I told you."

"Of course. You went with your father."

"I meant to send you a poem by Sir Walter Scott."

"Did you?" He stood, very stiff and self-contained, betraying only a slight embarrassment.

She might as well have said she'd intended to send him a dead fish. A tight band of misery constricted her throat but she would not let him see how he hurt her.

"We were invited to sup at the Olds'. Deborah was there."

His eyes flared open, full of something she did not want to see. A sickness attacked her stomach. All her misgivings rushed back like a noxious tide but she forced herself to smile. "We—we had a most interesting evening. Deborah has had good fortune. But, then, you know about that, don't you?"

"Do I?"

"She said so."

"Oh? I had imagined—"

"That she'd be more discreet? You cannot know her as well as you may think."

He picked at an imaginary thread on his cuff. "Will your father be long ?"

"Only a few minutes. But you need not bother to stay with me if you've something better to do, or if I make you uncomfortable."

"I did not say that. This is a place of business and not for personal meetings."

" Mr. Tully was more welcoming."

"You are angry, Miss Emma, that I am not as I was that day we walked together."

"Not angry. Disappointed, perhaps, but certainly not angry. I realize, of course, that you did not know on that occasion that Deborah was to come into a new inheritance. It must make a difference."

"Unfortunate that you should put such construction on the business." There was an edge to his voice. "Did you not stop to think how it would sound to your father if he came and found us—intimate? After all, it was you said he was so dead set against a—friendship. That we must not broadcast our meetings."

"It's not friendship he's against."

"Miss Emma—"

"Emma."

"I cannot bring myself to—"

"Compromise me? I confess I'd not care." She laughed at his discomfiture.

"Then you should. Once your good name is lost—"

"One's value depreciates?" In spite of the pain, it was good to see his control lost in exasperation. Even annoyance was a more acceptable reaction than indifference.

"Some people would think so."

"No one is going to come into my father's room without first knocking."

They faced each other and Emma saw that his irritation had turned to something else. Excitement? His quickened breathing might suggest that. She wished, impotently, that she did not find him so handsome. Someone had once said in Emma's presence that people were attracted to a particular type. If a widower remarried, his second wife was usually a facsimile of the first, and women must feel the same. Her own preference was for brown, lean faces with arrogant noses and blue, amused eyes. For hard, slim bodies. Strong, thin fingers.

"Oh, Lewis, you know what I'm trying to say." She moved closer, swayed by her own imaginings, dazzled by the light that made his irises clear and shining, his skin so smooth.

She put her arms around his neck and kissed him passionately, thinking for one heavenly, unforgettable moment that his lips had responded. Sure that they had, she clung to him happily, then was mortified to feel him grasp her wrists and put her away from him. "Lewis—"

The warmth left her and she was again cold and unsure, hating him for the volte-face and wanting to hurt him.

"Emma, I do advise you to take care. You know you conceal nothing. That is inviting trouble."

"What happens to me cannot affect you. I have been very foolish. I see it now."

"It is not as you think," he insisted.

"Do you want to wait until Papa returns?"

"I think I will not."

"Don't you want to hear about my visit to Newgate?"

He looked at her curiously. "I never thought you'd go. What were they like, those women?"

"They taught me a great deal. One thing I learnt was to rip my petticoat and cry rape. Shall I try it now, Lewis? What would happen to that splendid future then? I've a good mind to."

"Why should you do such a thing? Revenge, I suppose." His forehead was damp with sweat and he was pale.

"Then you *did* lead me on that day! I find you a broken reed, Lewis. You'd never have mentioned revenge unless I'd been given grounds for a grudge against you. Hoist with your own petard."

"I'll come back when you have gone, Emma."

"Very well." Her eyes met his perfectly steadily. "I'll tell Papa."

The door closed behind him. That would teach her to run after men who hankered after other girls. She closed her eyes against the onset of despair.

Wildford returned just as she had composed herself. She greeted him calmly, not allowing one trace of her unhappiness to show. He'd crow if he knew Lewis had set her aside, and say things like "I told you so." Emma was in no mood for homilies, and even in her state of rejection she had no wish to spoil Lewis's chances of promotion. Her own obstinacy and stupidity had got her into this situation and she had been well warned. Perhaps he had not meant it. But the seeds of hope refused to germinate.

"Will that be sufficient, Emma?"

"Quite sufficient, thank you. Did you know Tully is still full of forebodings about paper money?" She slipped the coins into her reticule.

"My dear Emma. If I have heard of the National Debt once, I've endured it a thousand times. He dins it into me that the annual payment is merely the transfer of money from one pocket of the nation to another. I feel he gives me no credit for sagacity. I am merely a figurehead."

"Oh, Papa! You a cipher!" In spite of her recent blow, Emma could not help laughing. Wildford was so vital, so strong in every way, that Tully must have a blind spot to miss his employer's very real qualities.

"And he has never forgiven Britain for presenting mass production to the world. Mass-produced is ill-produced. He fears craftsmen will vanish with the century and I suspect he may be right. There'll be a uniformity Cobbett would welcome. He'd sweep away all ownership. Oh, to the devil with Tully and Adam Smith, the whole boiling. Go and buy whatever it is you want and remember that, though I'll not be back till the small hours, I'll want an explanation from you tomorrow evening and a sight of Jess Ashcroft."

"Yes, Papa."

"You look pale, girl."

"Perhaps another trip to London would be beneficial. I should so like to go again with Mrs. Fry."

"To that sink of iniquity?"

"It might not be so if we were to persevere."

"Such cesspools can never be eradicated. Nor sweetened."

"I suppose not. And yet— She is so determined and you'd not believe the effect she had on some."

"And there would be others who'd spit on your shadows and stick a knife in your gullet."

"There are always those who'd crucify their mothers. Lie and cheat—"

"Who has crossed you, Emma?"

"It was not—personal. I think Mrs. Fry could be success-ful."

"The Frys have been singularly unsuccessful in other matters. The business. The matter of their children being brought up by others."

"But by relatives with the means and the love to wel-come them. It was not her wish to be parted from those daughters, that son. They say she writes to them most touchingly. I never had such a letter from Mama. Money does not necessarily make good parents."

Wildford's face assumed a look of weary experience. "Sometimes you sound so pedantic. So Quakerish. You'll not adopt her faith as well as her sentimentalism?"

"You do not see her as she is. There is no sham. No his-trionics."

"I remain to be convinced. I suppose you had better go."

She wanted to ask him about Mrs. Craven, only it was none of her business. But there was Jess, unexpectedly available, needing support. Her father might be more than interested in reclaiming the girl. He'd be a better catch than Ringan.

A worm of excitement uncoiled in her stomach. In retro-spect, she could not imagine what had prompted her to invite the captain to dinner this evening, unless it was a recognition of his determination to solve the problem of Jess. As if anyone could!

"Thank you for the money, Papa."

"Who else do I have to whom I can show generosity? There are gaps in my life, Emma. I'd have liked a son. Un-ashamedly, a son would have both pleased me and made the bank worth all the effort of building it up to what it now is, a success. As it is, you have assumed pride of place in the absence of son and wife. I hope you'd not feel differently to-ward me should I fill these gaps?"

She must not let him become aware of her sense of dis-quiet. "My feelings would never change. How could I love

you less because you let others into your life? Any more
than you would if I were to do the same."

He gave a bark of laughter. "Emma, you were not supposed to say that! To introduce your own ultimatum. Yet I
can recognize the justice of your remark, in spite of the fact
that it would still displease me if you were to form any major relationship with a man. I still consider you far too
young for such commitments."

"Many girls marry at sixteen. Younger than I—"

"Like your mother, and make dreadful mistakes. As she
did."

"I still find it hard to understand how she could not love
you. And even more so, to prefer Maybrick. Though, it has
not lasted, as I found out to my cost."

"Let him lay one finger on you and I'd kill him."

"He'd not have said what he did if he'd not been drunk
and rebuffed."

"I think he'll find it was his greatest mistake."

"He'll never come. Not to Norwich," Emma said. "Nor
to Staves."

"He'd best not."

"By the way, Lewis wished to see you. He came but
would not wait."

"Strange. I thought he'd have jumped at the chance of
having you to himself. "

"He is quite punctilious. Almost too much so."

"So it appears." Wildford clapped her on the shoulder.
"Buy yourself something pretty, my dear. And keep Jess out
of trouble. Oh, here is Lewis. Come in, my boy, Emma's
just leaving."

"Good afternoon, Miss Wildford." His clear eyes flashed
their message of brief contempt.

"Good-bye, Mr. Critchley."

He looked startled at this as though he had not expected
so final a salutation.

"Au revoir, perhaps?" he suggested.

He was keeping a door open she had just resolved to close forever. Why not allow him to do so?

"Good-bye," she repeated firmly and let herself out before she changed her mind. She had forgotten Miss Fallon. But her heart warmed itself gratefully on the unmistakable spontaneity of the woman's greeting, her look of pleased surprise as Emma apologized for keeping her waiting. Jess's departure had brought some good in its wake which was more than her reappearance threatened.

"Am I too early?" Ringan asked.

"Not at all," Emma said politely. "May I offer you a glass of wine?"

"You may."

He attempted to smarten himself up, she noticed. His shirt and cravat were clean, his coat was brushed and his boots were polished. She still smarted from her encounter with Critchley and wondered if that prickliness would make itself evident. Ringan could be very much more far-seeing than her father.

"Did you have a successful day in Norwich?" he asked.

"Very."

There was a silence which Emma broke. "About Jess—"

"Remembering that if the door opens we are talking of yellow dogs and gazebos?"

"It would be more discreet." She watched the firelight flicker against the wall and on the gilded picture frames. "I bought some clothes for Jess today. I'd intended sending some things of my own, discarded gowns and shifts, but then I thought that new garments would show her that I do —care. That I am making an effort."

"I see."

"Unfortunately, I had to account to Papa for the money I'd spent and I was silly enough to let out the fact that Jess was nearby. He was none too pleased that he'd been left out."

"Does he want my head on a plate?"

"Not necessarily on a plate. Next to mine, I think."

Ringan smiled lazily. "I'd not object to that arrangement."

"Figuratively speaking, of course."

"Of course." He swilled the wine gently around the glass. "Have you had some reverse today? Who has thwarted you?"

She was surprised by his perception. "Why should you think so?"

"You have blue shadows around your eyes. And there are similar glints in your hair. How wise of you to choose the same color of gown."

"If I am downcast I cannot say the same for you. I have never seen you so well-groomed."

"It's Jess you must compliment."

"What *are* we to do about her? Papa will insist that she comes here and I cannot feel that it's the best thing, particularly after what you said about her frame of mind."

"She needs time to lick her wounds. This household would oppress her."

"At one time it was just what she enjoyed. She domineered over the other women—"

"It's the knowledge that they'd kick her while she was at a disadvantage that worries her, I think. And there's always a man to take advantage."

"That's why my father is so angry that you and she are so thrown together."

"My dear girl, I am out all day and half the night! I've not the strength for orgies of that kind."

"And you say that the only cure for that dog is a trap?" Emma asked.

"Eh? What's that? Oh, the dog. We'll have to have a beat, I think. Drive it out into the open and fire upon it."

Jackson had come in quietly to replenish the fire.

"Bring in some logs, please," Emma said. "The captain

and I will be here for some time. And, Jackson, remind Cook the dinner is to be served at eight sharp."

"Do you agree that could be the answer? Invite some of Mr. Wildford's cronies and smoke the beast out. Welling cannot afford to lose lambs at this rate."

"I wonder where it came from?"

"Who knows? Like the riffraff from Napoleon's war, there's no one wants it. One can draw parallels, there. The law of survival being what it is, the brute must eat, only there's no one to feed the creature."

"That's—rather sad."

"Welling would prefer you to pity his sheep."

"He has others. The dog is solitary." She wondered what Ringan would say if she told him he reminded her of the elusive animal.

"Returning to Jess—" He finished the wine and she offered him more, taking some herself. It was a long time since she had eaten and its effect was strong. They tried to find alternatives to the girl's present way of life but there seemed no solution beyond having Jess at Staves.

In the dining room, Emma took her father's place at the head of the table. Ringan was amused, she could tell, but she could not resent the slow smile. The bitterness of this morning was cushioned by the floating comfort of the wine and the firelight, the sparkle of the chandelier and the table that gleamed in the dimness like a black lake. There was a perverse satisfaction in the knowledge that this man seemed to be attracted by her. Not that she believed his declaration that there had been no affairs since the obliging Frenchwoman. It would all be a matter of expediency, like Lewis blowing hot and cold. And how very arctic the cold could be.

"Stop thinking of it," Ringan said abruptly. "Whenever you touch upon that raw nerve, your eyes look like two holes in a frozen pond."

She laughed. "Your compliments are like my honesty."

"I'm not given to flowery speech as you well know. If you know me at all—"

"I don't know you. There are certain people one can't reach and you seem to fit into the category more than most."

"Are you certain that the summerhouse was illegally occupied?"

"Summerhouse? Oh, yes, Captain. If you remember, I reported the matter to you on the instant." Emma joined in the farce with a certain enjoyment. Almost anything seemed amusing after a glass or two of Papa's best French wine. Perhaps they should order some of the pale dry German next. It was particularly good and there was trout to follow the soup. They should combine excellently.

"You do not seem to find it so difficult to lie," Ringan observed softly when they were alone again.

"It must be the company I keep."

"Touché!" She saw that she had delighted him.

"You should tell me more of yourself, then perhaps I'd understand you better."

"What's there to tell?"

"I'm sure Jess knows more than I do."

"And that matters to you, doesn't it?" He smiled thinly.

This time his insight infuriated her. She bent her head over her soup, ignoring both him and the smell of the dark red roses that reflected themselves in the table's dark surface.

"I was not always an adventurer."

"Indeed?" Emma stared at him, her gaze beginning at the top of the scar and following it past his eye, his cheekbone, his jaw, to the corner of his mouth. His mouth was not so much like Lewis's as the rest of his features. She recalled the feel of his lips against her own with a combination of unreality and a desire that the experience be repeated, then was angry again that he so obviously read her thoughts. She and Ringan seemed to inhabit a vacuum where nothing else intruded except the rose scent that grew stronger by the second.

"You are wishing you'd not invited me."

"But I have and must stand by it."

"And you've been hurt and want to savage someone in return. Well, I'm tough enough to withstand the blows. A man, is it?"

"I'd rather not discuss it."

"So, there's you and Jess in the same pickle! Except that she has the badness out of her system while you are letting the wound fester."

"We were not to talk about me."

"Except that it would be a release of sorts. Why not let me be your confessor? I'm closemouthed as an oyster."

"Until it suited you to blackmail me for my indiscretion."

"And how, I wonder, did the intruder gain admittance to the summerhouse when you say you remember locking the door? The windows seemed untouched."

There was a different footman in attendance, Emma realized, curbing a hysterical impulse to giggle. These switches of conversation were so sudden and so ridiculous one could not take them seriously. She wondered where Jackson was.

"Perhaps I did forget, or left the key in some obvious place."

"Was anything disturbed?" Ringan was grinning broadly as though he enjoyed the pretense.

"More wine, please," Emma said, surveying the trout in its crisp coating, the almonds pleasantly brown on the surface.

"Miss Emma—" Ringan murmured warningly.

"You were to tell me about your family."

"Was I?"

"Yes."

He shrugged and watched her drink three-quarters of the contents of her glass before setting it down with a clatter beside her plate.

"My grandfather had an estate in Somerset, near the Mendip Hills. So my young life was bounded by the sight of the hills, of caves and stalactites, the rhines with willows overhanging, deer, curlews and whortleberries. Farther off were the deep, green combes, and the distant bulk of Glastonbury Tor—"

"And what," her speech was ever so slightly slurred, "made you leave this paradise?"

"Human nature." He shrugged and picked up his fork. "The usual thing."

She knew better than to offer to cut up the fish.

"My father's life was bounded by his land and my brother John. John was to be seigneur in his turn and must be taught everything. There was no place for a younger brother. It rankled that John did what he must so infernally well that I must make my presence felt by misbehavior."

"Misbehavior?"

The dark blue eye transfixed her. "Carousing, card-playing, wenching. I've a brace of sons in Priddy—with different mothers, of course. I'd not have known if it had not been that I saw them years later. Discreet women in Somerset. They looked bland and uncomprehending when I spoke of the matter and swore the lads were their husbands'."

"And—"

"And then John died. My father was past himself with grief and could not accept the fatality. He took a long walk in winter and did not come back. They found him frozen like one of the stalagmites." He threw down the fork and stared at the table.

"Then you were master."

"Aye. And did not know how to care for the place because of my former exclusion. Those I employed to help me traded on my ignorance. I did try, I swear it, but it was like fool's gold, vanishing with every dawn. I then tried to recoup my losses by gambling but lost most of what remained and had to sell to the only bidder, he taking the house and land for a pittance because there was no market for it at the time. With what remained I bought a commission into the army and swore I'd learn the art of the cards if it killed me. I did learn—and lost my liking for it. It's damned funny when you think of it."

"I don't think it amusing." There was a catch in her voice.

"Then you should!" he shouted. "D'you think I'm looking for a long face? You asked and I've told."

"Please do not shout. It is boorish." Emma, unable to eat the rest of the fish, finished her wine.

"I beg your pardon. Why are you not eating?"

"I am not hungry. It has been a trying day and we are still no further forward with the business of—"

"The dog."

"That's right." Emma caught sight of Harrison's liveried back. The plates were taken away to be replaced by the meat and vegetables. "I feel wicked. All this food to go out to the pigs and those children in Newgate scrabbling for crusts, heaven help them."

"Newgate?" Ringan sat bolt upright. "What do you know of that place?"

"I went with Mrs. Fry, the banker's wife. We took—comforts for the prisoners."

"Comforts!"

"It's true. Clothes and clean straw. Combs and suchlike. Bibles."

"And came out alive?"

She raised her chin. "Alive and ready to do it all again."

"I confess I am surprised. You humble me, Emma. Here am I trying to justify my failure and all the time you are hiding your own triumph."

"Mrs. Fry would not allow anything to happen. My only mishap was to lose a piece of my skirt. It was of no account."

"It was not so simple as you make out. I've been inside the jail—"

"Oh, no!"

"As a visitor A friend of mine was in debt. I took money."

"It's a dreadful place. No one who goes there can remain innocent. I—did not like to see the children forced to accompany their mothers."

"What else can they do? The workhouse might be worse. At least they are not separated."

"Some would be better removed from the women. I'm afraid—I cannot bear to think of one infant in particular."

"Do not upset yourself. Eat." The strong hand clasped hers briefly, roughly.

She did as he bade her but the food tasted of nothing in spite of its delicious appearance. Cook would be huffed if she sent it back. The fire crackled, the wind made melancholy noises. The whole episode was joyless. It was Lewis who spoiled everything.

"I've some things for Jess—"

Ringan coughed meaningly.

"Stupid of me. I mean for Miss Fallon. I must remember to give them to her."

"And I must go, Miss Emma. I've taken up too much of your time."

The door closed upon the last of the servants.

"Let me come back with you. My father insists that we have the matter decided by tomorrow or he'll deal with it in his own way. And that is usually forceful."

"And not at all what the girl needs at this juncture."

Ringan looked different since his divulging of the past. The rakishness was tempered with the hint of forces beyond his control, an irony of fate.

"Then I will fetch the clothes and walk with you to the cottage."

"I think it would be better if I took them. You should go to bed. All that wine on an empty stomach! The fresh air would have you flat on the ground."

"Perhaps it was a mistake. You'll find the bundle at the side door. I put it ready."

"Will you tell your father we dined together?"

"I hadn't thought—"

He rose and the long, thin shadow stretched endlessly. "Good night, then, Miss Emma."

"You called me Emma half an hour ago."

"A slip of the tongue. Who was the man who hurt you?"

"What business is that of yours?" Lewis had receded to a far distance. A speck in infinity.

"I'll run him through the next time we meet."

"I can fight my own battles, thank you."

"Good night, Amazon."

"Good night, Captain."

She was too weary to fend him off if he attempted to make love to her. But he did not. One moment he was there, the next he was gone like a wraith, the door swinging behind him. It closed with a final click, leaving silence.

Emma wondered how she would manage the stairs, but she must have done it, for she found herself falling down onto the bed, the canopy seeming to press down upon her, wrapping her in darkness.

Chapter Six

She thought she had met Ringan's father in some cold, arctic place. Her fingers reached out to touch the rime of frost on his face and hands and she knew that he was dead, yet still moved, lurching toward her like some stiff marionette. Emma screamed.

A hand came over her mouth but it was not frozen like the old man's. It was warm and strong. A voice hissed, "Be quiet, Miss Emma, or you'll rouse the household."

She struggled for a moment, the fog of sleep not blown away. Then the pressure of his breast against her own aroused nameless longing, nameless fear. The hand was removed. The breeze blew through the open window, stirring the hangings.

"Get out, Ringan. I should have known you went too quietly."

"Keep your voice down," he whispered, and there was nothing loverlike in the sound.

She drew back against the coarse linen of the pillow slip. She had no liking for satins and silks in bed. Better by far the linen and lavender sprinkled—

"Jess has gone," he said in a low, angry voice, "and—Jackson is dead."

Emma sat up, pushing off his restraining arm. Her head ached abominably after the overindulgence in Wildford's wine and her mouth was filled with acid sourness.

"What do you mean? Jackson is dead?"

"Just what I say. She is not there and Jackson is dead on the cottage floor."

"He could not—just die."

"There's a knife through his heart. The one Tom used for gutting fish."

The sickness rose. Emma flung back the thin spread that had covered her and stood by the bed. She had not found the way under the sheets and blankets and now she was cold as death.

"But what has Jess to do with Jackson? I know she once said he lied about her because she kept him at a distance." She took her cloak from the press and wrapped it around her. "She did not encourage the man, I'm certain."

"That's why he's dead. I think he knew Jess was there and took himself over when his duty was done. Then, when she repulsed him—"

"Do not say it!" Her brain still hammered against her skull, but her thoughts were clear enough. "It need not have been Jess."

"Who else? Why has she gone if not for some overpowering reason?"

She became aware of the import of his presence in her room. The open window, the possibility of Wildford having returned or Miss Fallon being awakened.

"My father will kill you if he finds you here. You know that."

"He has not yet returned. I checked the stables."

"Then it's possible he'll stay the night. He'll have had his share of claret and brandy by now. The Goswicks are old friends and often give him a bed. What have you done about Jackson?"

"Nothing yet."

"It was my fault, wasn't it, for being indiscreet? I know I mentioned Jess's name more than once."

"I think he knew already. She said someone passed by the window during your visit—"

"I remember! She was extremely upset, though she soon recovered. Thought it was you at first, but no one came— It seemed to frighten her."

"Perhaps it was inevitable she'd be noticed. She's not a girl one can overlook."

"I must come back with you."

"No—"

"But I am in charge when Papa is not here."

"I only came to tell you in case you found out more harshly tomorrow."

"Oh, God, Ringan! They'll say she murdered him." The pictures on the wall, the bed hangings shivered and swayed, were still as stone. She saw—Newgate.

"They need not know she was there at all. She's left no traces."

"But Papa knows. Because of me."

There was a long silence, then he said, "I'll hide the body, then. There are places in the wood no one would ever find."

"They might." She drew closer to him as if for comfort. "And then they'd look about and before you know it they'd be sniffing around the cottage. And you."

"I'd be no loss. A failed landowner. Failed soldier. Failed lover."

"But you're none of these things! Inexperience is not a fault. And you must have had many victories—"

"Killing country lads who'd never thought of the mud and the bullets? Only the pretty uniform? Hollow victories they turned out to be. Their last breath their mother's name and their eyes a child's eyes, surprised and shocked—"

"You said nothing of this tonight. Last night—" She was deeply moved.

"It was not the moment. You swamped with memories of

a bleak encounter. Your revelations of Newgate. Your thoughts centered on a man and you'd not love lightly. You are not a woman who does anything lightly—"

"Woman?"

"You'd more of a woman in you that first day in the Ring than many a matron who imagined she'd lived to the full."

"No one would call you a failed lover."

"It's the uneasy cock that crows loudest."

"Ringan—"

"Oh, leave off, woman! It's not sympathy I want. I've a corpse to dispose of and a girl's life in my hands. What in heaven's name am I to do?" All the planes of his face were taut with frustration and his mouth was set.

"I shall tell Papa that you came to see me about Jess and that I made you stay for the meal to decide what could be best. We went to the cottage to give her the clothes I bought and she was not there. I came back after we concluded she had made other plans for her future. It could appear that she refused to be dragooned by you and me."

"And—if Jackson's body comes to light?"

"We know nothing. Someone had a grudge against him."

"But Jackson's disappearance will be reported from the kitchen."

"They'll think they went together. It would be only a nine days' wonder."

"We cannot be sure his bones will not be discovered—" Ringan said doubtfully.

"Bones! Whose bones? Who could prove anything? Bones are so very anonymous."

"What a lawless creature you turn out to be," he murmured wonderingly. "I hope you are right, Emma. If the tale can be strung together, it could go hard with Jess Ashcroft or—"

"You?"

"Aye."

"No! Someone from the kitchen—"

"Do you not see yet? If he'd been going away not intending to return, he'd have packed his possessions. Jackson did not. He imagined he'd have an easy conquest since I was dining safely with you. And he shares a room with two others, so any question of retrieving the goods cannot arise. He may have dropped some hint that he had a prize in sight. He'd a big mouth, Jackson."

And now that mouth was silenced. But she'd never let Ringan take the blame! Only, how could she know that he hadn't found Jess and Jackson in some compromising position and attacked the footman out of jealousy or rage? Then given Jess some money to send her to London in search of a post? He had felt very strongly about the world's treatment of the girl.

Tiredly, she said, "I'll tell Papa what we decided. Someone else will tell him about Jackson. We will know nothing. Why should we?"

"As you say." His voice was heavy. "It's just that I cannot relish the thought of Jess thrown onto the tender mercies of the world a second time."

"What did you do with those new clothes?"

"I thought she might come back. I left them."

"Let me know if she takes the bundle. I told her I had some things and that she'd get them today. She had no shoes."

"I made her some out of skins. They were better than nothing."

"Oh, Ringan, I feel we are walking a tightrope! Yet I'd never forgive myself if Jess were discovered and tried for his murder. They have the most abominable cells for the condemned. Nine by six they measure, dark and the tiniest windows, double-grated, nailed planks for walls—"

"You must be quiet."

"Yes." Her voice dropped. "Yes, I must."

"So long as you stick by the story we both shall tell."

"I won't forget."

"Good night, a second time."

"Good morning."

He did not smile, only went to the window. His hair stirred in the draft.

"We are doing the right thing?" she asked.

"God knows."

"Be careful. No one must see you. Do, please, take care."

"Oh, I shall. I've a healthy respect for my own skin." He put one leg over the sill, gave a sudden, heart-skipping lurch, and disappeared from view.

She ran to the window and stared out into the darkness.

His voice came from the mesh of ivy below. "Good morning, Emma."

There was a rustle, a soft thud, a shadow quickly lost.

She tried to tell herself he had not come, that his revelations about Jess and Jackson were part of her nightmare about the old man who had frozen to death. But the load on her heart brought its own terrible answer.

She had sworn she would not sleep but she did eventually doze, waking at intervals to remember afresh, to wonder if Ringan had finished the grisly task of burial.

Pale and quiet she made an appearance at breakfast in order to give an impression of normality. Jackson usually served at this meal. This morning it was Harrison.

"Where is Jackson?" she asked. "Is he ill?"

"There's no one rightly knows," Harrison replied. "Didn't come back last night. He asked if I'd mind taking over the last part of dinner as he'd promised to see someone and dinner did last longer than usual. Afraid of missing the person, he was."

"Perhaps he stayed at their house—"

"Which house? There's only Wellings' and Captain Ringan's. And the captain was here."

So Ringan had an alibi of sorts, Emma reflected, but Harrison's remark had made her see how few suspects there could be should the body ever be discovered.

"He is friendly, perhaps, with one of the Welling girls?"

"Not him, Miss Emma." Harrison laughed. "None of us ever fancied one o' them, poor souls. Old maids they'll be, for certain sure. Not that they ain't *nice* girls—"

"Since that theory is destroyed, is Miss Palsey perhaps in residence?"

"Gone 'ome a week since."

"Then Jackson must have gone to Norwich."

" 'Ow?"

"Walked, I suppose."

"Lazy sort o' beggar, Jackson," the man objected and took away her plate.

"Some things can induce unaccustomed activity."

Harrison grinned. "He said something of the sort."

"But gave no clue as to the identity of—the person?"

"No, Miss Emma. Just that it was someone 'e'd fancied for long enough."

"Then the girl must live in the town. I shall want an account when he does come back. Jackson knows when he is entitled to his leisure and it was not last night or this morning."

"Very well, Miss Emma."

"Just clear away, Harrison. Papa will not be here until this afternoon and I am not hungry."

She left the man busy and wondered what they were saying belowstairs. And would Harrison, should there be an inquiry later, remember that she had not been herself this morning? She should have pinched her cheeks and eaten the kidneys and eggs, even if they'd choked her.

Leaving Miss Fallon with sufficient to occupy her until luncheon, Emma made her way toward the lake. It was such a grand name for so small a sheet of water. Few knew of its existence, enclosed as it was within the walls of the estate. Perhaps the lake would have been a better place for Jackson's body, and if he'd been washed up it might be thought that he'd missed his footing and drowned. But there was the knife wound in his breast.

She saw Ringan against the tapestry of trees. Picking up the hampering skirts she ran toward him, then warned by the slight shake of his head, slowed her pace.

"You should not let anyone notice a need for urgency. Behave as if nothing had happened."

"It is not easy. I feel—hagridden."

"It's none of your doing."

"Oh, but it is. If I'd not sent Jess to Lady Rayleigh."

"Jess was born to be a catalyst."

"Is—he—?"

"Buried? Aye. It took longer than I thought." He showed her his hands with the nails all broken and still blackened with soil. "I'll not be beat if I can help it."

"Where did you put him?"

"Best keep it to myself. Then, should things go wrong, there's nothing you can inadvertently give away."

"But they will not go wrong, will they!"

"Of course not."

She told him of the conversation with Harrison at breakfast and he laughed grimly. "Lying like a trooper, Miss Emma! You're scarcely recognizable."

"I've not taken a taste for it. It's expediency."

"You'd gull the greatest skeptic, my dear. You have only to widen your eyes and stare as you used to. Used to. A sad little phrase. We've all conspired to spoil you."

"That's nonsense. Did Jess come back?"

He shook his head. "And will not now. God knows what will become of her."

"What did you do with the spade?"

"Hidden it until it can be cleaned properly."

"Your hands. They are sure to attract notice. Let me see to them. I could not rest at home."

"And ate no breakfast, I'll be bound."

"No."

"Then I will see that you eat if you will attend to me."

The cottage seemed farther away than usual. Ringan

limped a little and there was dirt and green mold on his breeches and boots. Both were silent now and even the wood was quiet: no sound of birds or running water.

"No one saw you?" Emma ventured when they reached the door.

"A passing ghost, maybe. Nothing more."

She shivered. It was cold in the shade of the trees and tiredness chilled her.

"Come," Ringan said, and stepped over the threshold.

Once inside, Emma looked instinctively around the floor. The knives were kept by the chipped, shallow sink in the corner. Jess would have been there, her back against the wall, her hand tightening over the horn handle. In the place where Emma calculated that Jackson would have fallen was a dark, damp mark.

"It was there," Ringan told her, shrugging himself out of his coat, "and now you are going to resist the temptation to look again. Do you hear?"

"Yes." She turned her back on the stain, ignoring the terrible compulsion to disobey, the feeling that if she spun round quickly, Jackson would be lying there, his blank eyes staring at the roof beams.

There was water in a bowl and some pieces of white shirt. Ringan produced scissors from a drawer, dainty things that had not belonged to Tom Hunt. He sat in the chair and she knelt beside him, trimming the torn nails to some kind of neatness, using the scissor points to remove the muck behind them, washing the hands so that they were as clean as she could make them, then drying them carefully on one of the white rags.

One hand was lifted, the fingertips slid gently across her hair and down the side of her neck. The touch of the cold fingers on her skin made her aware of their isolation, reminded her of what had happened while she and Ringan ate and drank. She withdrew from him, emptied the water outside and stared between the recesses of the trees. He'd not have buried Jackson near the cottage. The grave would be far from this spot.

"Here!" Ringan called. "There's bread and cheese and a drumstick."

"Let us eat them outside. They'd stick in my gullet, otherwise."

He brought the food and spread it on a cloth on a tree stump, then set out the chairs beside it. Emma tried to feel enthusiastic about the picnic meal but the bread seemed dry and she found it difficult to swallow. She thought Ringan would take her to task, but when she looked at him, his head was tipped back and his eyes closed. A crust slipped from his hand. She pushed back an inclination to cry, whether it was for him or for Jess she could not decide. It might even have been for Jackson.

She fetched the coat and put it over him. He looked much younger asleep, in spite of the pallor and the stubble. Then she moved away and the shade quickly engulfed the cottage and the man in the chair. Somewhere a dog howled, but he did not hear it.

Wildford was in a bad humor when he returned. "You look sick as a cat."

"I'm tired, that's all."

"What's this tale of Jackson?"

"Nothing very dramatic. He went off to Norwich to see some girl and decided to stay away."

"He'll get short shrift when he gets back."

Emma breathed more easily. "Did you have an enjoyable evening?"

"It followed the usual pattern. Bob Goswick loquacious, his wife silent. Then Bob silent and Arabella noisy. Then a rather well-cooked goose, plenty of claret, the beef, more claret, brandy and the pattern on the ceiling coming and going. The chandelier plunging earthward and awakening to find myself in bed. Breakfast. Bob and Arabella both mute and rather green about the gills—"

"Why do you go, then?"

"Because—I'm lonely."

"You mean because Mother left you?"

"Lack of a wife." He shrugged.

"And Mrs. Craven?"

"What do you know about her!" Wildford's eyes narrowed menacingly.

"Oh, Father! Everyone knows."

"Kitchen gossip, you mean." His look boded ill for Mrs. Bott.

"Perhaps you were not very discreet. Masters are all of overweening interest to their servants."

"Then, since you already know so much, you need no longer fear Mrs. Craven. I grew tired of her jealousies. They were a yoke around my neck. Take warning, Emma. Jealousy is the devil. Better to be lonely."

Emma knew all about that destructive emotion. The thought was gall.

Wildford strode about and slapped his boot with his riding crop. "Jess," he said. "We'll see the wench before supper."

"It's—too late."

"What the devil d'you mean, girl?"

"She's gone."

"Again?"

"Captain Ringan came to tell me she'd taken fright at the thought of being compelled to return here—"

"And why should she do that?"

"You know how she put on airs. The servants resented it. Well, the women did."

"And they'd have taken it out on the returned prodigal?"

"I suppose it is human nature."

"I still mean to have it out with Ringan."

"He tried to help her. Leave the matter, Papa, please. It could do no good to go to the cottage and quarrel with him. It will not bring her back."

"The fellow's too secretive by half—"

"I asked him to join me at dinner. It was then we decided to take the new clothes I bought for her, but she was not there, nor has she come back. I asked the captain this morning."

"You seem to be making very free with him."

"Well, I am in no mood for anyone tonight but you. Let us sup together and talk a little. I have not seen you properly for some time."

Wildford looked mollified. "I'm glad you still want to be with me. But I still mean to speak both to Mrs. Bott and the captain."

"He did save my life and you told me I was ungrateful."

"I find you quite perplexing. But, then, it's the nature of woman. I suppose Jess has solved her own problem but I confess I'm uneasy—"

"Papa. Let us not badger ourselves with conjectures—not tonight."

Emma coaxed and cajoled him to a better humor, though she'd have preferred to be quiet and to have gone early to her bedchamber. Wildford responded to her obvious desire to make the most of their unaccustomed proximity, but Emma could visualize all too plainly the despair of Mrs. Craven, who, unkempt and uncaring, would be drinking herself stupid, listening for the knock that never came.

After a time, Wildford became red in the face and his voice grew louder. Sprawled in his big chair, he looked suddenly bulky and out of condition, his hair graying, his face puffier. The fingers that looped themselves so expertly around the stem of the glass seemed thicker and stubbier. Emma found the change in him pitiable. She had the conviction that, even if she had the chance to leave him, she'd not be able to bring herself to do so. He should not have burdened her with his loneliness.

He fell asleep and Emma rose, telling Harrison to be at hand to help him to his bed.

Wildford called her child, but she felt old. So very old—

* * *

Nothing was progressing. The dog was not caught and
Wildford was disinclined to organize a beat. He was not in
the mood for entertaining. Mrs. Bott was cold because of
the master's disapproval of the kitchen gossip that had informed his daughter of the existence of his mistress, so the
servants fell studiously silent when Emma put in an appearance. Captain Ringan kept away, obviously on Wildford's instructions, and no one mentioned Jackson in Emma's presence. She did try to draw Harrison on the subject
but he said the master had told him Jackson was no longer
in his employ and would be turned away if he came to the
door.

"But, his belongings?"

"Oh, he can have those, not that there's very much. But
men wi' little usually come back for what they own. It
seems queer that he hasn't."

Emma stared down at her plate.

"Anyway, no one believes he went to Norwich." Harrison was enjoying the sensation of being the cynosure of his
mistress's regard. "They say *she* were in the vicinity."

"She?" Emma was cold.

"Jess Ashcroft. Wymark's gamekeeper saw her."

Emma had forgotten the gamekeeper.

"Saw her with the captain," Harrison said slyly.

"*Thought* he saw her, Harrison. That's not the same
thing."

"Good sight, Jenkins 'as. Not likely as he'd make a mistake. And the only wench Jackson ever fancied was Jess,
beggin' your pardon, miss."

"It must have been someone else," Emma said through
dry lips.

"We don't think so, miss. It were just after she ran off
from Lady Rayleigh. You did find 'er an unbiddable girl,
Miss Emma. Remember?"

Breakfast suddenly tasted of sawdust and ashes.

"You know Mr. Wildford's views on gossip," she said, and Harrison's ears turned pink. It was not fair since she had instigated the discussion.

The arrival of a letter from Mrs. Fry, thanking her for both her own letter and the hamper of children's clothing, helped subdue Emma's wild restlessness. She would be welcome, Elizabeth said, and it was only right that she have the opportunity of distributing her own bounty. Wildford's soup and straw were very much appreciated.

Emma showed the letter to her father. "I can stay at the same hotel."

"You'll have more than your skirt torn off, this time."

"It wasn't as bad as that. A small tear only and Miss Fallon has repaired it. I'll wear the same dress."

"Oh, if you must!" Wildford looked out the money for the journey.

She saw Ringan as the carriage set off. He was riding, and the background of trees and the dark color of the horse gave him a curiously spectral look. Emma had never seen him so pale and drawn. It was no wonder he looked haggard, considering how he had been required to bury a man in the wood, then live in proximity to that secret. And the speculations of the kitchen staff could render his action useless because the Wymarks' gamekeeper had convinced everyone that Jess had been the person Jackson had gone out to visit. She wanted to climb out of the carriage and warn Ringan but the horses were moving fast and the captain had disappeared down the narrowest of the woodland trails. As soon as she returned, she must seek him out whether or not Wildford approved.

Miss Fallon enjoyed the journey if Emma did not. The watery sunshine was pleasant, reflecting off the brass-edged coach lamps and polished panels, the flanks of the blacks. The hint of rain kept the air cool and fresh and the occasional drops on the window sparkled like diamonds. Every now and again the maid would point out the beauties of the countryside in her gentle voice and Emma would drag herself from the memory of Ringan's dirt-encrusted hand, the picture of Jackson lying by the cracked sink.

London was at its busiest when they arrived, the streets full of drays and chaises, every corner with its political agitator. "It's not privilege we 'ates! It's tyranny and injustice!" being the universal cry. There were Punch-and-Judy shows, children playing shove-halfpenny in the dubious alleys that ran off the main thoroughfares. People shouted against bull and badger baiting, while a man set a dog about a sackful of rats that ran, with shrill cries, around a pen from which they could not escape. Miss Fallon averted shocked eyes from the bloody spectacle. A man in billboards proclaimed the delights of Astley's circus. A ragged boy stole a handkerchief.

The hotel, too, was crowded with travelers, though there was a room, they were told, if Miss Wildford wished to share it with her personal maid. Emma said that this arrangement would be suitable since it was so short a stay. They had supper in their bedchamber in order to avoid the congestion below, and retired early though Emma could not sleep. Miss Fallon made ladylike noises, soft and fluttery like the sound of the white moths' wings against the glass of the coach lamps. Emma, eyes burning behind the closed lids, saw Lewis with green shadows on his face, Deborah hanging on his arm, her wood-shaving curls brushing his cheek. Jess, heaven alone knew where, her feet bleeding and her eyes wild—

She thought of Ringan with a detachment she could not understand. He was so positive and he had done so much she considered admirable that she felt her reaction toward him should have been stronger. It seemed the studied numbness surrounding her abhorrence of the Jackson affair had spread to thoughts of the captain. But she remembered how his injured hand had stroked her hair and her neck, and with the recollection came a kind of peace.

Emma woke early and could not at first reconcile herself with her surroundings. Then the sound of Miss Fallon's breathing told her where she was and why. She rose and Miss Fallon awoke, exclaiming that she should have been up first to seek hot water and to order breakfast. Emma told her she must not fuss, that there was plenty of time and insisted that the maid take a walk in the park in the afternoon while she was with Mrs. Fry. She also gave her money to buy coffee and cakes at a smart establishment, or to go to Astley's circus which was so well advertised. Miss Fallon positively blushed with pleasure.

Mrs. Fry greeted Emma with her usual calmness and sense of dignity. The smaller children were in evidence but were to be looked after by Elizabeth's sister-in-law. They were pretty little things, apple-cheeked and fair-haired, but not very well disciplined, and Mrs. Fry seemed far less at ease with them than she had been with the Newgate women.

Emma and Elizabeth left the house after a dish of tea, the children waving good-bye from the window, all but the baby who was asleep in his crib. Emma had changed into her "prison" gown, the tear mended very neatly by Fallon. She was surprised that Mrs. Fry wore a gold watch on a chain on the bodice of her dress but presumed the lady would remove it on arrival at Newgate. They were both heavily laden with the usual bundles.

Once more they walked the echoing passages, listening to the filthy invective that rose from the jail yards, the shrieks and moans, pitiful supplications. Someone spat through the bars and the horrible slime touched Emma's shoe. She could not think what to do with it, the stuff seemed to corrode like an acid, yet she dare not stop to wipe it away. So she slid the side of her foot along the wall, her gait ungainly, until she was sure nothing remained. They reached the infirmary.

Emma noticed the clean straw of many of the sickbeds

and thought, Some of that is Wildford's. Her eyes wandered over the pale, listless faces of those who lay there. Even replenished straw and soup had not wrought miraculous changes. Then, and immediately forgetting Mrs. Fry's measured tones and quaint Puritan accent—it was all thee and thine—she saw the child who emerged from behind one of the hammocks.

She was no cleaner than last time and the marigold hair in a worse mess of tangles. She stared at Emma and the girl knew that she was recognized. The stupid look vanished in a touching awareness. Emma's heart beat faster. She had imagined the child gone, never to be a recipient of Wildford charity. One of the gowns had been specially chosen, just in case they met again, sunshine yellow with a white trim.

Mrs. Fry had finished. She was saying something about the contents of the parcels, and there was an immediate surge toward the two visitors. The child with the marigold hair smiled and held out her arms. But women appeared from behind the filthy hammocks, shouting and pushing. A heavy face with a dark line of mustache, a hand thrusting at the small girl. She was flung sideways to disappear in a stampede of legs and feet. There was not time for her to scream.

Emma dropped her bundles and began to run toward the place where she had last seen the infant. It was dark where she came upon the small body. The lips still smiled, but a thin trickle of blood ran from the corner of the baby mouth. Even as she gathered the little girl to her breast, she knew that it was too late.

"Don't take it so much to heart," Wildford said uneasily. "You know that the Fry woman said the child died in what was probably the one happy moment in her life."

"If it had not been for my charity," Emma's tone was bitter, "they would never have rushed toward us in that undisciplined way. It was I killed her."

"Rubbish! It was her mother's greed, Mrs. Fry finishing at that precise moment, the position of the moon, the fact that it was the thirteenth day of the month—"

"No. I shall never forgive myself."

"For saving her from a daily routine of filth and brutality? From an accelerating corruption? From prostitution, the clap, from becoming men's prey? From the river when things became too much to bear?"

"Please—do not—"

"You know it is true. Look the facts in the face."

But she was not to be so easily consoled. Her white face disturbed her father more than he cared to admit.

"Look here, puss. You wanted to have a supper party. A rout. I mean to give one. And if there's enough claret and brandy we'll have a hunt for that yellow cur. I'll invite Lewis Critchley if it'll bring a smile to your face. He leaves for London at the weekend. In fact, if you're really set on him, I'll let you marry him. I know I'll rue it as soon as it's done, but I cannot abide to see you so desolate."

"You cannot buy me a husband. Grandpapa thought he could sell you a wife."

"I'll offer him a partnership now instead of in a few years' time. Now don't tell me that won't please you."

"You were right, Papa. He wants Deborah."

"Did he say so?"

"She did. And she's as good as the Olds' heiress."

"She tried to put your nose out of joint, that was all." Wildford lit a fat cigar. "Old won't be able to offer him advancement and that's what he is avid for."

"And you'll tell him that if he is a good boy and puts a ring on my finger he'll be suitably rewarded?"

"I know you want the lad. And, in spite of my reservations, I intend to see you get him. You glowered at me for separating you and now you question my desire to mend matters."

"It's your *way* of doing it! As if money could accomplish everything."

"But at least I'm treating you as a woman and that was what you wanted most a few weeks since."

Emma shrugged. "It's ridiculous, is it not, how things one craves for can seem unimportant in retrospect?"

"You sound more like my Emma, thank God. Dictionary pie. It's a good sign. I'll arrange the rout. You needn't trouble your head about anything but enjoying yourself."

"Enjoying oneself is not the be all and end all of existence!" Emma's eyes flashed and her lips were set.

Wildford grinned and relit his cigar. He had succeeded in prodding the girl out of that unnatural self-castigation and her color was better. "I'll see that rascal Ringan about the beat. He's been trying to interest me in it for long enough."

Emma sat up straighter. She had intended to seek out the captain the minute she came back from London but the terrible business of the overrun child had pushed every other thought aside. He must know what was being said.

"I'll take a walk by the lake," she announced carefully.

She fetched her cape, for the evening was dull and cool, and slipped out by the postern. The smell of the grass and aromatic shrubs was strong. The sorrow engendered by the traumatic visit to Newgate dulled into an ache a shade less than intolerable.

She knew Ringan was in the cottage, for his horse was tethered outside. The beast raised his head and whinnied and the captain came to the doorway, waiting.

"Does your father know where you are?"

Emma shook her head. "But I had to come."

A queer little spark jumped in his dark blue eye. "And what is so urgent?"

"The staff know about Jess. I'd forgotten the Wymarks' gamekeeper, Jenkins. And they seem sure Jackson meant to see her. They wonder why he's not been back for his traps."

"I see. But they'll still think they went off together."

"It's the business of his possessions they can't understand."

"Sticks in the craw, eh? Come inside."

She did not want to but she made herself enter the dark little place. The shadow of the loft rail fell across the wall like prison bars. But the stain seemed gone from the floor.

"Take a glass of wine with me."

She sat on the nearest chair, her body suddenly weak. Ringan stared at her. "What's wrong? It is not only the Jackson business, is it?"

Emma shook her head.

"It's worse than being set aside by that man of yours, isn't it?" He pushed the glass of wine into her hand. She found herself telling him about the trampled girl, then sobbing, trying to repress the ugly sounds of grief while he knelt and set the glass on the floor, then put his arm around her shoulders. She laid her head against his coat. "I'd thought," she said painfully, when the worst was over, "that I might somehow get the child out of Newgate. Bring her here. Then I imagined she and her mother might be gone and I'd never see her again. Papa and Mrs. Fry warned me not to become too involved but I find I cannot remain at a distance. Even when they spit at me and tear my clothes I can understand how galling it must be to see someone clean and free to leave at the end of the afternoon." She lifted her wet cheek from the breast of his coat and saw the material stained with her tears. "I've spoiled it—"

"You've spoiled nothing. I shall wear the mark like a trophy."

She laughed shakily. "What a trophy! You should have something more worthwhile."

"Drink your Madeira. You'll feel better."

Emma obeyed. Some of the despair receded. The shadows of the bars grew dim as the candle flame guttered, then sprang into renewed blackness as it flared high in a prelude to dying. "At least I have been promised a husband and this constitutes what could be called a victory. Papa has been disinclined to face the fact that most women are made for marriage and children."

"Oh?" The candle flame expired with a sigh and she could not see Ringan's face.

"He could not thole my long face and decided he preferred me wed and smiling than the other way."

"And how will this be achieved? If—the man has previously rejected you?"

"I thought he had, though it was not clear. Perhaps I misunderstood."

"And—?"

"Papa is to make him a partner."

"Then he is a banker?"

"I was sure you'd have wind of it from Mrs. Bott or Harrison. Gossip! They seem to know everything. It is Lewis Critchley and he's to take charge of the new London office. A relative of the Wymarks."

Ringan made a noncommittal sound.

"I nearly forgot. Papa will be arranging the beat for the dog after all. He's to invite Lewis and some cronies and when they're charged with brandy, they'll hunt for the beast in moonlight. That will be unsuccessful, of course, so they'll continue next day when their heads are clear and they can see what they are doing. So you'd best take care you're not in the woods after the rout. They'll be so drunk they'll shoot one another."

He laughed and the sound was empty. "Perhaps I *should* stand in their way. Who's to miss one more scallywag!"

"I've worried you over the Jackson affair. It was only true that I thought forewarned—"

"Is forearmed? Yes, you acted quite properly, Miss Emma. And now I must make my evening patrol so you'd best be off. Shall I light another candle?"

"No need. The moon's up." Emma stepped out into the blue dimness and thought it, for a moment, magical. Then recollection of imprisonment returned to spoil the brief enjoyment. People could be shut up for such small crimes, and for worse they could be executed. She felt a sudden cold griping of the bowels as she realized what she and Ringan had done.

She turned, afraid, but the captain was not there. He would be priming his hunting rifle or some other such necessary task. But there was no sound of breech locks or cartridges, no noise at all. He must be standing quite still in the dark beyond the open door. Unnerved, Emma began to run along the track which showed plainly, since the cold light fell on the small stones. Ringan had not moved but some strange force seemed to follow her.

Miss Fallon, who, because she was so detached and ladylike, heard none of the buzz of gossip about Jess and the former footman, was excited about the coming rout. She considered the big drawing room, which was cleared of much of its furniture and the floor polished to glass, most beautiful with its plants and sconces and shining mirrors in gesso frames decorated with fat cupids, flowers and leaves. She loved the eau de Nil paint, the touches of gilt, the chandeliers that hung heavy and glittering, the dull gold hangings at the windows. The silver and napery—

"It is quite lovely," Emma agreed a little sharply, not sharing the maid's expectations of the evening.

"And the gown is so pretty even if it is not white."

"I wanted something more sophisticated."

"Well—the emerald green is very striking against your dark hair. What a pity we can never quite get it to curl."

"That's what my mother used to say. With annoyance, I may add."

"Oh, she should not have blamed you for it."

"Some people like straight hair and I am not mad for curls."

"It does suit you," Miss Fallon decided belatedly. "You have so much character, feminine fripperies might seem out of place."

That made Emma laugh and she prepared for the event in a better humor than she had expected. She could almost forget Jackson and the child with the orange-yellow hair. Harrison slid sly looks in her direction as he went about his tasks. Guests began to arrive and Emma had no time to brood. She stood with Wildford at the double doors, the light splintering off the crystal doorknobs, managing to smile as though nothing disturbed her and the only people who mattered were those who came to dine and drink and exchange chitchat.

Wildford had invited the Wymarks but she would be spared Deborah who was with the Olds, making a new life for herself in the city. To which Lewis was bound in a day or two. The thought of Lewis did not bring either the accustomed thrill or the taste of bitterness. Emma blamed the catastrophic events of the past week or so. So much had happened. Could still happen—

The griping in her stomach had barely subsided when Lewis was announced. She received the impression of a studied simplicity of dress that clashed sharply with the magnificence and ornateness of most of the materials used in the coats and gowns of the other visitors to the house. And, with that shadow over his face he looked more than ever like a younger, less shop-soiled Ringan. The same high-bridged nose and bone structure.

"Glad you could come, Critchley," Wildford said, gripping him by the hand. "I want a word with you before supper. Come to my study in half an hour. I must wait for the rest of those invited. All your plans made for Friday?"

"Indeed they are. Good evening, Miss Emma."

She smiled and offered him her fingertips. No currents passed between them at the delicate touch. Emma frowned. It was not long since she had wanted to die for Lewis. His longish face, the clear eyes and white teeth still pleased her but there was something lacking. He was too good at concealing his emotions. She must arrange that he forget these inhibitions.

"There's no need for you to remain, Emma. Remember, Lewis. Half an hour."

"Why does your father want to see me?" Lewis asked, guiding Emma across the room. He smelled of soap and cleanliness and his shoes were elegant.

"I know," Emma told him, "but I do not think it is my place to tell you."

Lewis smiled. "Shall we walk in the garden? It is too early for dancing. And immeasurably too soon for supper."

"Very well."

"You will not be cold?"

"I do not think so. How is Deborah?" The night air touched their faces lightly with just a tiny bite in it that made Emma shiver.

"Deborah? She is back home. For the present."

Emma was amazed. "But—the Olds! She was to live there."

"I am afraid Deborah—provoked Mrs. Old." Critchley's voice was edged with annoyance.

"Oh. I did not think all would be well in that quarter. So she is not to be adopted after all?"

"No. Not at the moment anyway."

"If I had been Mrs. Old I'd not have relished a pretty girl twisting my husband round her little finger. I might have felt—insecure. After all, they were not related."

"I think you make too much of it."

"There's the moon, above the trees."

"So it is." There was no pleasure in his tone.

"I think I will tell you what Papa wants." Emma was touched by perversity. "He wants to offer you a partnership—"

"A partnership! But that is splendid news." The handsome profile relaxed into a smile that was far more genuine than the previous one. "I honestly had not hoped for it at this stage."

The emerald silk was making whispering noises, rubbing against her petticoats as she walked. "Of course there are provisions. Well, at least one."

"And what is that?"

"That you propose marriage."

He stopped abruptly. "Marriage to you?"

"Why, yes. He is not likely to reimburse you for wedding a stranger."

"No."

"You do not sound ecstatic."

"It is not that. It was a complete reversal of what you told me so recently."

"You still could have sounded pleased."

"It is too much like—buying and selling. A business transaction."

"How very Puritan. But wasn't that what the Wymarks were doing? Or is that different?"

"I held you in higher regard."

"Did you, Lewis? Then you'd want to marry me even if Papa was not about to bribe you?"

"If I gave you any other impression, it was that I had nothing to offer you but prospects that might not have materialized, banks being what they are, notoriously unstable."

"There would always be Rothschilds. They never put a foot wrong."

"It's a family affair. A strong, talented family."

"Wildford's could be. Gurney's and Fry's were."

"There's a solidarity about a family firm if it's properly administered. Yet, I hardly like to ask you to marry me for such mercenary reasons."

"Lewis, have you any connection with a family called Ringan? A John Ringan? of Somerset?"

"Not that anyone has mentioned, though it's not impossible there's a distant connection. My mother's from Glastonbury."

"I see. Then it's reasonably likely. He mentioned Glastonbury."

"Who did?" Critchley was understandably confused.

"Oh, no one who'd matter to you."

"Not even if he's my second cousin once removed?"

"Not even then." The candlelight was shining through the leaves so that they were pieces of glowing sorcery, and where the shadows of the leaves fell they were black flakes, lifting and falling, never still. She always associated Lewis with green magic.

"It's not too late," she said softly, "to forget all the past and start afresh. If I have been jealous and suspicious, then I apologize unreservedly. Perhaps being starved of a mother's love and the company of brothers and sisters has made me the kind of person I am. Vulnerable. If you can forgive my hatefulness and sharpness of tongue, you might find something worth having."

"Why, Emma." He looked so kindly and so surprised that she could not help laughing, even though there was a catch in the sound. It was as though, for the first time, she had discovered him off guard.

"It's not words I want," she whispered. "Give me something more than those."

His shadow blotted out the leaves and the pillars. "You do trust me, Emma?"

"Of course I do."

His face came down toward hers, familiar and yet touchingly strange. She felt his arms around her, the pressure of his mouth. The kiss did not arouse her as much as she had expected, but they were new lovers and had much to learn. There was plenty of time.

He released her.

"He will not offer you the partnership if you are not willing to take me as part of the—"

"Bargain?" Lewis suggested, his fingers drumming against a pillar.

"If that is how you are determined to view it."

"But I do have a great affection for you that has nothing to do with ledgers and sums. Will you marry me, Emma?"

Acceptance meant Lewis, London, easier access to Newgate. Ironically, she could not keep away from the place
that had broken her heart.

"I suppose I must."

"In your own words, you do not sound ecstatic." He drew
away and stood with his body outlined against the luminous green of the leaves.

"It has nothing to do with you, Lewis. I have been hurt
lately by so many things. In spite of what you may think,
it's no lame excuse. We have always been open with each
other."

"I cannot accuse you of reticence," he admitted.

"But you know that I love you and need you."

"I did think so."

"Nothing has changed. It will all come back."

"Come and dance," Lewis said.

Lady Rayleigh had arrived, red-faced and black-browed as
ever. They said she had a meek maid now who cried herself
to sleep every night and hated the dawn that presaged
another day under her ladyship's heavy thumb.

Worse still, the Wymarks were there and Deborah with
them, her blue eyes shrewd, her pale, bouncing curls indestructible as always. Already, most of the young males
gathered around her like bees at a particularly succulent
honey-pot. How enticingly small her waist was inside the
white dress with its ruching and ribbons.

"How very virginal you look," Emma said insincerely.

"And why not?" Deborah retorted sweetly and lan-
guished, reminding Emma of her mother.

"Why, indeed? Lewis and I are to be wed. I wanted you to
be first to know."

What little color there was in Deborah's face receded.
"You—and Lewis?"

"Isn't that so?" Emma prompted. Her gown looked so
vivid against the simplicity of Miss Wymark's. The baggage
had done it on purpose.

Lewis opened his mouth to speak. Wildford called, "Emma? Emma!"

"I will come back," she said and went to answer the summons, her gown drawing a great deal of attention from the matrons and older gentlemen who had obviously already had a fair amount to drink. Old Pugh-Hailey leered at her and called her a "fine, striking filly," and Wildford laughed, well pleased. He introduced her to recent acquaintances from the other side of Norwich, then drew her aside to say, "It was a blind to ask you to send young Critchley to me now. I've had enough of the posturing idiots for the moment and intend to fortify myself with some of the French brandy I keep in my study. I suppose you've sounded him out?"

"You could call it that."

"Very well, Emma. I'll wait for the boy."

She returned to the corner where she had left Lewis but he was not there. Neither was Deborah, but the door to the conservatory swayed as though someone had just passed that way. Emma, oblivious of stares and the increased sound of the voices and shrill laughter, passed across the room and went quietly through the doorway and into the green, shadowy region of the glass house. The candlelight penetrated here, showing her great, dark fronds, drifts of delicate leaves and curled petals. Damp, exotic smells drifted in sweet waves, hanging in the air. The rising moon laid a patina on the floor.

She heard them before she saw them. "Damn to all that," Deborah was saying, "she shan't have you."

"I'm afraid she must."

"No, no, Lewis—" She begged.

Emma saw them now, where the yellow light streamed in from the ballroom window. For a moment they stood apart, and then Critchley reached out, pulling Deborah toward him violently. She was passive at first, letting him fondle and kiss her roughly, then slamming her against the glass wall and thrusting himself against her so that she gasped with pain or pleasure. Then his hand was delving into the neck of the white gown, probing and pushing until the material tore. Deborah moaned. Her own hand came up to press Lewis's harder against her breast.

Cool, correct Lewis was unrecognizable, Emma thought. Then her foot touched a clutch of plant pots, overturning them with a clatter, and Critchley turned, his face clear in the glow from the large windows opposite. The shadow of a tendril of vine lay across his right cheek so that he looked, at last, exactly like Ringan, alive and lusty. As he would never look for Emma Wildford.

"That must be the shortest betrothal I ever had," Emma said and left them.

Ringan was with Wildford when she returned. He appeared vagabondish beside the other guests and his face, in spite of the wet summer, was beginning to brown. He looked better.

"Mr. Critchley will not be coming to the study, Papa."

"Why ever not, puss?"

"He is engaged with Miss Wymark. I did not care to interrupt."

Wildford frowned. "Later, then. Ringan, keep your eye on Miss Emma. It's supper soon and she needs a partner. I am too much of a coward to play the part."

"Will you sup with me, Miss Emma?"

"Do not feel you must be dragooned," she said as Wildford left them.

"Will you join the beat? It's to take place after the refreshments."

"Refreshments, Captain? Everyone will tear and slobber, demolish all that's in sight and wash it down with Papa's claret and Madeira and belch and unbutton their waistcoats, then start all over again. I would not call that refreshment."

"You are at an age when a rout is an adventure, or should be."

"I fear I have outgrown them. I used not to think overmuch about food and the waste of it, but now I see how wrong that can be. If there were only a quarter of what's displayed, it would still be extravagance. But he did it to please me."

"Has Mr. Critchley done his duty?"

"It depends which duty you mean."

"How very oblique. Did he propose marriage?"

"He did. I should like some of that lobster. I will take enough for us both. Hold out your plate. Fowl? Beef? Game pie?"

"What did you say? To Mr. Critchley."

"I accepted."

"No more food, Miss Emma. I do eat sparingly and I must do what I can a little later to prevent your guests from killing one another. I cannot afford to be sluggish."

"What in damnation's name is that accursed noise?" Pugh-Hailey shouted, dribbling a little stream of port down his blue satin waistcoat.

Emma's skin goose-pimpled. One by one the voices died.

The yellow dog was howling eerily from the trees above the lake.

CHAPTER SEVEN

The night air streamed against their faces. Wildford's
guests milled around the stables, lurching and laughing, the
moonlight on the wigs and beauty spots, on half-bare shoulders and glistening materials. A woman fell, shrieking,
picked herself up.

"Dear God," Ringan muttered, "it puts me in mind of
Newgate."

There was a distorted similarity, Emma agreed silently.
Some of the women in that notorious jail were drunk, but
on penny ale, and they wore rags and tatters. Yet these
wealthy county folk acted in much the same way, even if
their accents were a trace more refined. They shouted and
jeered and pawed one another, screamed with inebriated
laughter, showed bosoms and legs, ogling and jostling for
notice.

A few of the women were pushed unceremoniously onto
mounts. The whole scene was becoming bacchanalian.
Pugh-Hailey, looking as though he'd been stabbed in the
chest, was astride and trying to put a short, thin arm around

189

a well-developed lady Emma did not recognize. Papa had made a lot of acquaintances recently in order to fill up the loneliness ahead. The buxom lady seemed unused to a horse.

Emma used the mounting block to arrange herself side-saddle. It seemed preposterous to go riding in one's new gown, but the whole idea of a hunt at night was ridiculous except to those who were fuddled on Wildford's claret. Men were mounting, one back to front, and fowling pieces and pistols handed up. All to dispatch one pariah!

She would not have gone if it had not been for the sight of Lewis Critchley pawing Deborah in the conservatory. Anger had sent her out.

Wildford came out of nowhere, the moonlight kind to his increasing weight and the marks of dissipation. The white stock gleamed against dark face and dark coat. The light breeches molded themselves to his thighs. He looked very handsome.

"Ringan. Emma. Shall we lead? These poor fools may follow if they can." Then he laughed at the tipsy man who sat facing the tail. "I've a mind to put a shot across his bows!"

"You'd hurt someone," Ringan warned and secured his weapon.

They began to ride toward the lake path, the moon swinging from branch to branch and the stars freckling the sky. The dog still howled. Emma saw the captain's face, grim and drawn. "What is it?" she whispered.

"It's in the wood. Just where we do not want the ground trampled. I could wish your father had not been so enthusiastic."

"You mean—where—*it* is buried?"

"I'd say so. The cur shifts about, sometimes down by Welling's, then on the other side of the water. But there are numerous small creatures in the wood if it's hungry now that Welling has more men by the sheep pastures to protect the lambs."

"There will be little to see in the trees."

"Let us hope not."

Wildford was ahead now, his big body outlined against the lake, his stock and his thick hair flying in the breeze. Emma's body was licked with the same cool fire and her skirts rustled where they were blown on the wind. It was, suddenly, marvelously exciting.

They were past the dark little summerhouse, thudding up the trail, avoiding the spreading roots. Behind them someone was blowing on a hunting horn. The sound, the drum of hooves, the dark shape of Wildford crouched over his horse, the taste of the wind, were intoxicating as nothing else had ever been. Ringan rode beside her as though that were his place. Lewis was nowhere to be seen. Pugh-Hailey jogged along doggedly, his pale blue satin reflecting the moonlight, his wig askew. Every now and again he gave vent to a high-pitched squeak, like a small animal. If it had not been so serious a chase, Emma would have laughed immoderately. The whole tone of the occasion was extravagant.

The beech roots were silver snakes writhing and the face of the moon inexplicably mysterious. Emma longed to ask it the answers to her future, only there would be no solution there. Beside her, Ringan gave a grunt of apprehension but she took no notice. The sensuous feel of the wind and the touch of the dark green silk around her body was intensely satisfying. She had never lived until Newgate and tonight but she could not understand the relationship. This mad ride could only open up vistas of danger but the realization did not deter her. Rather it exhilarated her in the way that a hunt did, except that she could never accept the death of the fox or the hind. The race was wonderful, the end abominable. She supposed life must be like that. There was no picture now of the girl-child cast aside, no remembrance of Jess's lovely face and appealing breasts. There was only cold moonlight and a sharp breeze, the tree roots putting out their own tortuous impediments. It was all wildness and beauty but she knew there must be an end and so she shirked thinking of it since the present was what she had always hankered after.

Black lances of shade lay across the path and the white moths were there, small blossoms swirling out of the pits of obscurity, drawn, in the absence of flame, to the lesser obsession of moonlight. Somehow she became one of those moths, she and Jess, even Deborah, aware of the pull toward the masculine, unable to resist.

The knowledge that Lewis did not want her refused to strike too deeply but she suspected it would tomorrow or the day after. There was something so insulting about being offered the gentlemanly kiss when she'd have preferred the burrowing in the bosom, the touch of his fingers around her nipples. The magic was turning to reality as the effects of Wildford's wines wore off and the elation began to die. She was no longer alone with Wildford and Ringan and old Pugh-Hailey. The more energetic and efficient riders were catching up with them. From the edge of vision she saw more bent backs and hair streaming. A small animal raced for cover and an owl hooted. In that moment of the recognition of freedom she understood all the bitterness and frustration of a prison existence where, often, the only escape was by bribery, either by money or one's person. What kind of liberty was that?

The howling of the dog had grown louder. Emma saw Ringan press forward, now on a level with Wildford, now gone ahead in a blue shimmer of horse flanks and taut thigh lost quickly in darkness.

"Wait!" Wildford shouted, spurring the harder. The moon, disconcertingly, went behind cloud, casting the scene into obscurity. Riders plunged and floundered, cursing. A woman screamed in terror. There was a spurt of flame from the direction in which the captain had ridden, a choked-off howl that was almost human, then a lull in which could be heard only the shuffle of mounts and a cracking of twigs. Then the moon emerged, showing tight, white curls and black ribbons, the line of a woman's back under a satin bodice, breeches that encased a full bottom, a shiver of light up long boots. A horse's hocks—

Wildford galloped in the direction of the shot. Everyone followed, evading root and overhanging branch. There was a sour, rotten smell as if the wet summer had blighted every growing thing. A sudden, startling glimpse of Ringan, his arm hanging by his side, a sprawled shape at his feet.

"The dog!" The words passed from mouth to mouth and then there was a hush, a crawling horror, a disbelief. "What's that he's uncovered?"

Emma was swept with fear. The captain was so still—so defeated.

Wildford dismounted, the blue light picking out soft gleams of leather, the flounces of the frilled shirt. He knelt by the body of the dog. His hand went beyond it, pushing at the crumbling soil and loose stones. A branch dragged across his head. Ringan's hand clenched. Wildford raised his head. "It's Jackson," he said very quietly, "Jackson," and his eyes were raised toward the captain.

Emma kicked at the mare's flanks. "It has nothing to do with him! Everyone knows. Everyone but you. It was Jess. Jess Ashcroft. He only tried to help. It was Jess."

There was a silence. A hard knot of misery gathered in her breast. But she could not have watched Ringan accused. She could not.

"I see." Wildford had not moved. The handful of soil rattled over the dead face. The dog's fur stirred in the unquiet air.

Ringan was staring at her as though he had never seen her before. The expression on his face moved her profoundly. In the pale clarity of the moon's light he looked young and unspoiled, the youth who had seen his brother indulged, who had been driven to rebellion as a result of his father's indifference. Emma felt an overwhelming pity.

"I had to tell the truth," she said painfully. "I had to."

"Of course." No one heard Ringan but herself.

The atmosphere of the house was heavy with conjecture and suspicion. Emma moved about the mausoleum with a sense of complete unreality. Ever since the grim discovery—the dog had unearthed part of the body in its shallow grave—she had regretted her outburst. If only she had remained quiet, the murder might have been attributed to some passing vagrant, the flotsam and jetsam of the war. But there would still have been the gossip that was inevitable. Mrs. Bott's outspoken condemnation, Harrison's sly remarks, the reminders of Jackson's unclaimed possessions. They'd have blamed Ringan because of the proximity of the cottage and the fact that the wood and the lake were his domain.

Jenkins, the Wymarks' gamekeeper, was produced to tell his story of having seen the captain and Jess Ashcroft talking. Ringan admitted having sheltered the girl, but he said nothing of the finding of the body, only that she had gone during his evening with Emma at the big house during Wildford's absence. Emma knew that he had refrained from saying more in order to protect herself and not to incriminate Jess.

She told of having known that Jess was sheltering in the cottage after leaving Lady Rayleigh and that she had gone back with Captain Ringan after the extended meal was over, with clothes for the girl, only to find her fled. They had not known that Jackson was missing until the following day, and had presumed, as the kitchen staff did later, that the couple had run off together.

It was hard to listen to Mrs. Bott railing about Jess's undoubted guilt and how she had always led on the men who

worked at Staves before Miss Emma sent her to Lady Rayleigh because of her inability to submit to discipline. "A
bad girl who'd led a squalid life before Mr. Wildford be-
friended her. We know. She talked—"

Harrison reinforced the verdict that Miss Ashcroft had
been a tease and probably worse. Had she not encouraged
him on more than one occasion? Not that he had suc-
cumbed, though that was not Jess's fault. She had all but
enticed him to her bed—and her room was not shared—but
he had not forgotten himself and the responsibility of his
position.

Humbug, Emma thought angrily, then called herself a
hypocrite. She was the Judas.

Emma, remembering the ill-fated child, saddled her mare
and set off for the lake. Lewis had, only yesterday, set out
for London without the partnership. Wildford had been surprised by his daughter's volte-face but patently relieved.

"I do not want to share my husband," Emma told him,
her voice hard. "If I cannot appeal to him at my age, I'd be a
miserable old woman."

"He seemed fond enough—"

"Fondness is not sufficient. Nor for me. I want—passion."

"There might be passion—later."

Emma had shaken her head. One-sided relationships
were not for Wildford's daughter. It became a matter for
concern that her desire for Lewis Critchley, which had
seemed so strong and enduring, could change, so swiftly, to
a sour regret. She was terribly afraid that all violent affec-
tions would have the same end, a few weeks of burning anticipation, then the leaden flatness of disillusion.

It seemed a lifetime since she had been in the summerhouse. Dismounting, she tethered the mare and found the
key above the door. The place smelled of dust and mush-
rooms. Emma opened the window. Here she had heard Jess
singing and seen her dancing as though the little dwelling

had been her own. She could almost see the girl now, smiling secretly, reveling in her unbound hair, saying uncomfortable things about the differences between gentlewomen and servants. All the agony that should have come with Lewis's rejection—even his acceptance had seemed that—came over Emma in a black tide. The sky was purple with rain.

She sank to her knees and laid her head on the arm of the nearest chair. The grief was not to be assuaged. A few sparse tears squeezed themselves from behind burning eyelids. "Please, God, let me cry." But she could not, and it was as though knives twisted inside her body. She writhed on the floor, arms clasped over her breast. They all mocked her. Jess, Mrs. Craven in her ashen despair, the baby girl whose name she would never know, the dog. Even Jackson with leaf mold on his face—

He was standing in the doorway, faceless against the muted light. Emma was suddenly still. Even when he moved toward her she could not utter a sound. A foot trailed in the dust. The figure dropped to its knees. Reached out for her.

"Emma?" The voice was thick. Unrecognizable.

"Go away," she said. "Please, go away."

"But you do not want me to go, do you?"

She still did not recognize the voice or the dark silhouette. It was not until the strong arms came around her that she knew it was Ringan. But it did not seem presumption that he held her, lay close beside her in the neglected room. She never knew how long they stayed there, bound together by dark secrets of complicity and a macabre attraction. Yet he was the better character. He had protected Jess Ashcroft. She had betrayed her. She was not fit for Lewis Critchley. Perhaps she was meet company for an adventurer, a man who had once saved her life and to whom she owed an obligation.

"Ringan—"

"Who did you think I was?" he whispered, his hand against her hair.

"Jackson. Jackson—"

"Nightmares only. Thank you for your partisanship. I'd have been prime suspect if it had not been for you."

"But Jess. What if they find her?"

"She'll have sense enough to keep out of the way of Bow Street runners and the parish constables."

"I should have looked after her better. We spoiled her, Papa and I—"

"You meant well, I'm sure."

She put her arms around his neck and was disturbed to find him straining away.

"What's wrong?" she asked.

"It's not gratitude I want." He was still, his arms falling away so that she felt insecure without their firm clasp.

"I would not have called it gratitude."

"Then, what? What would you have called it, Emma Wildford? Critchley does not want you, but you, or your body, needs him. Oh, I know he made a play of asking for you but he's bound to that Wymark wench and she's not one to release her prey without a struggle—"

"How did you know?"

"Listened. Asked questions."

"Then—you care?"

"Oh, I care, Miss Wildford."

"Really care? Or is it that you scent a conquest? A hold on my father?"

"Does it matter?"

"Oh, Captain, believe me, it does matter." Emma raised herself onto one elbow. "You would not find it onerous to be bound to me as Lewis is to Deborah?"

"I'd not find it in the least burdensome. But he has made you suspicious."

"Then why don't we—?"

"Because, Miss Emma, I am still in your father's employ.

And should Jess be caught I could face the charge of burying a corpse in order to cover her tracks. And you have abetted me. There are all kinds of reasons why I should not seduce you because you are unhappy and fear there will never be a man to give you solace."

"Not solace! More than that, I hope."

"I will always remember with gratitude that you made me such a proposition—"

"Damn you, Ringan! I want none of your patronage."

He laughed and rolled away from her, rose to his feet gracefully and became faceless, anonymous as before.

"I think I hate you," she whispered.

"Tell me when you are quite sure." He walked away. The doorway stood empty and the first drops of rain fell like the sound of rats' feet. Emma got up from the floor and smoothed her skirt. The pain was gone and in its place was something more alive. Disturbing but preferable to emptiness.

There were posters up for Jess. Turning a corner in Norwich, the black lettering obtruded from the thick, white paper. *Wanted, for the atrocious murder of Edward Jackson, the notorious Jess Ashcroft of Staves, near Norwich.* There followed a description of the murder and the burial in the wood, some scurrilous comments on the character of the girl and the inducement of a reward for any communication that would lead to her arrest.

Sick to the soul, Emma blundered away from it, arousing the curiosity of Miss Fallon who had not noticed the poster, being very shortsighted. "Are you not well, Miss Emma?"

"I am perfectly well. I tripped over an uneven paving stone, that is all." Yet a cold chill took possession of her. Only Wildford knew that she and Ringan had been party to concealing the body in order to protect Ashcroft. None of the other members of the drunken foray had been close enough or sober enough to take in the import of Emma's indiscreet words over the dead dog in the wood. And Wildford had taken care that she spoke to no one without his being present. But if Jess were apprehended and questioned, she would deny having buried Jackson. What fools she and Ringan had been.

Color returned to Emma's face at the thought of the captain. She had long since ceased to feel angry with him over the incident at the summerhouse, only intensely aware of him in a way she had not previously suspected. Like some old maid behind curtains she had taken to spying on him, watching him from upper windows if Wildford mentioned the captain was calling at the house on estate business. Following at a distance if she saw him around the lake or the copse. He had given no sign that he knew but she had the notion that he laughed at her behind her back.

She had seen Elizabeth Fry again and had promised to visit the school, taking with her such useful things as slates and chalk. Mrs. Fry had been distressed about a woman prisoner who had murdered her infant and was executed in spite of Elizabeth's endeavors on her behalf. She described how she had spoken twice with the unfortunate creature who had been driven by force of circumstance to the awful deed. It had done no good, though, to point out to the authorities the extenuating features of the sad case, but Mrs. Fry still did not think that God truly believed in the doctrine of an eye for an eye, but hoped rather that the sinful could be converted.

Again, Emma experienced that tightening of the stomach muscles. There would be no reprieve for Jess and her punishment would be too awful to contemplate. Small beads of sweat broke out on her nose and temples. Her hands were clammy.

"I shall speak to Papa," she told Miss Fallon. "I've a notion to go to London again."

"Not to that dreadful place!"

"It is not so awful now. There is a school started with

thirty or so pupils and Mrs. Fry says many older girls crowd
the doorway of the room, crying to be taught. It's not possible, of course. The women are given things to sew, so they,
too, are taken care of in another, more practical way. I find
it rather touching that such underprivileged women should
want instruction."

"It seems natural," Miss Fallon said, but she enjoyed
learning because her life was empty without knowledge.

Emma broached the subject to her father at supper and
Wildford immediately made objections.

"You were hurt sufficiently last time. I'd prefer it if you
declined the invitation."

"Would you let go of a prospective client because you'd
had some previous unpleasantness?"

"I might." Wildford smoothed white cuffs, then applied
himself to the claret. The candlelight shone through the
liquid so that it resembled rubies.

"I think you'd overlook it because of the ensuing benefit," Emma persisted.

"And what benefit would there be in your case?"

"Good for my soul, Papa."

"I think I do not believe in souls. Only in the flesh and
mortality."

"You cannot mean it! You sit in church, when you remember."

"Only because the squire is meant to set an example. But
it is meaningless, I assure you."

"Papa!"

"No need to worry, child. I'll be satisfied if I've extracted
all there is to be had from this life. One grows tired as one
grows older and the effort of wanting to last forever seems
pointless. I'd prefer a long, comfortable sleep with no waking."

"But earthly pains and disabilities would not exist— So
they say."

"Don't preach to me, girl. All I know is that I think London is bad for you. If only you'd go to Astley's or to the opera or playhouse, I'd be enthusiastic—"

"Then I will."

"With that dried-up old maid for company?"

"You've changed, Papa. Only a short time ago it was all, 'I shall never willingly see you go out with a young man.'"

"Damn Critchley for awakening you! If he were not so good at his work, I'd send him packing."

"I made a fool of myself, I agree, but I'll not find a husband stuck here at Staves, will I?"

"I'll not object if you set out to enjoy yourself. But if you come back moping as you did last time, I'll never agree to another visit. So think well."

"I knew you'd say yes." Emma kissed him.

Wildford had not expressed his fears about Jess and Emma was thankful. It was as though, ostrichlike, he preferred not to see the incipient danger. Jess could tell one story and Emma and Ringan had told another. It did not bear thinking about.

Miss Fallon and Emma set off the next day. The humidity of the summer had given way to the first chill of autumn and tiny sparks of frost were struck from the stones by the wayside. Spiders' webs stretched ghostily from twig to twig and the sun was red above a frieze of dim trees that thinned to nothing beyond the curve of the road. Miss Fallon tucked a rug about her knees and stared about her with her customary pleasure. Any moths that Emma saw were small and gray. The hay stocks had been spoiled and the fields were mildewed and windswept. There had even been freak storms of snow and hailstones to batter the crops and now there were the fogs and mists that shrouded the countryside so that the carriage seemed to ride through limbo. She had read in the morning's newssheet that people were so hungry because of the crop failure that a poor widow from Lincolnshire, who begged at doors, was offered two guineas by a chimney sweep for the son who accompanied her.

London was its usual vociferous self when the carriage finally rolled over the cobbles beyond the suburbs, and street corner orators were calling for the Elgin Marbles to be sold back to Greece and vilifying the Regent's intention to build a new palace. The price of wheat was to reach an incredible 103 shillings and more widows would be prevailed upon to sell their boys to chimney sweeps. The potato crop had failed in Ireland and folks ate nettles and grass. Astonishing, Emma thought, how living in a country house like Staves immured one from reality. It was sobering to realize that some country people were burning ricks and barns because of bread prices, and all because of the wet summer that had seemed merely an annoyance to Wildford and his cronies.

The crowds were so threatening that poor Miss Fallon cracked several knuckles before they reached the hotel. Now that Papa had a London branch, Emma reflected, it would not seem out of place to suggest a permanent suite of rooms, or even a town house. A stone struck the door panel and she had a glimpse of a pale, distraught face, more skeleton than human, and was jerked out of complacency. But it did not matter how much one gave to relieve the distresses of the poor. It was never enough, and the contribution sank into the great sea of need as though it had never been. Almost automatically, she threw the coins in her purse out of the window and saw the accusing face vanish in a plethora of others while she and Miss Fallon made their escape under cover of the ensuing brouhaha and the carriage was driven to the inner courtyard. Their chamber seemed a haven.

She went to Mildred's Court the following morning and Elizabeth Fry told her there was to be a Newgate call that afternoon. Her babies had colds and were confined to their room. Two of the older girls had only yesterday left after a homecoming and Mrs. Fry was low-spirited. The school visit would give her some motive.

Newgate looked different in cold and mist. Emma forgot

the box of slates and chalks she carried. In this shadowy place, beautified by its present insubstantiality, dwelt more unhappiness than was good to think about. The figures of Liberty and Plenty became travesties and Dance's building an unholy mirage. No sounds penetrated the windowless facade. A tendril of vapor clung to the horn of Plenty and was sucked into the gray sky as though not even that must be left to give visual pleasure.

Emma, conscious of the gap left by the little girl with the yellow hair, was suddenly unwilling for the key to be turned. The door yawned open, the gap beyond filled with a confusion of faces, arms, fingers, bodies thrust forward and smelling of unpleasant things. But, miraculously, most of the faces were not unfriendly, and the pushing and grasping tailed off into a sort of order and an unaccustomed show of respect.

"Can't rightly understand it, ma'am. Raging tigresses they were. Now look at 'em. Mild as milk," the second turnkey grumbled, his rheumy eye singling out a girl in blue at the back of the crowd. A trickle of saliva showed on his underlip. He watched her as he stepped back and locked the barred door, leaving Elizabeth, Emma and the box in the middle of the floor. Emma thought of tonight and the girl who could not escape, unable to concentrate on the prayer and the reading from the Bible.

" 'Oo's Christ?" one woman asked. " 'Oo is Jesus?"

"Must a' been a fool to let 'isself be nailed to a bit o' wood. Catch me!"

More inmates had heard of God. The carpenter's son was too difficult to understand. God was like the King, only sane. -

It was hard to reach the school. Mrs. Fry called upon the strongest women to carry the slates, promising them something for themselves next time. The box was lugged along, not too unwillingly, and a way cleared by the schoolroom door. Emma, peering over the nearest head, saw that the room, formerly a laundry room, was small and crowded, but the children astonishingly neat. Close by, some women were knitting like the old harpies around the guillotine during the French Terror.

The corner where the hammocks swung lazily, casting fishnet shadows on the plaster, reminded Emma of the child who had stolen her heart. She moved away from the doorway and the press of young girls who watched, fascinated, the progress of the class. There was a pool of urine on the floor in the spot where the little girl had been trampled. She wanted to clean the place and put flowers there but it would be an empty gesture. Far better to give something to someone who was still alive.

The girl in blue who had attracted the attention of the jailer was sitting in the darkest corner, crouched against the wall. The gown was torn in places and the riot of dark hair matted. But there was something familiar about the line of the neck and the curve of the slender back.

Emma could not speak. The girl, suddenly conscious of being observed, turned a face that was cut and bruised, the eyes huge with a mingling of fury and despair.

"Oh, it's you, Miss Emma." Jess's voice was flat. "Saw you doing good deeds just as that turnkey marked me down for his bed warmer tonight."

"What are you doing here?"

"Got nabbed for stealing a loaf. Well a loaf and some other things—"

"Not—not because you—killed Jackson?"

"That swine!"

"Keep your voice down," Emma urged, disquieted.

"Sell the hide off me back if they knew." Jess peered into the shadows, relaxed, satisfied. "But there is nobody knows who killed Jackson 'cept the captain and he'd not tell."

"Everyone knows. There are posters displayed, describing you and giving details of—of what you did—offering a reward. You were seen by a man called Jenkins visiting the farm, remember? And the kitchen staff have testified against you. Harrison in particular."

Jess was sheet-white. Even in her fear, her eyes were wonderfully blue. There was a bruise on her throat, another on each of her forearms. "Harrison was always a pig!"

"What—what name did you give," Emma asked, "when you were arrested?"

"Not mine! I 'adn't forgotten what I'd done. I ain't that daft. Said I was called Betsy Smith. And stop staring at them marks!" Jess had become slovenly in her speech and Emma suspected it was a defense of sorts against the women among whom she found herself. Any sign of gentility would set her apart, make her a butt for the others.

"Oh, Jess. Why did you have to kill him?"

"He wouldn't go away. Wouldn't take no for answer."

"You won't be able to kill that jailer if he comes tonight."

Jess covered her face with her hands. There was a large sore on the inside of her wrist that had begun to suppurate. The sticky mess gleamed in the light of someone else's tallow dip. Out of the corner of her eye, Emma saw a middle-aged woman asleep against the wall not far away. Asleep or foxing? She tried to remember if she had said anything incriminating.

"That woman—"

"Ale drunk. She had some money."

"Jess. Are you sure? We've spoken of the captain and Jackson. Jenkins. The posters. I wish I'd spied her sooner but it's so dark over there and she looks like a parcel of rags. She'll know I came with Mrs. Fry—"

"She's beyond hearing. Anyway, I don't know if I care. I'm to be transported because it wasn't only a loaf I took. There were several things. There would of been no need if I'd done all the things I was asked to do, but I do 'ave certain standards and a weakness for gentlemen. Not that I met any after Wildford. And it's no use asking if I really did sleep wi' 'im, Miss Emma , for I won't tell."

"It doesn't matter. I thought it did—"

"You'm become priggish, Miss Emma." Jess smiled for the first time and it was an amusement filled with malice and mischief. She had not changed. "What did you do with Jackson? I never thought Ringan would tell on me."

"We decided to bury him in the wood so that everyone would think he'd run off but we forgot the things he left at Staves. Harrison and the rest did not."

"And—?"

"My father decided to have a beat for the yellow dog you said you saw. It very quickly became a grim reality, killing off lambs and a sheep or two. Then, the creature sniffed out the corpse and ate half his arm. But his face was intact."

"Then why are they hunting me and not him?"

"He would not implicate me, and I could not see him blamed."

"So you said I'd done it?" The vivid blue eyes were dark now with some emotion that was not entirely hatred. "A fine friend you've been, Miss Emma."

"Ringan was not the murderer. Why should he hang for you? Why should you expect it?"

"Shouldn't, of course. But I thought he'd 'a been grateful—"

"Grateful for what?" Emma was conscious of a pit before her feet.

"Oh, come, Miss Emma! Never looked green, you didn't."

"He said he'd not touched you. He swore—"

"Well, 'e'd 'ave 'ad to, wouldn't 'e!"

"Why should he lie?"

"Because you'd be more of a feather in 'is cap. Needs money, the captain does, and that factoring won't do much to provide it."

"You're lying, Jess. Aren't you?"

The girl smiled. It was the old, tantalizing reflex. "Make up your own mind, Miss Emma. If you can. Now, you'd best go. Wouldn't do to be seen being familiar with criminals, would it? A transport."

"I'll say—I was asking how you'd come here. What you'd done."

"Funny it had to be for taking such small things. When all the time I'd stuck a knife in that ram, Jackson. I'm not sorry."

The woman by the wall stirred, fell quiet again.

"They said you'd led the house servants on. I know they were struck with you."

"Honest, I never encouraged them."

"Too busy—" Emma stopped in time.

"Luring on your pa? 'E was a lovely man but I'd like to 'ave wed the captain. 'E was real special."

"He stole. Gambled—"

Jess snorted. "What's that matter? A very loyal gentleman, Ringan. That counts more."

"There's Mrs. Fry looking for me. I have to go, Jess."

"Bring me something. Some rhino, please! If you've ale, you can stand it. I 'eard tales of the transport ships, the things that 'appen when you get to Botany Bay, if you ain't dead of the fever first. There was a woman 'ere, went out two days since, and she'd been transported. There's nowhere to shelter when you land on the beach and you 'ave to go wi' the first man as asks you. Not that they do much asking! Whipped like bitches if you don't do all that's required of you and some of that unnatural. A bit of food thrown at you, if you please, and more hard work than you can cope wi'. Nothing but work. Sold to any brute—"

"Jess. Don't, please. I'll do what I can, I promise."

"You *could* say 'oo I was. Make it easy for you to get rid of me proper this time." Again that infuriating, soul-searching smile.

"Don't you know me better than that?"

"There's your saintly friend. Tall for a woman, ain't she? Easy to be good when you've all you want."

"Her husband is bankrupt and her children adopted against her own wishes."

Jess looked skeptical. "Don't trust nobody 'oo's as good as that. Why should she bother?"

"Those others seem to know."

"Makes you doubt everyone, 'avin' a pa like mine and being pretty and 'avin' men like Jackson around you. You won't forget? Money for drink. To bribe the jailer to look at someone else another night?"

Emma felt in her purse and found it empty. "I threw coins to the crowd and forgot to replenish it."

"And Mrs. Elizabeth Fry?"

"I told you. She and her husband have nothing. Babies to keep."

"You want me to suffer! I can always say you and Ringan helped. Burying 'im."

"Don't talk nonsense, Jess." Emma was very pale. "I'll be back tomorrow. It's the best I can do."

Jess curled up suddenly, like a child inside its mother, and wound her arms around her head. The neglected hair covered her features like a shroud.

"Emma!" Mrs. Fry called.

"Coming." Emma hardly had the strength to go. She looked back once but Jess had not moved.

She could not sleep. There had been no one to ask for advice about Jess Ashcroft. Mrs. Fry would very quickly have uncovered the whole terrible story of her interest in the girl who called herself Betsy Smith, and so far, Jess was only accused of theft. Wildford was too far away and Ringan with him. Lewis? Instinctively, she knew Critchley would never jeopardize his future in a bid to salvage the remnants of a Cockney servant's life. All he wanted was his partnership and Deborah Wymark. The knowledge hurt more than it had at the time of the rout.

All men were the same. Ringan had lied about possessing Jess. If the girl was to be believed. And why bother to stir up trouble when she wanted money and aid from Emma?

The strange room became a rack, Miss Fallon's ladylike snores a Chinese torture. Dawn was an age in coming and when it did, Emma was exhausted. Miss Fallon was concerned by her appearance but her mistress was determined to accompany Mrs. Fry a second time and she herself had arranged to visit her distant relative and could not cancel the appointment at such short notice.

Once at Mrs. Fry's house, the cries of convalescing infants in her ears, Emma was aware of a great relief. She had money enough with her and it should not be impossible to let Jess have it without attracting notice. Quietly, she listened to Elizabeth, fondled the head of one of the blond, little Frys. She liked the feel of the round, small head, the trust that flowed between them. This was something Amelia had never experienced. She had not been equipped for motherhood and wanted only to fob off her child onto someone else. She had never cuddled or kissed Emma. That had been left to Wildford.

Emma and Mrs. Fry left after a frugal lunch. The girl was distressed that one so worthy should be forced to live so modestly when Wildford's one thought was of self-indulgence. But she did love him in spite of his faults, and he had been generous toward Elizabeth's cause. She herself would never again waste a penny if she could help it. Then the heaviness of the purse in her reticule reminded her of the reason for her journey.

The carriage stopped to pick up Anna Buxton, Fowell's sister, who was to accompany Mrs. Fry, and Emma saw that this could be to her advantage. Sometime while Anna and

Elizabeth were absorbed, she would seek out Jess in her dank corner. Pray she would not be indiscreet with the other prisoners! Emma saw the shadow of a rope.

It took her all her time to follow Anna and Mrs. Fry into Newgate. She was not a coward, far from it, but the thought of public execution for aiding murder was not the stuff of which bravery is made. Jess had been a fool to steal while under threat of being apprehended for a greater crime. But if she were starving, who could blame her? And then the thought of last night, and what had happened to that pretty, arrogant girl under cover of darkness, sickened her afresh. She would not think of Ringan having done the same thing, yet the thought obtruded in spite of the resolve. Emma wished he had not lied. Lewis never had. He had prevaricated, but that did not seem so damaging. She took a deep breath and allowed herself to be shut in with all the smells and screams, the aura of fear and slyness, all the desperation.

Today, her gown was not immediately torn. Miss Fallon would be pleased, as she found it increasingly difficult to cope with invisible repairs and it was not fair to inflict them upon her. Emma intended to see that she was provided with some proper spectacles, otherwise she might not be able to enjoy books.

Mrs. Fry forged her usual, assured way past thief and harlot, forger and cheat, toward the schoolroom. The sound of children's voices issued from it and the calm tones of Miss Mary Connor, her brown hair smooth and—deceptively?—virginal. Emma could not quite lose her mistrust of anyone who stole. But she had always been cushioned against want and work. What could she know?

The unaccustomed feelings of humility reminded her of Ringan. Poor captain. He had obviously adored his father, wanting always to be allowed to share the responsibility of the estate with his spoiled brother only to be continually shut out.

Who would not have turned to available pleasures and fulfillment? But, why lie to her? It seemed that Jess's version of the proximity in the factor's cottage was the truer. Ringan was a strongly sexual man who had lived in the same confined space with a beautiful and desirable girl who, by her own admission, was experienced and wanted him into the bargain. Emma tried to close her ears to the devil's voice but it remained persuasive.

She saw Jess just at the moment that Elizabeth and Anna bent their heads over the slates and schoolbooks. She looked worse than she had yesterday, one eye all swollen and her gown deplorable. Emma swallowed. If she had not been so jealous and suspicious, if it had not been for the Rayleigh fiasco, Jess would have been spared this indignity.

"Miss Emma—" Jess clung to the strands of the dirty hammock, her one good eye enormous and brilliantly blue. She seemed to have twice as many bruises and she did not move easily.

"Oh, Jess—"

"Did—did you bring the rhino?"

"I have it here." Emma patted the heavy reticule. She could not bring herself to ask about the previous night. Jess's appearance was sufficient.

"I shall need—more."

"More?"

"You were right, Miss Emma. We were not careful enough. She 'eard, that ale drunkard. Seems she 'ad no money left for drink and she was sober for a change. Pretending to be tipsy. Listened to every word. I could 'a killed 'er when she came up to me after you left. Wants fifty guineas, she does, an' I knew you'd not bring that much. Just when I was thinkin' I'd be surely transported for theft an' maybe 'ave a fresh start in Australia. Could meet someone my own kind. Can't prevent myself being shipped, I sees that now. But I'm sore afraid o' being topped." She dropped to her knees and clasped Emma around the calves of her legs. "Please, Emma—"

"Oh, my God— Where is she now?"

"Over there. You'll hardly see her in the dark, but she repeated it all. The posters. Staves. Remembered Captain Ringan, Jackson's name and the fact that I stuck a knife in him. Remembers that Mrs. Fry knows you well. Even recalls Jenkins and Harrison. And I mentioned Wildford—"

"Jess!" Emma was seized by cold fingers of panic on her father's behalf.

"Lucky your friend's such an attraction, and that school of hers, or you'd be spotted over here wi' me. Can you bring the fifty guineas? Can you?"

"It won't stop there."

"It might. We got to try! It could be your neck as well, Miss Emma. Your neck."

"Stop it! You're hysterical. That won't help either of us. Anything Ringan and I did was to help you. Because we were concerned."

"Except that *you* told them *I* killed Jackson."

Now that her eyes had become adjusted to the dimness, Emma could see the woman by the wall. She had her eyes open and her smile was malevolent. A filthy shawl, on which she had vomited, was pulled up to her chin, the dried encrustation sour and stale in the enclosed space. The girl felt sick but more angry than afraid.

"I should have to ask Lewis Critchley for so much money. It's too far to go back to Norwich. Lewis is at the new branch. I could try to explain."

"He's a tricky gentleman, Miss Emma. I did try to warn you."

"He's better than no hope at all."

"If I'd a knife I'd get rid of her for good. For both of us. A quick shove in the dark. No one'd know who or why. She could talk once she's drunk enough—"

"You don't know what you are saying!"

"We both know quite well. Your neck and mine safe. But

I only 'as to wait till I'm transported. Could be anytime now. No runner will think to look for me here."

"You could be held for some time, awaiting transportation, if there is no available ship."

"Once I was away, I'd be all right. No one'd know. I'd be Betsy Smith, off to a new life in Australia. All I need is money and you got it. You or Wildford's bank."

"She—that woman could speak out afterward. You'd leave her round our necks, Ringan's and mine—"

"Should 'ave left Jackson where he was then!" Jess's eyes were feverish. "Didn't ask you to interfere."

"We couldn't. We wanted to help—"

"Until Ringan was threatened and you're lusting for him, aren't you! Pretending to yourself that it's that cold-as-a-fish Critchley when all the time it's the captain you're bedding in that cool little mind o' yours! That's why—" Jess stopped abruptly, flushing.

"That's why he didn't try to bed you? I knew he wouldn't lie! But you did because I gave you away. I suppose I deserved it. You know I'm sorry, that I'd never have said anything if it had not been a question of someone else being blamed unjustly."

"It was because it was me. You turned against me," Jess accused.

"No. Why do you think I came back? Brought you this? What's that woman's name?"

"Lily. Lil Morris."

"Wait here. I must speak to her. Tell me if Mrs. Fry or Miss Buxton come this way."

"Emma—"

Emma went over to where the old woman was sitting. The sick, acid smell of the shawl repelled her but she made herself stay. "You want money for ale," she said. "I can give it to you."

"If I keeps me marf shut, eh?" The gray face was twisted with vindictiveness.

"You know what will happen if my friend comes to any

harm. Say one word and I'll say you were part of it. They'll believe me sooner than you. They always take a lady's word first, especially anyone who helps Mrs. Fry and supplies comforts to the prison."

" 'Ere, are you threatening me?" The pouched eyes stared, surprised.

"Advising you, that's all. You blab about—about Betsy—"

"Betsy! Ha!" Stumps of teeth were shown in a mirthless grin.

"In that case," Emma said, jingling her purse, "there's no more to be said."

"Didn't say I *would* say nuffink." The old crone scrambled to her feet with hideous alacrity and grabbed at Emma's arm. Emma heard the sleeve tear under the armpit. Her look of fury must have sobered the old woman, for she drew back. "Sorry, miss," she said placatingly. "Such a pretty dress, too."

"What you ask is impossible," Emma told her, looking over her shoulder to ascertain whether Mrs. Fry and Anna were still busy. They were, the majority of the women clustered around the schoolroom door, only a few furtive groups left in this part of the room, all bent on mischief, she was certain.

"Fifty guineas would buy me out an' a good livin' after."

"Then blabbing to Bow Street when you've drunk it all? As you will."

" 'Twill probably kill me first, little miss. You've not much to fear."

"I'll need time to get it."

" 'Ow long?"

"Two days?" Emma could not count on assistance from Lewis.

"I want some now." The old voice turned ugly. "Got a thirst, I 'ave."

Emma took several coins from her purse, hoping desperately that no one was watching. "For God's sake have the sense to hide them."

"Wasn't born yesterday. No one won't get these. Now don't you forget me, will you, miss? Or your friend might be sorry. Pretty neck she's got."

Bruised as it was, Jess's neck was still beautiful, and if Jackson had been intent on ravishment, she did not deserve to have it stretched for defending herself against violation. But no one would believe her since the servants at Staves had their revenge for Jess's former arrogance. One or two might even think they'd spoken the truth and they'd never be shifted from their testimony.

"They'll not let me in without Mrs. Fry so I must wait until she returns."

"Best not take *too* long," Lily Morris warned, her hand scrabbling inside the ghastly shawl to thrust each coin into a different place. Emma noticed that one of a small group on the other side of the next line of hammocks was watching the old woman, scratching a curly red head at the same time. She had a brazen face and a voluptuous figure that still looked attractive under its covering of Newgate rags. The woman looked away again, laughing stridently at some remark made by a companion. Neither paid any further attention to Lil, and Emma breathed more easily. This place made one suspicious.

"If you open your mouth too wide you'll never get your fifty guineas," Emma said. She hated this unpleasant woman who had spied and intimidated without any feeling for her victims. She'd not hesitate to make Jess miserable while she waited for Emma to return.

"Just see that you comes tomorrer."

"It may not be possible. I explained—"

"You got ter try 'arder, then." The toothless smile was totally evil.

Emma went back to Jess before she was tempted to lift something and batter the woman to insensibility. She was suddenly afraid of the passions that could be aroused by a blackmailer. It was the basest of crimes, far worse than the murder of a rapist. The loss of a worthless life seemed to pale with insignificance before the taking of a woman's self-respect. Giving one's body was not the same as enduring the brutal possession of what should only be offered. She could understand now why Jess had behaved as she did in the bad time after leaving Lady Rayleigh. It had been cruel to send her into the kind of life she had endured with her own father.

"Have you bought the old bitch off?" Jess whispered nervously, pulling her shawl over the worst of her bruises.

"Only temporarily, I fear."

"Just let her try her tricks again!" The girl's face was distorted with hatred.

"Jess. Oh, Jess, don't do anything you'll regret. I'll be back as soon as I may. I came unprepared. Here's money for yourself but don't let them see you accept it." She indicated the strident woman with the auburn curls and the sly couple with whom she consorted. Their eyes flickered everywhere, moving from one place to another with unbelievable rapidity, but Emma was sure they missed nothing.

Under cover of the shawl, the purse exchanged hands. "I must go," Emma whispered. "Already, I've been here too long. Take care and do not lose heart."

"Easy to say!" Jess laughed discordantly. "You won't take it amiss that I said Ringan had been with me? 'E's the only one I fancied who didn't feel the same, blast his eyes. Only wanted to make you sweat as much as I'm doing—"

For a moment Emma thought of nothing but the captain, the way he had lain with her on the floor of the summerhouse, his hand tracing the line of her throat, her breast. She experienced a second of such extreme happiness that she lost count of time and place. There was only the sensation of a quite delicious warmth that stole along every nerve, leaving her in a lassitude that she wished would go on forever. Then the harsh strings of the present pulled her back to find Jess staring at her jealously.

"You do lust after 'im, don't you!"

"I'd use another name for it."

"There's no such thing as love," Jess said bitterly. "Not for the likes of me, there isn't."

Emma could not help herself. She put her arms around the girl and briefly a comfort passed from one to another. Then Jess laughed unevenly, pushed her away. "Are you encouraging me to forget my place, Miss Emma? No good can come of it. You taught me where my place is. In the gutter, and I got to remember that."

"I have to go into the school. That's what I came for. Be brave, Jess." Emma left her without another look. Not even when she had gone the round of the children and listened to Mary Connor's voice—she was good with the pupils—and helped gather up the equipment after the lessons and the prayers— Not when the barred door was opened and the same rheumy-eyed turnkey let them out, did she turn her head. Yet every sinew of her body wanted to go back. She had a hideous premonition of disaster that spoiled the realization that she loved Ringan very deeply. She tried to tell herself it was only the atmosphere of Newgate that depressed her, but all the time an inner voice said that it was much more than perception or intuition, more than the beastliness of Lily Morris. She set herself to find out exactly when Mrs. Fry intended to return.

Lewis's office was very handsome. Emma had forgotten how fine the fittings and decorations were. True, there was a large number of files, but they were neatly set out on the shelves. The ebony desk contrasted with the light colors that surrounded it so that it was the most important thing in the room. Lewis leaned back in his chair and surveyed her through narrowed eyes. He looked capable, indeed, almost ruthless, and she did not envy Deborah the furrow she must plow to reach this man so unexpectedly strong. Ringan must never be encouraged to be too ambitious.

"Well, Miss Emma?" Lewis stared at her, taking in the

simplicity of the dull green gown she wore, the bonnet that was the exact color, the pelisse with its narrow edging of fur.

Emma was not sure how to begin. The last time she had seen him he was burrowing inside Deborah's gown, his breeches tight with desire and temporary frustration. That such a lusty gentleman existed inside that cool, contained skin had surprised her beyond measure. How well he was hidden at this moment.

"I need some money and have not time to return to Norwich to obtain it from my father."

"Indeed?" His lips curved satirically. He was enjoying the moment of triumph.

"Papa perhaps made some mention of sums of money that may be required by me from time to time? Unexpected calls upon my purse?"

Lewis shook his head. "Mr. Wildford made no such provision. Rather, I had the feeling he frowned upon any softness on my part where anyone was concerned."

"I am not anyone. I am Emma Wildford."

"Of course you are, and should have more sense than to plead with me to break your father's rules—"

"You said he'd made none!"

"Unspoken rules."

"If they were unspoken, they cannot exist."

"There are—understandings in business. You bend words to suit yourself."

"I think it ridiculous that my father owns this place and I cannot obtain money you know will be returned as soon as Papa is aware of the transaction."

"You mentioned a sum. How large?"

"Fifty guineas."

"I cannot help but think that had you a legitimate need, Mr. Wildford would have entrusted you with that amount before you left home. Why do you need it?" His fingers twisted upon a quill pen that lay on the dark surface of the desk.

"For a friend. Someone in trouble."

"What friend, Miss Emma! I'm well aware of the extent of your social activities in London, and they are, your mother and Maybrick, the Olds. And Mrs. Fry with her Newgate commitments. You and your father have both subscribed to those. Neither of you have any traffic with Maybrick and Mrs. Wildford. The Olds do not need fifty guineas." His mouth quirked into a grimace she took to be of resentment.

"The money is for none of these."

"I should know far more before permitting such a sum to leave the bank."

"My own father's bank!"

"I could be assisting you to run away, to gamble. To put yourself into the hands of rogues or moneylenders." How cold his eyes were.

"It is for no such reason," she murmured stiffly, hating him.

"Blackmail?"

The question came so quietly and unexpectedly that Emma could not hide her shock.

"You are wondering how I know?" Lewis asked, letting the quill fall with a soft thud. "There are only a few reasons why a banker is asked for certain sums and we grow to recognize them all."

She sat pale and silent.

"There is one way to make me change my mind and make you a personal loan. One that need not involve the bank."

"Oh?"

"Renew our engagement and ask Wildford to offer me the partnership."

"And an allowance for Deborah panting for you in some discreet little house not too far away?"

Lewis smiled unpleasantly. "Well, Emma?"

"How do you know that I'd not retract as soon as I had the fifty guineas?"

"Because of your stark honesty."

"I am not so scrupulous nowadays."

"I suspect you are. And I know you must be desperate because otherwise you'd be racing back to Norwich where your papa may, or may not, indulge you. No moneylender would take you seriously. You know that."

"Let me have it, I beg you." Her voice was low with pain for Jess. For Ringan who was receding from her with every passing moment.

"If you let me call in the rest of the staff in order to announce our betrothal."

Emma stared into a future where she was old, seated in an empty chamber where her face, lined and unhappy, was reflected in dusty mirrors, and somewhere Lewis lay abed with Deborah, both replete as satyrs and as merciless.

"I could go to Mr. Old. Throw myself on his good graces."

Lewis shook his head lazily. "He is on a tour with his wife. At her bidding."

"Deborah *must* have disturbed her," she could not help saying.

"We are not talking of her." Lewis looked angry. "It's you we are discussing."

"I—cannot do it."

"I used not to repel you."

"That was before I really saw you."

"Come, Emma. Make up your mind. I've an important appointment in half an hour. You know you want my fifty guineas. You need it badly, don't you?"

She thought of the sterility of being tied to Lewis, forced to become his wife when he wanted children to reinforce his claim to Wildford's Bank, neglected when it was not necessary to breed. And all for fifty guineas! Then she remembered Jess and the turnkey, Lil Morris with her whining malevolence and the very real threat the woman represented. Ringan could still answer for that night burial—

It was the concern she felt for the captain that decided her. Dryly, she said, "And do you have wine for the celebration? It is not every day you are betrothed to the future you thought had evaded you."

He laughed very softly, and she wondered however she could have imagined him pleasant or attractive. She saw him all too clearly and the discovery was like touching ice or wet stones. He went toward the door and she said sharply, "Not until I have the money in my hand! Say not one word."

"You do need it badly, my sweet." Lewis bent and kissed the side of her neck. She flinched. "I am not dirt!" he said furiously. "You'll not behave so with me."

"I cannot help it."

He stared at her angrily.

"You have what you want," Emma reminded him. "I am not obliged to pretend what I will never feel."

"Why have you changed?" Now he was curious.

"I prefer to keep the reasons to myself. May I have what I asked for? If not, I may as well go. I must have it for this afternoon or it is useless." Mrs. Fry was to be away for three weeks or more and today was her last visit for some time to the newly formed school at Newgate. She was to take sewing for the adult prisoners who had expressed interest in the occupation and Emma must take the opportunity while it was offered. She could not afford to fail. In one hour she must be at Mildred's Court.

Lewis sat down at the great sarcophagus of a desk. Slowly he took out a key and put it into the lock of one of the drawers. The light shone down one side of his face. He looked like an angel. Then he raised his eyes and they were shallow with dislike. Lifting his hands he spilled the contents onto the shining black top. They rattled and clinked like Judas's thirty pieces of silver. "How will you manage them?" he asked.

Emma could not imagine. She had not visualized the weight and capacity of the gold.

"I'll cope somehow. Wrap them in something strong and

I'll put them in my reticule." God alone knew how Lily Morris would keep such a hoard secret in that crowded place. The turnkeys would make their own investigation when she tried to exchange the first. And if she were robbed, she'd squawk like a dozen hens.

"Could you change it into silver?" she asked, recognizing the futility of presenting Lily with this money. Silver would be far less obtrusive.

"That will be even more unwieldy. Why not a promissory note?" The curiosity persisted.

Emma shook her head. There was the smell of doom about the whole affair.

"Very well." Lewis fetched a leather bag and counted out the amount in silver as she had requested. She stared at the bulk in desperation. She'd have to pretend she was taking some clothes for the prisoners and fold a dress or two on top for camouflage.

"May I invite my colleagues now with the joyous tidings?" Lewis asked, relocking the drawer and surveying Emma with satisfaction.

"If you must." That day of the green shadows she would have cried out with joy, only the soft summer magic was long since gone. But she'd not present an abject figure of despair! As she listened to Lewis's voice beyond the opened door, she bit her lips to restore the color and rubbed at her cheeks. If she had not after all bought Ringan's life and Jess's passage to Australia, then would be time for mourning.

Chapter Eight

The prison seemed quieter. Emma, the bag, from which folds of material protruded, heavy on her arm, stood still and listened. Normally the women made ten times as much noise as the men, but today there was a curious hollowness within Newgate. Mrs. Fry lifted her head, the cap incongruously white and fresh against the dark stone of the passage. "Something is wrong."

Emma's spirits plummeted. Jess was discovered. Old Lily had drunk too much ale and had made a scene, let out secrets. For a moment she thought she must plead illness and go back to the carriage, then her courage reasserted itself. She was in the mess now for good or ill and at least she'd be spared the mockery of a wedding night with Lewis Critchley.

"Something wrong all right," the turnkey grumbled, and Emma had a quick glimpse of prison officials hurrying across the end of the passage, faces grave. A spider dropped on the end of a filament of web and touched her cheek. She screamed soundlessly. "Some old 'ooman snuffed out in the night, like a bit o' candle."

"Died, you mean?" Elizabeth asked. "Poor soul."

Oh, God, Emma thought. God. Lil Morris's face was before her eyes, still twisted with wickedness and greed. She'd baited Jess a fraction too far and the girl had carried out her threat. Where had she obtained the knife? Bought it, probably, out of the money Emma had given her.

"'Elped on 'er way."

"You mean—someone murdered her?" Mrs. Fry could not conceal her repugnance.

"Lot o' bad feeling, allus, in jail. Got ter expect it, all 'em bitches shut up together. Try to control 'em, but you see 'em for yerself, Mrs. Fry. Can't stamp out all the wickedness wi' a few prayers and a new fichu. 'Appened in the night it did, when we was nowhere near the place."

"I always understood that some of you *were* there at night." Elizabeth could not altogether conceal her bitterness. This was the constant complaint of the women.

"Not that late, ma'am," he replied virtuously. "Got ter make sure they've settled down, 'avent we? Stands ter reason."

A horrid, hot discomfort had risen up inside Emma. She bit her lip to prevent herself from shouting.

"Was there no outcry?" Elizabeth asked, hastening her steps.

"Not a sound. Must a' been someone wi' a bit of strength. Young."

Emma almost fainted with reaction. They did not know. Yet—

"Someone must be in possession of the facts. Has no one said anything?"

"Not them. Try to get summat out o' the women first, then if that don't work, they'll say they was too scared to tell for fear of gettin' the same as old Lil."

"Lil?"

"Woman callin' 'ersel' Lily Morris."

"How," Elizabeth asked carefully, "was it done?"

"Smovered wif 'er own shawl."

Emma turned her face away quickly, almost smelling the filthy object. Lil must have bought ale with the money she was given, then Jess only had to wait for dark to come. But in such close proximity, another prisoner must have been aware of what was happening. Even an old, inebriated woman would have thrashed and kicked, disturbed somebody— Blackmail was a hideous chain.

"We will be allowed inside?" Mrs. Fry asked.

"You'd best ask the governor, ma'am. 'E's there at present."

"This will be my last opportunity, as I told him the other day. Besides, we should have a service for the dead woman. What had she done?"

"Attacked a Robin Redbreast with a gin bottle while she was tipsy, ma'am. He was trying to arrest 'er."

"Not a massive crime, however you look at it. Why was she killed, do you think?"

"Money, ma'am. We found silver 'idden in the straw and inside 'er clo'es."

"Then why was it not taken?"

"Ask them as did it, ma'am! Blest if I know. Cunning 'iding places she 'ad, but they was missed. All the others was searched and two of the rest 'ad similar coins on their persons. A woman called Molly Darke and a girl, Betsy Smith. Smith said she'd been given 'ers by a lady 'oo came wi' you yesterday— I wasn't 'ere so I couldn't say yea or nay. Did you 'ave a lady companion yesterday, ma'am?"

"I had two. Miss Buxton and—and this young lady, Miss Wildford. Emma? Did you distribute money to the prisoners?"

Emma's voice was surprisingly steady. "I know it was foolish, Elizabeth, and you warned me against it, but I have to confess I did. There was a poor girl, badly beaten, and I was touched by her plight—"

"Emma! You promised you'd not be involved! Not in that way. Not personally—"

"But you know me, Mrs. Fry. I cannot help myself. It's happened before."

"And the old woman?"

"I gave to her also. I have so much, you see. She wanted ale for comfort."

"But only those two?"

"Only those two."

"Then we must tell the governor. You could identify the girl Smith, Emma?"

"I certainly could."

As soon as she had spoken, Emma was conscious of a feeling of dread. If she exonerated Jess, she would be practically accusing the other of old Lily's killing. In a nightmare, she followed the hurrying figures of Mrs. Fry and the turnkey. As they turned the corner, they could see the governor and his secretary in deep conversation by the door of the women's quarters where the school was now held. Inside was a confusion of low voices and hushed whispers. The door opened to disclose two men carrying a stretcher upon which lay a sheeted form. A portion of the shawl obtruded.

By this time the governor's attention was drawn toward Mrs. Fry and her companion. "Mrs. Fry. Your visit had escaped my memory. This *dreadful* business—" The rest of his conversation was lost as Elizabeth hurried toward him in order to pass on the information she had elicited from Emma.

Emma listened to the ringing footfalls of the turnkeys as they bore away their awful burden. The governor turned to look in her direction. His secretary raised a quizzing glass. Mrs. Fry beckoned, her face kind. Emma, her gaze fixed on the governor's middle waistcoat button, told her story a second time.

"You've no objection to identifying the person to whom you gave the silver?"

Emma shook her head, not trusting herself to speak.

"Then both women will be brought out and we can clear up the miserable business."

The weight on the girl's arm became more than she could bear and she had to set the bag on the ground, imagining she heard the coins clink, that everyone would hear.

A turnkey opened the door and Emma saw, held by her arms between two of the prison staff, the flashy woman with the red curls. The woman's eyes were dark with terror. "'Twasn't me!" she screamed, struggling with her captors. "'Twasn't me, I swear. Tell them, 'twasn't me. For the love o' God."

"I gave her no money," Emma said, "but that's not to say she had none already."

The face under the bright hair was ashen. "Course I 'ad some 'id away. We all got a bit somewheres. I never took nothin' from old Lil. Never!"

"Take her to be questioned further. Solitary confinement for the present," the governor said without expression.

"No!" The shriek was enough to raise the hair on one's neck. "No. I'll never come back from there! No-o-oo." The cry died away as the woman collapsed and was dragged away, her heels scoring marks on the flags.

"Is that necessary?" Elizabeth asked, white-faced.

"She had no money when she was searched two days ago."

"Theft is not the same as taking life."

"No, but never fear, she'll be questioned until we get to the bottom of the affair. Fetch the other prisoner."

It seemed an age before Jess was brought out. She looked strange and quiet, her eyes fixed on distance as though she neither saw nor heard. Neither did she struggle as the woman called Molly had done. Her calmness impressed the governor.

"Did you give silver to Betsy Smith?"

"Y-yes." Emma was far from self-possessed.

"Can you remember how much?"

"I'm not certain. You see, there was the old woman—I gave to both."

"How much do you think?"

There was expression in Jess's face now. Her hand went up to her hair and Emma saw that all her fingers were extended.

"Five," Emma said. "I'm almost certain it was five shillings."

"That was the sum found on her, I believe," the secretary said, consulting a paper. "No. I am wrong. Four shillings. What did you do with the other one, girl?"

"Paid the turnkey to tumble someone else," Jess replied with some of her old spirit.

"Watch your tongue, girl!"

"It's true. You said we must tell the truth. But it was a waste of money, for he took it, then 'ad me just the same, the swine."

Mrs. Fry flinched then looked first angry, then compassionate. "You know that these complaints have foundation," she said to the governor. "Time and time again we are told the same—"

"But today we are concerned with the taking of a life," he reminded her, "not a tumble."

"Are you sure it was the other woman?"

At Mrs. Fry's quiet question, Emma stared hard at Jess for some affirmation of her own doubts and suspicions. Jess's eyes seemed to repudiate the suggestion. "Must 'a been Molly," Jess said, though the question had been directed toward the governor and not herself. "I never touched the old biddy. Anyways, I 'ad company all night. Not very welcome company at that. I swear it was not me." It was to Emma that she made the declaration and her tone had the ring of truth. Emma remembered the red-haired woman's scrutiny of Lily, her remarks to her two cronies, the studious attempts at disinterest. Yet, she could never be certain.

"I must say that everything does point to the woman, Darke's, guilt. She was stripped to the skin only two days since, and her pallet examined most minutely when she was accused of theft by another prisoner. She has had no visitors who might have brought her money. Smith had even less than she was given by Miss Wildford, though I have only her word for what happened to the fifth shilling. Who was the turnkey you say ravished you?" The governor's voice betrayed only a cold distaste and Emma was tempted to turn on him.

"Jerrold Stamp. Ain't left me alone since I came."

"Was Stamp on duty in the women's ward last night?"

"Aye, sir. But them harpies will say anything—"

"That's enough! I know my own prison! Let the woman, Smith, be returned for the moment. Watch your step, girl. If there's one more cause for complaint—"

"Won't be anything, guv'ner," Jess said, dropping a mock curtsy, "unless them cronies of Moll's decides to make trouble 'cos I get back and she don't."

"See they are warned," the governor snapped. "Make it plain they'll join Darke if they as much as raise a finger against Smith."

Jess was seized and hauled upright. The warder's fingers bit cruelly into her upper arms but she managed to smile. "Thanks, miss, for your help. Might a' been topped if you 'adn't come today to bear witness. Remember that, I will."

She was pulled away roughly, oddly touching in her rags and down-at-heel shoes, head held high in defiance.

Emma, the useless money bag at her feet, had an inclination to weep at the futility of her capitulation to Lewis. She had bargained away her future to no good purpose. Then she wanted to laugh, but the urge was quenched by the governor's obvious annoyance over the disruption of his routine and by Jess's accusations against Stamp. There was also Mrs. Fry who was a persistent thorn in his flesh.

"We may go in now?" Elizabeth asked.

"I think you should not—"

"But I know we should! It was arranged. And I promised the women. It is bad to make promises and then to break them, especially in a place where there is so much unhappiness. And so little hope."

The governor gave a grunt of irritation. "They are here

because they have committed crimes. You seem to forget that."

"Mostly such small ones, and always because they have been driven by circumstances into wrongdoing."

"They can sound pitiful when it suits them, madam."

"They know we are here. It can only lead to trouble if you deny them."

"Well—" The governor knew she was right, yet disliked giving in too readily. The prisoners would end up making impossible demands, anticipating privileges as their right. This Mrs. Fry was disruptive and he could not be expected to show any great enthusiasm for her breaching of his former prison discipline and regulations.

The murmuring behind the door grew in volume. "Very well, Mrs. Fry. But a short visit only and there must be no repetition of the events of yesterday. What have you in the bundle you carry?"

"Comforts," Mrs. Fry answered. "Combs and ribbons, Bibles and some children's clothes. Handwork."

"And you?" This to Emma.

"A few gowns. Some of the women who were not in rags when they arrived are most certainly in them now." Emma knew better than to mention Jess by name.

"There must be no money doled out. They would cut one another's throats for a farthing. You've seen the truth of that today."

"I promise there will be no gifts of money."

"They'll all be searched so it would be useless."

"I have already said—"

"Yes, Mrs. Fry. Open the door, turnkey. And I should like to see Jerrold Stamp."

The governor turned away, his mind already on other problems. Emma picked up her bag and hoped it did not look as heavy as it was, that the coins would not rattle.

They were inside the women's ward and the prisoners crowded forward, subdued, faces anxious. "Thought they'd keep you out, lady."

"Tell us a story."

"What did you bring us for carryin' the slates?"

"Promised, you did!"

"Gawd bless yer, missus!"

"Want summat to sew, Mrs. Fry. Never 'ad any last time."

"Please. Something for my baby. 'E was cold last night."

"One at a time," Elizabeth said, her Quaker cap seeming, suddenly, a kind of halo. "Here's a baby shawl. It belonged to my Elizabeth and I kept it apart. But far better it's round one of your children than put into lavender in a drawer."

Elizabeth was the Fry child who had died young. It seemed that the women knew of the tragedy, for the shawl was not snatched but taken quietly, and put about a wizened infant with a face prematurely old. It seemed hardly to breathe.

"I wanted the shawl," another woman said.

"I have another, newer."

All the time Mrs. Fry distributed her largess, Emma searched the motley crew for Jess, spying her at last behind the hammocks, leaning against the wall, her face a mask of weariness. She wanted to leave her the leather bag, but if it were not stolen here it would be discovered on the voyage to Botany Bay. The thing was suddenly a millstone from which Emma would never be separated.

She held up the best of the gowns she had brought. Jess shook her head. Silently, Emma begged her to accept the parting gift but Jess made no move. It was as though she was severing the last link with her past life. She was Betsy Smith, soon to sail to the other side of the world where her secrets would die along with her old identity. She had killed Jackson. Had she told the truth about Lil Morris? If she had not, then the red-haired woman would hang for someone else's crime.

Slowly, Jess shook her head. Shook it again and turned her face against the wall. It was the only surety Emma was likely to be offered. It was also a farewell.

* * *

Miss Fallon had not returned when Emma went back to the hotel. She was to be brought back at eight of the clock and it was only six.

Emma set down the heavy bag and took off her bonnet. The streets were not quiet. People still ranted against the price of bread and the Regent's extravagance. "Wot's 'e want another flaming palace for?"

Emma took off her cloak and her gown, then lay down on top of the bed in her petticoats and bodice. Tiredness descended and a weariness of spirit. She closed her eyes gratefully. Thoughts of Lily, Moll Darke and Jess came and went like fish in an overgrown pond, sometimes seen clearly, then murky shadows. Lewis smiled from a cave filled with stalagmites and he seemed harder and colder than they were. Ringan's father lurched his way across a snowy landscape.

From an immense distance she heard the opening of the door, the soft click of the latch. Emma did not move. It must be eight and Fallon would see that supper was brought. How tired she was, and there was a taste of salt against her lips as though she had cried in her sleep.

The bed moved as someone sat on it. A hand grasped hers. A mouth was against the bare flesh of her shoulder and a thrill of warmth ran through her body. The mouth transferred itself to her throat, her breast. She let the lips do what they would.

"I could be Bluebeard," Ringan whispered eventually.

"I knew it was you."

"Even with your eyes shut?"

"Even then."

"But you didn't know I was in London."

She did open her eyes then. "Why are you?"

"Your father expected you back two days ago. He could not come himself so he sent me."

"An emissary. Do all emissaries behave like you?"

"I doubt it. Where's Miss Fallon?"

"Visiting. Until eight o'clock."

"Indeed. And it is not yet seven."

She was wide awake, gloriously alive. Everything was forgotten except that he was here.

"I thought you hated me," he said, correctly interpreting her pleasure in his presence.

Emma shook her head and a strand of black hair fell across her bodice.

"Oh, God," he whispered, "I intended none of this."

"None of what?"

"What I think I am about to do."

"I love you, Ringan. I love you terribly. You must know that now."

"I'll lock the door. That woman might come back early." He got up from the bed and his foot kicked the bag. The silver pieces clinked together. Emma remembered everything. The warmth receded into flatness.

"What's this?" Ringan asked. "Your father said you'd be short of money by this time and gave me a letter for you to show at the bank."

"I wish—how I wish you had come this morning!" Emma got up from the bed. It did not matter that she was half-naked. She rejoiced in the look in his eyes. Caught against him, the pulse of his heartbeat plain against her breast, she said, "I have told Lewis I will marry him because of your tardiness, or Papa's."

Ringan and the setting of the room froze into a tableau. Her ribs hurt under the pressure of his encircling arms.

"Why?"

"I needed money. Fifty guineas."

"And you had to go to Critchley?"

"Yes."

"Suppose you sit down and tell me all about it." He pushed her into a chair and watched her moodily from his stance at the fireplace.

"I'll ram his silver down his throat!" he threatened violently when she had completed the wretched recital.

"There's no need for you to keep a promise made under duress."

"He told everyone we were betrothed."

"Then he can tell them you are not. Wildford's not likely to agree in any case. Is he?"

"If I say that it's what I want."

"But it is not, is it, Emma?"

"No."

"Then I'll go visit Mr. Critchley and return his loan."

"I thought you had some other plan for the next hour?"

He shook his head. "I'd not counted on seeing you lying there half-dressed. You tempted me out of my customary caution."

"Damn caution!"

"It was as well I kicked that illicit hoard. It would all have been over and your life spoiled—"

"Not spoiled! I wanted you—"

"And a bastard brat into the bargain? Most of my affairs seemed to end in a confinement and I'd not want to saddle you with the same result. You're a child—"

"Oh, go and see Lewis! Miss Fallon will be here when you return so you'll be quite safe. I am now going to put on another gown."

"Not quite yet." Ringan seized her by the arm and drew her toward him. He kissed her mouth, her neck, the hollow of her shoulder. Then he bent his head to kiss the rise of her breasts above the white bodice.

"Oh, Ringan." Emma knew that there was some intolerable pleasure to be explored if he were not so gentlemanly. She tried to restrain him but he set her aside.

"That was to keep you from straying. The minute you go out of sight you engage yourself to someone else."

"It was for Jess and you."

"I know that and I am suitably impressed. Wait. Wait for a little—"

"I think it will prove too difficult."

"There is your father's letter for the bank."

"Shouldn't you show it to Lewis?"

"You may do that tomorrow. My visit to him is of a different nature. Am I to sup with you later?"

"Miss Fallon and I will be delighted to see you. Hurry back."

"What's the fellow's address?"

She told him. Ringan picked up the bag. He had groomed himself very carefully, she noted, for his call at the hotel, and was touched. The words she had intended to speak stuck in her throat in a rush of tenderness. There was such comfort in the knowledge that there was someone to fight her battles, to extricate her from awkward predicaments.

She heard Ringan's boots on the stairs, the slam of the front door. Running to the window she was just in time to see him mount his horse, glance up as if he knew she was there, then laugh as he saw her state of dishabille. He motioned her away from the glass, then kneed the horse into motion and was swiftly gone.

The room was doubly quiet now that she was alone. Everything was falling into place. Jess out of the worst of her trouble, Ringan safe, Lewis about to be thwarted. Then why was she aware of a sense of impending doom?

Staves loomed up out of the mist. Emma leaned from the carriage window, shivering as the damp air licked at her face and neck and crawled over her fingers. Ringan was riding alongside, straight and spectral. A dim glow outlined a hunch of shrubbery, the tall yew at the corner of the drive.

"How gloomy everything looks."

"It will be different inside, Miss Emma," Miss Fallon replied.

Emma, conscious of an urgency to see her father, could not descend from the vehicle quickly enough. Though it was cold and damp, there was a sense of brooding oppression that disturbed her. Not waiting for the others, she hurried up the steps and past Harrison who was in the hall. She had pleasure in ignoring the man.

A light showed under the study door. She pushed it open, not waiting to knock, and saw Wildford half-asleep in his favorite chair. He had removed his stock for comfort and the brown column of his throat rose from the open shirt neck. Emma watched him move, the struggle for comprehension, the final recognition.

"Emma! Where the devil have you been? What've you been up to, eh?"

"Are you all right, Papa?"

"Do not change the subject."

"Are you? I've had such misgivings—"

"Of course I am" They could hear Miss Fallon's soft, precise voice, Harrison's gruff tones, receding footsteps. "Now, young miss, let's have an account of yourself." Wildford reached for the decanter and poured himself a good measure.

"I saw Jess Ashcroft." Emma let the green cape fall over the arm of a sofa.

"The devil you did! And she was the reason for the delay?"

"Yes, Papa."

"Suppose you begin at the beginning."

Wildford's color receded as the story unfolded. "Murder and blackmail," he said. "That's what your precious Newgate has brought. Terror and unhappiness. And as for Critchley—!"

"He suffered enough," Emma told him. "The captain beat him and threw all his silver back at him. But he did not have it all his own way. Ringan had some bruises of his own."

"I'll send Critchley packing," Wildford raged.

"Is that wise? The bank. Lewis 's contacts."

"It would never do now he's put this wedge between us."

"He'll make a bad enemy, Papa."

"I've a mind to close the London branch. I can never trust Critchley again. We managed perfectly well before I engaged him."

"Think well. I feel that I put you into this situation. But at least I am cured of my infatuation."

"I always said you were too young for marriage."

"I am not. " Emma wanted to tell him about Ringan but could not decide how best to begin. "I am in love, Papa. Truly in love this time."

"Is this some joke, Emma? How can you be? If it's some young jackanapes you met in London, you'd do well to forget it. You've not had time to know anyone sufficiently well."

"It is not someone new."

"Then who?" It was obvious from his frown that Wildford had no idea.

"Someone here—at Staves."

"Here? You don't mean Ringan? He's too old for you! Too dissolute." Wildford was outraged.

"He's gentle and honorable. In spite of me—"

Wildford leaned across and struck her across the face. "Don't talk like that. Like a whore!"

"Like a woman." Her cheek burned painfully.

"Go to your room, Emma."

"I am too old to be sent to my bedchamber. Most girls are married at my age. Mistress of their own homes. Why should I be different?"

"If you wed that profligate you'd be mistress of a cottage."

"I tell you, I'd not mind—"

"Piffle and fiddlesticks!" Wildford's face was unhealthily red. "It's not impossible he's a wife already. A parcel of brats. In spite of his denials."

"He saved my life, Papa. You said I should be grateful."

"Not to the extent of taking him as husband. To your bed—"

"You gave in about Lewis—"

"Because I imagined you genuine. And you were so miserable over that first Newgate affair. Now, in the next breath, almost, you have an undying love for an adventurer.

A likable man, but still a scamp with a past that does not bear investigation—"

"He's told me all about it."

"And you believe him, of course." Wildford's skin was unpleasantly mottled and he was pacing the room like a caged beast.

"You've grown insensitive, Papa."

"And you've let your wits grow addled."

"Papa, this time I mean it. You were right about Lewis. It was a wildness that burnt itself out before there was harm done."

"I'll not see you possessed by a man near old enough to be your father."

"You're jealous, Papa. Jealous."

They stared at each other, afraid to face the truth.

"Go away!" Wildford said roughly. "Leave me alone." His lips had turned an odd blue.

"It will not change anything."

"Get out!"

Emma, recognizing his desperation, let herself out of the paneled room. She thought she would always be aware of the smell of books, the tang of logs on the fire. She met Ringan in the hall.

"Please stay away," she begged. "He's beside himself. I told him I loved you. He's never intended that I break away from him. I know that now. He'd have found some way to separate me from Lewis before any actual ceremony. I think I will—never be free."

"It was a mistake to be so honest."

"You know how I hate to lie."

"My poor Emma. But I'm no great catch, am I? I do see his dilemma."

"Let him seek you out when he's had time to become used to the idea. I do not intend to change my mind. May I visit you?"

"Wait. I advised you to wait awhile."

"But I am all impatience!"

"All the better reason to think well."

"Do you think Lewis will seek revenge?" She touched his sleeve, hoping that he might embrace her, but he made no move to do so.

"Possibly. But he is in London and I am here."

"He'll not leave the bank unless he must. Papa means to close the new branch. That worries me."

"Aye. It's a blow Critchley will not easily forgive."

Harrison appeared from the kitchen stair and Emma disliked him anew. If it had not been for men like Jackson and Harrison, Jess would not be where she was, condemned to a transport ship and an uncertain future.

"I'll go," Ringan said.

"But we must be with each other."

"We'll see." The captain was evasive.

"We must," she whispered, conscious of Harrison busy with candles and the fastening of window catches, the burning sensation in her cheek where Wildford had struck her.

"Good night, Emma."

"I want to kiss you—"

"You cannot."

"Ringan?"

"Good night." He bent swiftly as Harrison went into a side passage to place a lighted candle on a table, kissing her hand, striding for the door. Banging it after him to show his own frustration.

"Damnation," Emma whispered viciously. "Oh, damn!"

Her fire was lighted when she went upstairs and Miss Fallon had turned down her bed.

"I ordered supper, Miss Emma."

"I'm not really hungry."

"Eat a little. And have an early night."

"That's what I want more than anything."

Emma ate sparingly, conscious of Wildford's empty place. He'd have drunk himself into a stupor by this time. It would be useless to try to cajole him into the dining room and she could not bear another scene like the one on her arrival. Let sleeping dogs lie. She wondered what had happened to the yellow dog. Thrown onto a bonfire, probably, and the animal had always reminded her of Ringan. It was like imagining him destroyed.

Even when she was in the sanctuary of the four-poster, she was not at peace. Lil Morris invaded her mind, grinning and beckoning. Moll Darke scraped her heels against the flagstones, screaming. Once more, Jess Ashcroft refused the gift of the gown, shook her head twice and turned her face against the wall.

Emma could not wait for morning, then when day had broken, she could not bear to encounter Wildford. At ten, she ordered the carriage for Norwich and tried to think of an excuse for going. "I want to buy something for the Fry children," she told Miss Fallon. "Their mother has been so kind." It seemed preferable to acquiring new gloves or a purse when she already had so many.

The leaves were drifting as they drove to Norwich. The blacks stepped out bravely in spite of the rising mist that all but drowned the landscape. Church spires barely showed against the sky and the River Wensum slid, sibilant, against its dim banks.

Emma bought some gifts for the little Frys, then a shawl for Miss Fallon. She tried to think of a suitable present for Ringan but his life-style was so simple that she dismissed most of the articles that came to mind, settling on a silver flask that would, no doubt, be useful on a winter sortie around Staves.

"For Mr. Wildford?"

"No, Miss Fallon. For—a friend."

"It is very beautiful."

"Yes. I wanted something special."

There was some sort of incident ahead as they began the homeward journey. A lantern shone on a group of murmuring people standing around an unseen object on the riverbank. Emma had the carriage stopped in case she could be of help.

Descending, she walked through the damp grass. "What is wrong?"

"A poor soul drowned," a countrywoman said. "Drowned in the Wensum."

The figures parted to let the girl through. The woman lay on the bank, a bundle of sodden rags, the lardlike skin streaked with fronds of brown hair. Her hands had been crossed over her breast. They were not swollen and callous as a workingwoman's in spite of the dull gown and the bedraggled hair. Touchingly, the feet were bare though most of the face was covered by the wet tresses.

"How will you get her to town?" Emma asked, goose-pimpled.

"Dunno, miss. Coming over the bridge we was, then saw her floating."

"The carriage—"

"Nay, miss, but you'd have the seats spoiled. They'll use a litter."

"Who is it?"

"Woman called Craven. Been acting queer she 'as, for a bit. Talking to 'ersel'. Not takin' care o' 'ersel' as she used."

"You—are sure?"

"Oh, yes. Live in the same street."

"Put her in the carriage," Emma ordered. "I know Mrs. Craven. It's only fitting she is taken home with some dignity. Is there anyone there to take care of her? See she is properly buried?"

The woman shook her head. The lamplight shivered over the still body.

"I will see to it," Emma said. "Someone must."

Two of the men picked up the drowned woman.

"Miss Fallon," Emma said when the cortege reached the carriage, "do you mind riding with a corpse?"

Knuckles cracked once. Twice.

"Don't worry," Emma told her, "it's someone I know. Someone to whom my father was once obligated. He'd not want her to end up in a pauper's grave. So you won't mind traveling a mile with a woman who had nothing left to live for, will you?"

Miss Fallon shook her head. Mrs. Craven was placed on a rug and the carriage began its second entry into Norwich. The motion of the wheels over the ruts in the road dislodged one arm which hung over the edge of the seat, flapping with each movement as though it beckoned them to limbo.

Wildford was rattled by Mrs. Craven's death. He seemed to shrink and grow old overnight. The suicide filled his horizon so that he seemed to forget his intention to close the bank and to censure Ringan. But Emma knew that when the worst of his guilt was over, he'd rectify these omissions. She did not want to think of Staves without the captain. Once gone, she could never find him.

He had not been there when she rode over to the cottage. It was as though he evaded her. If he left the district she would go with him, so certain was she that this time her feelings were not misplaced. Wildford would never be persuaded a second time to allow her the freedom she wanted so badly. Even Miss Fallon seemed to watch her more closely, trying to dissuade her from the ride to the copse.

"Papa has told you to spy on me," Emma accused her.

"No. Truly—"

"I do not believe you."

The look on Miss Fallon's face had softened her. She had run to the woman and hugged her. "Forgive me. There is a problem I cannot solve. May never—"

"All problems can be resolved, Miss Emma. With time."

"Not this one."

"You'll see."

"I hope you are right."

Next day Emma had seen Miss Vera Palsey in the vicinity

of the lake. She was wearing a lavender-colored cape and her hair looked suspiciously fair. The sight of her in the dun-colored landscape did not arouse the usual dislike. If Miss Palsey was infatuated by Wildford, there would be no happy ending. Emma wondered if the news of Mrs. Craven's suicide had reached the Wellings.

The kitchen staff at Staves had talked of nothing else since the topic of Jess had palled so she was reasonably certain that the farm folk would be acquainted with the news that not only had Wildford's mistress drowned herself but his daughter had taken it upon herself to pay for the funeral.

Miss Palsey passed out of sight and Emma was sorry for her. If she had indeed come from London at regular intervals just for a fleeting glimpse of Wildford, then that was really sad.

She returned to Staves thinking that her life was, once more, without purpose. It was impossible to go back to Newgate until Mrs. Fry returned from her journey, and Wildford would be sure to put obstacles in the way. Emma was not even sure that she wished to visit the jail again. Moll Darke was still on her mind, and though she now believed that Jess was not guilty of Lil Morris's death, she still shied away from the certainty that her desire to help Jess Ashcroft had led to the certain hanging of the woman with red curls. There must be someone she could aid in Norwich or around the estate. Miss Fallon would like nothing better than to take calf's-foot jelly and chicken broth to sick villagers, and sew aprons for poor children. She'd not be averse to teaching like Miss Hannah More. Why not?

Wildford put in an appearance at supper. His eyes were bloodshot and his hands trembled over his spoon and fork. Claret slopped onto the floor. He looked cold and unwell. Emma could not bear to see his disintegration.

They ate and drank in silence until Wildford said harshly, "I suppose you've been hanging around that rascal! In spite of my strictures."

"You mean Ringan?"

"Don't put on those brazen airs with me, my girl!"

"I have not seen him for several days."

"I saw you go, yesterday. To the wood—"

"A pity you'd not stayed at your window. You would have seen me come back soon after."

"Only because he was out!"

"Had he been in, I'd have stayed longer, I admit."

"And done what!"

"I do not ask you what you've done with your doxies."

"You go too far." His eyes were furious.

"Ringan would not allow me to forget myself. Believe it or not as you choose. I wanted him. He would not take me. I'd swear it on the Bible."

"He's never laid a finger on you?"

"I could not say that. But you could have me examined by every doctor in the land and they'd tell you I was a virgin, albeit unwilling."

"I do not like such remarks from you."

"It's the truth, Papa. I am too much like you to be content with permanent chastity. You'd do better to let me wed. I'll wear him down one day. You'll see. Let me marry him honorably, please? I beg you."

"You'll swear on the Bible?"

"A hundred if it would convince you."

"There's one in my study."

"What better time?"

They rose from the table, Wildford staggering a little as though he were half-tipsy. He had not drunk a great deal, Emma reflected, hurrying to keep up with his lurching pace, afraid that he was ill or mad. But he could have been drinking all day before she saw him take his place at the supper table. Drunkenness was preferable to madness. He'd throw off the effects of wine and brandy. Derangement was so much more final.

He threw open the study door with such force that it struck the wall. The firelight showed up his unsteady form. "Light—the—candle," he muttered and crashed into a chair. Again there was a faint, bluish tinge around his mouth.

Emma, deeply disturbed, did as she was bid.

"The—Bible."

She stared around the shelves at the soft leather spines with the gold tooling. The big black volume evaded her. "Where is it, Papa?"

"Where is—what?"

"The Bible."

He peered about him, his head thrust out, bull-like. Wildford looked dangerous and Emma experienced a moment of fear. "I remember. I took it to my chamber. It was—when you said you wanted—Lewis Critchley. I wished to read the inscriptions—see how much room there was to add—another—for your marriage. Children "

"I'll fetch it if you still want it."

"I—want—it. Give me some brandy before you go, there's a good girl."

Emma obeyed. His broad hand fastened around the stem of the glass. She did not want to leave him in his present strange mood, but this swearing on the Holy Book seemed the only thing that would pacify him.

Taking a candle from the hall, she mounted the stairs, aware of a great disquiet over Wildford's condition. Her feelings of rebellion were always modified by the love she bore her father. But how often would this situation be repeated, each time her reaction more bitter than the last? She could see no end to it but to leave him and then who would care for him?

She could not find the book at first, then discovered it beneath a waistcoat flung carelessly over the bedside table. It was very large and heavy. Out of curiosity Emma opened it. The flyleaf was half-filled with cramped entries, the last two being her father's wedding to Amelia, followed by the record of her own birth. Wildford had been an only child and so was his father and grandfather. She had a brief panic in case she should prove barren. Ringan would think little of a wife who could not provide what his mistresses had done in apparent abundance. But she would be different from the rest of the Wildfords! She'd have at least a brace of boys and a girl or two.

Picking up the book, she held it against her chest. The edge of gold leaf glinted dully as she picked up the candlestick. It still seemed foolish to make a promise in God's book for a man who admitted he was an atheist. A long sleep was what Wildford wanted, nothing of heaven or hereafter.

It was when she approached the study that she heard voices and supposed that Harrison had been sent for to fetch something for her father.

"I should have thrashed you harder," Wildford said, shocking her to immobility. The Bible slipped so that she had to set down the candle to catch it before it could fall.

Someone laughed. It was a man's laugh but she did not recognize it. Lewis, perhaps, complaining of his treatment from Ringan? Ringan himself? Harrison?

"You'll not touch Emma. I'd—kill—you first."

"You're in no fit state to kill a fly." The voice was so repressed with hatred that she still could not tell who her father's visitor was. "Her first, so that you see her dead. Then you—when you've had time to suffer a little."

"You're—mad."

"You should not have marked me. People laugh at me. Turn from me—"

She knew who was in there with Wildford but if she called for help her father was doomed.

"Empty threats," Wildford muttered. "Months ago, I expected you."

"I was—ill."

"You should get out before my man comes. I sent him for —more brandy."

"With the decanter half full?"

"Damn you, Maybrick. May you roast in hell if you hurt Emma."

"I shall kill Amelia, too, when I find her. Only they've hidden her too well."

"You—are—mad."

There was the sound of a blow and a cry from Wildford. A crash.

"Do not say that again."

"Father!" Emma called out. "Are you all right? Harrison! Someone! Come, please."

"Oh," Maybrick said, "dear Miss Emma. Are you ready to die?"

She looked swiftly around the hall but there was no weapon, no sound of footsteps coming to their aid. Emma could not stop herself from running to the doorway. Her father hung back in his chair, eyes closed. Maybrick looked ghastly, the mark on his cheek almost purple, the rest of his skin gray and stubbled. His clothes hung on him. His smile was a rictus and there was a pistol in his hand.

"Taken to Bible reading, have you, instead of troublemaking?"

She could think of nothing to say. Her wide eyes were fixed on Wildford.

"He'll be all right in a minute or two. Come inside."

"No."

"Then I'll blow his head off. Didn't want to kill you yet, not until he saw it, but if you persist in staying there, I'll just have to forgo that pleasure."

She did as she was bid, moving very slowly to draw out the process in the hope that someone would appear. No one came. Maybrick shut the door after her and locked it. Emma continued to think, without much feeling, that when her father came out of his unconsciousness, he would sign her death warrant.

The logs in the fireplace shifted eerily and Maybrick swung around, expecting to see someone there.

"It was the fire," Emma said and noticed the brass dogs in the fender. She could never reach them, of course, not without some major diversion. She made a motion to set the Bible down but Maybrick leveled the pistol so that she gazed into the dark hole of the barrel. Her breath caught on a gasp.

"Do not move."

Wildford was so still that Emma feared he was already dead. Panic was slowly overtaking her initial shock. "You've hurt him badly."

The logs crashed and Maybrick started, the pistol wavering. Emma closed her eyes and felt the sweat burst out on her brow. Her hands were sticky against the musty leather of the Bible. Nothing happened. She opened her eyes again.

"I told you it was the fire. You see, I was right."

"Clever Emma! I saw the hope in your face when I did not discharge the pistol. But no one will rescue you. You know that in your heart of hearts, don't you? The moment Wildford sits up, I shall fire. Not before. Not now that we are so cozy."

"And what if he is dead?"

"There must be a part of him left that will shudder, even in hell."

It was useless to reason with Maybrick or to expect mercy. "Let me go to him," she pleaded.

"No."

Someone was walking overhead. Harrison? One of the maids? Dare she cry out?

"I should not do it," Maybrick warned her, his fingers tightening on the trigger mechanism. "You have an open face, my dear."

"So I have been told." Emma tried to keep her voice level. She was certain she had seen a movement at the window behind Maybrick. It was not a large window and the garden foliage grew almost as far as the leaded panes. Something flickered, came closer. A face was thrust against the glass and a thrill ran through her. Ringan was outside and she was conscious of a pale relief. But kept where he was by the smallness of the panes, unaware that only Wildford's coma kept her alive, what could he do? But his presence comforted her.

She must try to distract Maybrick until Ringan had time to evolve some plan. Emma watched the long, scarred face retreat and vanish.

Maybrick half-turned suspiciously. "What's over there that's so interesting? Ah, you had some idea of escaping into the garden. How optimistic, my dear—"

"Don't call me that!"

He stared full into her eyes. "I'll call you what I will. It was your fault that Wildford struck me and did this." He touched the red blotch with careful fingertips. "Amelia never liked it. Then she came to hate it—and me."

"People do not condemn other people for physical flaws that are so small. It was you, your nature, she came to detest. You were cruel then and you are worse now. She was afraid of you and that is why she hides from you. She'd have done better to stay with Papa."

"Be quiet!" A vein stood out in Maybrick's forehead.

"I have no intention of doing so. If I am to die anyway, I may as well go in my own fashion. Can't I put down this book? It begins to hurt my arms."

"No. It will keep you out of mischief. You cannot pick up potential weapons."

Emma listened intently. There had been the tiniest sound from the study door but Maybrick put it down to the collapsing fire. He backed toward the fireplace and kicked out at the crumbling logs. Sparks flew in a wide radius. Emma gave a little scream as several settled on the skirt of her gown and one burned her wrist.

Maybrick cursed, knelt to brush his breeches' legs, the pistol still directed at the frightened girl. Her wrist hurt and the sparks had made ever-growing black circles on the green material. But there was no burst of flame, just the smell of scorching fabric.

Desperately Emma ventured another look at the window. Ringan had not returned and she could not hope for the situation to remain static for much longer. There was someone beyond the locked door but whoever it was could not alter events.

"What's that?" Maybrick asked suddenly, satisfied that he had dealt sufficiently with the scorching fragments.

"I don't know what you mean."

"I heard something."

"Staves is full of people, all going about their business. They know nothing of what's happening or they'd have come when I called for help."

Maybrick grunted. He had not once relaxed his vigilance in spite of his undoubted abnormality. Emma had infused bitterness into her voice. He'd recognize that as a natural reaction to the nonappearance of any servants to her plea for assistance.

The leaves near the window parted and this time she saw Harrison duck from one side to the other, then vanish. Staring, she made out the man's profile in the dimness, faintly yellowed by the light that issued from the room.

The door handle turned with infinite slowness. Maybrick saw it move on the edge of his vision and straightened angrily.

"Are you all right, Mr. Wildford?" Ringan asked quietly.

"Say something," Maybrick hissed softly. "And make certain it's reassuring."

"Papa is asleep," Emma said. "We—need nothing for the moment."

"I thought the fire would need replenishing by this time."

"The noise would wake him."

"Very well, Miss Emma."

In the painful silence that followed, Emma saw nothing but Maybrick's passionate face, the cruel, searching eyes. The light was suddenly on Harrison who was now standing close to the window, holding something above his head. The ax struck the window with heart-wrenching suddenness, scattering bits of thick glass and strips of lead across the floor. Wildford groaned and shifted in the chair.

Almost simultaneously, a shot splintered the lock and the door was thrown open to reveal Ringan, pale and accusing, the new footman beside him looking green about the gills. Maybrick, who had begun to rush toward the window, flung himself around again.

For a moment Emma thought herself safe, then she became horridly aware of the pistol still trained on her body, the whitening knuckle. She screamed, "Papa! Papa—!" then her mind was filled with a deafening roar. There was a terrible pain in her breast. For an instant she saw them all, Ringan jumping through the doorway, Wildford struggling up in his chair and Maybrick backing away so that he had a clear view of both door and window. Then her senses whirled and spiraled, turned into fog and darkness.

Chapter Nine

She was looking into a golden haze, infinitely beautiful. It must be heaven, Emma thought, except that they said there was no pain there. She could not move for the torment. But the diffused light was lovely. Her heavy eyelids closed and shut it out, but she could not shut out the pain. She moaned.

A hand closed over hers. Miss Fallon said, "Miss Emma?"

"Why do I—hurt so?"

"That dreadful man—shot at you."

"Shot?" Emma had only confused recollections of some major event.

"That man Maybrick who had the grudge against Mr. Wildford." Miss Fallon's voice wavered.

"Oh! I do recall. I thought he killed me—"

"You escaped by the merest chance. The ball struck the Bible and did not quite go through. But the impact was very great. Another inch higher and it would not have been stopped. I am so glad you are safe, Miss Emma. But I should not be talking to you. I should go to tell the doctor who is downstairs. He insisted I fetch him immediately—"

"But you can't go!" Emma's eyes were open again, blinking against the flood of early autumn sunshine that replaced the time of mist and cloud. "I want to know about Papa. Ringan. Even Maybrick."

"I will fetch Dr. Joseph."

"Why can't you tell me?"

In the ensuing silence Emma knew that the answer was death.

Dr. Joseph took his time to come upstairs, and all the time Emma was thinking that if Papa had not sent for the Bible, she would have been vulnerable. Maybrick would have come just the same and found them together. She would have died immediately and then Wildford, in some horrible fashion, beaten or stabbed.

The doctor was at her bedside, watching her with guarded sympathy. "I should like you to take this medicine." He held out a glass containing a bitter-looking liquid.

"Why?"

"It will make you feel sleepy."

"If you have bad news for me, I would rather know without the soporific."

"Young lady, I do not agree. You may have escaped death but you must be in considerable discomfort. You have badly bruised ribs at the best, cracked ones at the worst, and here you'll have to stay till I decide which." His florid face endeavored to look kind under the untidy wig. His nostrils were stained with snuff. She tried to concentrate on all these small details while her mind kept repeating what her heart already knew.

"My father is dead, isn't he?"

"How—?"

"Oh, don't blame Miss Fallon. She said nothing, but her voice trembled as she spoke his name. She is not a good actress." Emma tried to move but her rib cage would not allow it. She gasped with agony.

"You see why I should have preferred that you did not

suffer mental pain as well as bodily torment? The combination of both—"

"Must be faced if they are to be overcome," Emma said bravely. "Why shut it out now to leap out on one later? How did he die?"

"He was a sick man—"

"I had noticed a deterioration."

"His heart was not good—"

"He never mentioned it."

"It was his express wish not to distress you. I had advised him several times to prepare you, to live more—sensibly."

"Papa would not relish giving up his greatest pleasures. I—I presume his mistress was one of these—sacrifices?"

"Miss Emma!"

"One does not enter Newgate without growing up twenty years in an hour."

"I heard you had gone there."

"Poor, poor Mrs. Craven. He blamed her jealousy but had endured it for quite some time regardless— He found it less easy to drink less or to fly into rages."

"We must decide what must be done about you."

"About me? I'll stay here. I have Miss Fallon."

"I thought more about the business. You are not fit—"

"For the moment, no. Mr. Critchley will continue to take care of the London bank for the present. I will look after Norwich."

"Are you sure?"

"With the help of someone very able. Mr. Tully *is* the Norwich branch. My father always said so. He was not a man to exaggerate."

"No. And the estate?"

"I have the utmost confidence in Captain Ringan." Ringan was intelligent and determined. He might replace Lewis at the bank quite adequately. And there were bound to be sons—

"The staff express doubts."

"Bother the staff!" Emma was close to tears with inadequacy and frustration. "They'd best behave themselves or there will be considerable changes. I'd sack the lot as soon as look at them. I am mistress here."

"Do not distress yourself."

"Do you expect me to overlook my father's death? But he did not suffer through Maybrick, did he? Tell me there was no violence used against him?"

"He had a collapse and rallied only for a moment when he heard the sound of the pistol being fired—"

"But he couldn't have known the pistol ball hit me? He couldn't, could he?" The answer seemed more important than anything she had ever known.

"He could have known nothing. I examined him soon after."

"He acted so strangely—"

"That was why. His poor condition, exacerbated by drink."

"I feared—madness."

"It was not that. His brain was perfectly sound."

"I'm so glad. At least he was capable of reasoning even if he was tormented."

"Take the medicine now. Any movement you make will add to your troubles. Impede progress."

"I must see him buried. You'd not bar me from that. I'm his daughter. His only kin—"

"It would be madness."

"I must!"

"Rest, then, or I could not guarantee it. I should not."

"Oh, give me the beastly stuff!"

She drank, then saw the choleric face blur and recede. Dimly aware of the return of Miss Fallon, she let her eyes close. Wildford smiled down at her, brown-skinned and vital, his dark eyes flashing as though he were amused. How white his shirt was and how the stock flattered him. She reached out through a maze of lethargy and took his hand.

* * *

The hand was still there when she awoke but the face was not Wildford's.

"Ringan—" I am free, she thought, conscious of a release, but as quickly she recognized the pain of losing her father. But she would remember Wildford at his best, and that best was immeasurably good.

"He tried to cling to me while he was able," she whispered. "I know it now."

"He knew nothing after Maybrick hit him. It was over very quickly. One blow."

"As I should want to go."

"You're strong as a horse," Ringan said sardonically. "It would need Staves to fall on top of you."

"But it never will."

"What a woman. You'll always require the last word."

"I'll kick my heels on the floor if I don't get it."

He gave a bark of laughter. "There speaks Wildford's brat."

"What happened to Maybrick?"

"He's in Bedlam."

"I thought—you might kill him."

"You think I didn't want to? But he—crumbled. I could not revenge myself upon a—thing. A cabbage."

"Mama did not have a good effect on her men. Papa. Maybrick."

"Frigid women never do. They like a man to hang around them with roses and promises of undying love, but they give little in return. Nothing of value. Only a sentimentality that's worse than rejection. Anything real and they shy away as if they'd been shown something monstrous. You are not like that, Emma, are you?"

"Not in the least."

"Thank God."

"Stay. Stay, won't you?"

He smiled, his dark blue eye very dark, the pale blue very

pale. It would be like being made love to by two different people and very suitable for people born at the end of May. She'd mourn her father for a little, then take the captain as husband. There was no one to object. A warmth almost overcame her pain.

"A letter came for you this morning."

"Oh?" She took it anxiously.

It was from Mrs. Fry. "I am back from my journey and I find that all is not well at Newgate. There are men about to be executed who are made to sit in the condemned pew with a coffin on a table close by. Folk pay a shilling to go and gloat over the sight. Then they are remonstrated with by the clergy who make miserable their last hours. I am minded to change all this."

"Ringan?"

"Yes, Emma."

"Do you mind if, after we are wed, I go to Newgate from time to time?"

"Not in the least. So long as you come back."

"Oh, I will. I will."

"Then that's settled." He leaned over the bed and kissed her very carefully so that her ribs did not hurt at all.

"I shall expect better than that in a little while, Ringan."

"You shall have better, I promise you."

"Good."

She closed her eyes and the autumn sunlight danced for a moment then was still.